Books by

MW01240963

Bonded (Book 1)
Tothars (Book 2)
Tilted (Book 3)

Books by my Alter Ego
Dawn Greenfield Ireland

Nonfiction

The Puppy Baby Book   Mastering Your Money

Puppy Adoption and Beyond   Writers Preparation Handbook

What's Breaking Your Budget

Fiction

The Alcott Family Adventures   **The Thol Series**

- Hot Chocolate   - Prophecy of Thol

- Bitter Chocolate   - Gifts from Thol

- Spicy Chocolate   - Love of Thol

- Boxed Set   - King of Thol

Stand-Alone Science Fiction (for now)

The Last Dog (dystopian)   Forced Dreams

Coming Soon

Katz' Cat   Texmexzona (TMZ)
                              Book 2 in the Last Dog Series

Unforeseen by DG Ireland

Published by Artistic Origins Inc.

Copyright © 2020 Dawn Greenfield Ireland

All rights reserved.

Cover image: Sandy Penny and Brandon White

Cover design Marcha Fox / Kalliope Rising Press

Interior layout by Yours Truly (me)

ISBN 978-1-940385-31-0 (eBook)

ISBN 978-1-940385-32-7 (paperback)

Dawn Greenfield Ireland

Artistic Origins Inc

www.dawngreenfieldireland.com

Publisher's Note: This is a work of fiction. Names, characters, places, and incidents are a product of the author's imagination. Locales and public names are sometimes used for atmospheric purposes. Any resemblance to actual people, living or dead, or to businesses, companies, events, institutions, or locales is completely coincidental.

Please visit my website: http://dawngreenfieldireland.com/

Sign up for my newsletter and get the latest news before the public.

I'm on Patreon! https://www.patreon.com/dawngreenfieldireland

 Created with Vellum

BOOK 4 OF THE BONDED SERIES

Unforeseen

DG Ireland

ARTISTIC
ORIGINS

An Artistic Origins Publication

ACKNOWLEDGMENTS

Sometimes it takes two to tango the cover image. Sandy Penny captured the cover image from the vast Internet, and my first born, Brandon White, redesigned it.

My two secret weapons attached their eyes like lasers to the pages and kept me out of trouble.

Great appreciation goes to Jeff Gonyea, and Grasshopper (Richard Stone) who caught last minute blunders. The student teaches the teacher a thing or two.

CONTENTS

CHAPTER ONE

B ig Bear Muchisky manned the front desk of the OPERA and Panther Industries office building on the private property that Ari Davis inherited from an uncle she never met.

A couple of months after Ari took the helm of her uncle's company, she changed the name from O'Briain's, to O'Briain Petroleum and Energy Resources Amalgamated. She played with words until she came up with the acronym OPERA.

The bear shifter at the front desk was an imposing sight in the Panther Industries Security Division's black formfitting uniform. At six-foot five-inches tall in his human form, not many challenged him. There was a hint of hidden weaponry in several places on his rock-hard, solid body as uniform pockets bulged slightly. His dark brown eyes swept the empty lobby and the front entrance into the parking lot.

Marcha, the human receptionist and up-for-grabs admin, made copies at the new copier in the recently renovated secured lobby. She was one of a handful of humans among the various shifters employed by the OPERA company. She loved her job and the unique people she worked with.

The building was so reinforced that once someone entered through the bulletproofed front doors, they couldn't get beyond the lobby. A badge and a personal code were required for access to anywhere else. If someone tried to access the building illegally, they'd have to get through the onsite shape-shifter employees, a next to impossible feat.

Panther Industries was known worldwide for their security business. If anyone wanted their people protected, they only had to make one call. Prior to Ari taking over her uncle's company, there had been no safety or emergency procedures to follow if a problem arose. The company had been vulnerable, and after only a couple of hours onsite, Panther Industries employees had discovered an embezzler in the O'Briain's workforce. That would never happen again.

Big Bear's brow scrunched as he spotted six individuals approaching the building on foot. They weren't coming from a vehicle in the parking area out in front of the office building. He wondered if they had parked over by the garages or the house. Ari wasn't with them, nor was Pablo, the groundskeeper, so they weren't being escorted.

He stood with feet firmly planted, taking on a defensive stance as the group approached the building. Big Bear's eyebrows rose as he took in the size of the males. He sent a silent shifter mind-message to the Panther Security Division, and his kings.

Six unescorted individuals approaching the building on foot.

The front door opened, and the group entered, led by the biggest man Big Bear Muchisky had ever seen. The olive-skinned man with hair so black it looked blue, was more than a foot taller than the bear shifter. If he had to guess, Big Bear would say the man was just short of eight feet tall.

Big Bear took in a whiff to identify the people. His head

silently clanged alarms to his kings, Roman Davenport, the CEO of Panther Industries, and Gage Stryker the president. Sherman Foo, the head of the security division, received the alert. The OPERA heads under Ari's domain, silently picked up on the alarm.

The sampling the bear shifter took was unidentifiable. He couldn't even make a guess which animal family this group belonged to. They were definitely shifters. He just didn't know what kind.

Marcha returned to the front desk from the copier with several documents stacked for distribution, unaware that anything was brewing. "Good morning, may I help you?" She bubbled over with friendliness, but in a professional manner.

Big Bear gently pushed Marcha behind him. He was trying to keep his grizzly bear under control and didn't want the human to get caught in an aggressive shift and get hurt.

Marcha peeked around the bear shifter. She saw nothing alarming with the group of visitors, but since she wasn't a shifter, she didn't know what was wrong, or what had the bear shifter so riled up.

"Identify yourselves," Big Bear growled out, his hand slipping inside a pocket of his uniform. His fingers tightened around the grip of a Glock 19. He noticed that these people bobbed their heads—not nodding—while slowly taking in the entire room, and that their tongues kept sliding between their lips. It was the most bizarre thing the bear had ever seen.

The elevator doors opened and Roman, Gage, Sherm, and Lonnie, Sherm's second in command, walked over to the reception center. A door clicked open and the OPERA heads, Chewy, Viggo, Roger, Booker, Melly and Judy poured into the area. They flanked the Panther group in a semi-aggressive stance, ready to shift and jump into action, if necessary.

The four strange men bowed to Roman and Gage, their

kings in the shifter world. The two women curtsied deeply. They all gazed on the kings with reverence.

"King Roman, King Gage, we come seeking asylum," the large man said, with more than a hint of an Indonesian accent.

"Who are you?" Roman asked.

"I'm Acawarman. This is Eyo, Kartodirdjo, Sopan, Novi, and Inggit. We are from a small island in Indonesia."

Roman sucked in a long breath. He was just as stumped as the grizzly. He had no idea what these people were, animal-wise. "What are your animals? I don't recognize your scents."

Acawarman stood proud and tall. "We are Komodo dragons." He showed his animal face.

Marcha peeked around Big Bear. Her hand went to her heart. "Komodo dragons? Oh, my!"

Sherm came forward. "Let's get you badged so we can meet inside and sort out the problem that brought you here."

After several minutes, the dragons had badges and were led into a conference room. Marcha entered a few minutes later.

"What could I get you to drink?" Marcha asked.

"Water or tea would be most welcomed," Inggit said.

"Nothing for us," Gage said.

Once the door shut after Marcha, the questions started.

"What is going on in your homeland that prompted you to travel such a great distance for this meeting?" Sherm asked.

Acawarman lowered his head a bit, his face splintered in pain. Then he met Sherm's eyes across the table. "Our numbers are dwindling to the point where we are in danger of becoming extinct—we as shifters, and our natural animal brothers and sisters. We've been hunted and captured relentlessly. We couldn't think of anywhere we would be safe until we attended one of your online meetings."

"Would you be able to survive here? The humidity is very high," Melly said.

Lonnie raised a brow at his girlfriend. He wondered how she knew about what they could tolerate. Melly winked at him. She liked to keep him on his toes.

"We will adapt," Eyo said. "The heat is good. While we are used to a hot, dry climate, this humidity won't harm us."

A tap on the door sounded Marcha's return. Ari was behind her. She held the door for Marcha, who set a tray on the side table and served cups of hot tea to the guests.

The Komodo's shot out of their chairs when Ari entered the room. The men bowed deeply and the two women curtsied low to their queen.

"Queen Ari!" Acawarman said, with a hint of reverence.

Ari took a seat at the table between Roman and Gage. "Please sit and enjoy your tea."

They sat across the table from the royals and the others in the room.

"We need to find a home as soon as possible," Acawarman said. "Novi and Inggit will lay eggs soon and need to build nests."

Ari's eyes swung to the two women. "Can we help you with the nests?"

Novi shook her head. "No, this is something we shall do in our natural forms."

Gage pondered. "Back in your homeland, did you have residences, or did you live in the wild? You said you saw one of our online meetings, so I'm sure you had some interaction with the civilized world."

"We split our time between the two worlds," Acawarman said. "Eyo, Sopan and I worked for a security company. Our size is a bonus in that field. Kartodirdjo and Inggit ran a restaurant. Novi was a homemaker and looked after all of us in our house."

"If you were so well established, I don't understand why

you felt you needed to leave your homeland to come here," Roman said.

"We couldn't shift!" Novi wailed. "One of our brothers was recently captured. No matter where we went, people hunted for our kind. Even though it's illegal to capture Komodo dragons, that hasn't stopped anyone! There are less than six thousand Komodo dragons left in the world."

"I'd die if I had to live in a zoo," Kartodirdjo said. "We are on the endangered species list, but people travel to Indonesia to steal our eggs and capture us illegally. The government doesn't really do much to protect us. The local officials take bribes and look the other way."

"We will find a place for you," Ari said, adamantly. "This estate is vast with a lot of acreage. I'm sure Pablo, our groundskeeper, will be able to help find the right location."

A tap sounded low on the door, then the door opened a couple of inches. Eyes at the door handle level peeked through the open slit. A hand up above the eyes by a good foot or more, pushed the door open.

"Come on, Eddie, you wanted in the room, so move," Phoebe June Blassingame said.

A tiny, four-year-old blonde girl walked into the room, followed by her nanny-slash-tutor. She stared at the strangers sitting at the table.

"Eddie, what are you doing here?" Roman asked.

She shrugged.

"Come on, out with it," Roman said. "I'm pretty sure you didn't come to the office building because you had nothing to do."

She placed her small hands on her hips and let out a huff of exasperation. "If you must know, I came to meet the Komodo's."

Ari introduced her wayward daughter to the guests. "This

is our daughter Edris, but she likes to be called Eddie, and her nanny, Phoebe."

"Nanny-slash-tutor," Eddie stated.

"Yes, that too," Gage said. He reached out and captured her hand in his and hauled her to his side. "Eddie, this is Acawarman, Eyo, Kartodirdjo, Sopan, Novi, and Inggit."

Eddie rocked on her heels as she took in the Indonesians. "I'm going to call you Warman." She glanced at Kartodirdjo. "I'll call you Dirdjo!" Next, she looked at Novi and Inggit. "There are some really great places on the other side of the property where you can build your nests. There's a house over there too."

Ari, Roman, Gage and Sherm stared at Eddie, then glanced over to Phoebe.

Phoebe shrugged. "I don't have a clue. We haven't explored that far away from the house."

"Okay, it's one of those things she knows," Gage said, with a shake of his head. They were getting used to the fact that Eddie knew things she shouldn't know and couldn't explain, as if she had the ability to see through time or something.

"You can help Pablo find the place," Sherm said. His phone twerped. He pulled it out of his pocket and studied the screen. He scrolled through some documents for a long moment, then clicked out of the app.

They are who they say they are, Sherm sent to Roman, Gage, and Ari silently while blocking everyone else in the room.

Roman stood. "Let's see if we can find this place my daughter seems to think is perfect for you."

"I'll have Pablo meet us out front," Gage said.

The OPERA group stood.

"Welcome to the estate," Chewy said. He and his group filed out of the conference room and returned to their area.

CHAPTER TWO

E ddie sat on Sherm's lap in the seat beside Pablo and guided him through the property. The large golf cart buggy held ten comfortably, but the Komodo dragon men were large people, so Lonnie drove the second buggy.

"Go that way," Eddie insisted, her finger pointing to a heavily treed area.

"Are you sure?" Pablo asked. "I haven't been over here in a while, but I don't recall seeing any houses or cabins."

"You'll see," the girl insisted.

Pablo drove on, taking the buggy over bumpy areas where a road might have been years ago. The property on this side of the estate was not used, and quite frankly, he didn't think he'd ever been where Eddie was leading him.

"You can stop here," Eddie said. "We can walk the rest of the way." She looked at her family. "It's not far!"

Everyone disembarked from the two buggies and followed their pint-sized guide. After a few minutes they emerged from the trees into an opening where an old, two-story house stood, frail from the elements. It had endured with no loving attention for what looked like decades.

"See? I told you there was a good place for you!" Eddie boasted, as she looked at the dragons, then her family members.

"The house direly needs maintenance, honey," Ari said.

"Let's take a look inside," Roman said. He walked over to the house, climbed two steps and grasped the door handle. The door fell off the hinges. He had to grab it and set it aside before it clobbered him.

"It's okay," Eddie said. "We can fix it up."

"Honey...," Gage began.

"I'm telling you it's okay. Some things need to be fixed, but the inside is still good," Eddie said. She led the way inside, against grumbling rebuffs from her fathers, mother and Sherm.

Once they were inside the house, it was as Eddie had stated. Other than cobwebs and dust, the house was solid. They went through all the rooms, climbed the stairs, and determined that it was large enough for the six dragons.

"Let's get some of our service providers over here to put the place back in order," Ari said.

"Oh, you shouldn't go to all that expense," Novi said. "We can tidy it up."

The dragons nodded emphatically. They didn't want to be a burden to their royal family.

"Nonsense," Roman said. "We have the resources to put this place back together again. In the meantime, you can stay in the apartments in the building."

"I'm on it," Lonnie said.

They walked back to the golf buggies and returned to the office building.

MARCHA WAS WORKING on the apartment spreadsheet when everyone walked through the doors. She registered the three vacant apartments on the sixth floor to the dragons. "These should be comfortable. I figured two per apartment." She looked at the guests. "Whose names should I appoint to each unit?"

They got that settled, and the dragons followed the royals to the elevators with their cardkeys in hand. Ari showed them the units and made sure everyone was familiar with how the appliances and the air conditioning worked. She didn't know what they were used to overseas, or what that type of living was like.

"Did you bring luggage with you?" Sherm asked.

"We rented a room at a hotel and left everything there," Warman said.

"You walked from downtown?" Gage asked.

"Yes. We're used to walking," Eyo said.

"Why don't I take you back to the hotel and we can get you checked out," Lonnie said.

"Stop at the house when you're finished," Ari said. "Dinner should be ready by then."

The dragon men bowed to their queen.

Novi, Sopan and Inggit stayed behind in the apartments, while three male dragons accompanied Lonnie.

ARI STUDIED her spreadsheet of shifter service providers and made a phone call. "Butch? It's Ari Davis. Are you busy?"

They had a lively conversation, then got down to business. Ari detailed what needed to be done to the house in the woods. Butch agreed to meet her the next day at nine in the morning to assess the house and property.

Ari sent a message to her son, Jason, who handled many of the financial details for the Panther businesses. He would set up an account for the refurbishing of the dragons' house. She detailed what it needed—all the appliances, possibly plumbing and electric, the dilapidated porch, stairs and front door. Butch and Joe would also assess the condition of the roof. She would send Butch over to see Jason after he saw the place, so he could provide a preliminary budget until he could work up a bid.

She wondered how quickly the dragon women needed to build their nests. Maybe they could find locations that would not be near where contractors could stumble across them. Ari pressed a hand against her stomach. She knew how important it was to have everything arranged for birthing—even if it was laying eggs. Mothers had to be ready for everything.

Her own pregnancy was a big mystery. No one knew whether she would go full term like a human, or a shorter span because of her liger and her Tothar heritage. As she contemplated the issue, a tap sounded on the doorframe of her office and pulled her out of her daydreaming.

"Hi, Dad," she said, as she rose out of her chair.

Kenneth Porter entered the room as Ari came around her desk. They embraced.

"Every day I get to see you is a day to rejoice," Kenneth said.

Ari's eyes got misty. "Will you join us for dinner tonight?"

"Marcha said there were Komodo dragons here?" Kenneth asked, mystified.

"Six of them! You can meet them at dinner," Ari said. "They're beautiful people—very large, beautiful people."

"I'll be here!" he said. "Honey, I was unpacking some of my boxes and came across some of your mother's things, and paperwork." He mulled a bit before continuing. "There are documents I've never seen before. After she left, and I gave up on her ever returning, I packed everything away without going through the contents and making an inventory. I figured if she wanted out of our marriage that bad to not take these things with her, they must not be important."

They shared a look. It was a subject that brought out powerful emotions in each of them. Kenneth for being abandoned by his new young wife, and for Ari being isolated from her family on both sides, then not actually meeting her father until recently.

"What did you find? Something important?" Ari asked.

"You mother owned considerable property in Ireland," Kenneth said. "There's land, farms, even a village. I'm sure the family over there have been taking care of things in her absence. You're going to have to go there eventually and meet the clan and determine who owns what."

Ari thought things through. "Dad, as her husband, you should have claim to that before me."

"Let's go through all the paperwork, then we can have Roman and Gage take a look at it," he said.

"Good idea," Ari said.

DINNER WAS a lively affair with almost twenty people around the large dining room table. Ari's aunt Aileen helped Mr. Butler get the spread onto the table. Everyone realized Aileen and the butler were a couple. Ari thought it was only a matter of time before the housekeeper's apartment upstairs was vacant, and her aunt had a live-in partner at her house in the woods near Pablo's place.

"Mr. Butler, I think the time has arrived where you need to hire someone as kitchen help," Ari said.

"I'm helping him," Aileen said, with a little huff of exasperation.

Dirdjo cleared his throat softly to call attention to himself. "Inggit and I could help with whatever you require—we owned a restaurant back home."

Mr. Butler looked down to the other end of the table where the Indonesian man sat. "As you can tell, the family gatherings are quite large. I'll gladly accept your offer of help."

"Maybe at some time in the near future you will want to open a restaurant here in San Marcos," Gage said.

"We couldn't consider anything until after I lay my eggs, and they hatch," Inggit said.

"Oh, that reminds me," Ari said. "Tomorrow morning, Butch will be here to look at the house and see what it needs. I've had Jason set up an account for the work, and to check with the utility companies about service."

Roman nodded. "Butch has turned into quite a resource."

"I wish you would let us pay for any renovations," Warman said. "We have money to spare—we lived frugal lives back home."

Gage sat forward. "We appreciate that, but as your rulers, we have granted you asylum here on the property. We will look out for you and no one will ever hunt you again."

"This is sacred land," Eddie said, from her little table in the corner.

People waited for her to say more, but that was all she was contributing.

"What do you mean?" Sherm asked. "Sacred, how?"

Typical for Eddie, she shrugged.

The family stared at the little girl. They were used to these things popping up out of nowhere. The dragons weren't on board. They just looked confused.

Roman thought about how to explain the situation. "The

easiest way to explain our little girl's pronouncements is that we can't explain any of them. She's just got these gifts."

"She's psychic?" Novi asked.

"I don't think that's the right term," Aileen said. "I thought maybe prescient, but that doesn't seem to fit."

"She just knows things no one else knows," Gage said. "She told us that we were having twins, a boy and a girl, and sure enough, they showed up on the ultrasound."

Novi leaned forward toward the little table. She and Eddie made eye contact and smiled at each other. "I have these same little quirks."

The five other dragons nodded.

"She saved our townspeople from a tsunami," Warman said. "Novi got this little twitch, and we spread the alarm. Everyone got to higher ground. An hour later, there wasn't much left of the town."

All eyes were on the dark-haired, smiling dragon lady.

Novi's eyes darted over to Eddie. They shared another knowing smile.

"I don't want anyone mentioning Komodo dragons to anyone," Roman said. "They are here for asylum, and we will protect them." He turned to Ari. "Butch doesn't need to know someone will move into the house right away. He just needs to know we want it renovated."

Ari nodded. "That's a good idea. Shifters will just have to be curious about the scent they can't identify. I hope the OPERA people haven't told anyone!"

"If they have mentioned the Komodo's to anyone in our world, I'll make sure they contain it," Sherm said. Everyone knew how effective the wolverine shifter was with security. He worked his phone and sent messages to the OPERA team.

CHAPTER THREE

B utch arrived the next morning with Joe, one of his employees. Ari rounded up Pablo to drive them over to the house in the woods.

"Pablo, you can stay and wait for us, or I'll text you to come pick us up. It may be a while," Ari said.

"No problem. I'll inspect the surrounding property," Pablo said.

Ari, Butch, and Joe walked the rest of the way to the house.

Butch and Joe stood in front of the house and eyed it, taking it all in, assessing.

"Ari, we're going to have to rebuild the stairs, the entire porch and the doorframe," Butch said. He stepped onto the porch and looked up. He didn't see any rot, but he knew he'd have to poke around more. He tapped on a window.

"Single pane windows from the fifties or earlier," Butch said. "We should replace them to keep the house cool in the summer and warm in the winter."

Joe noted everything Butch mentioned on an iPad with an Apple pencil.

They entered the house and Ari flipped the light switches right inside the front door. It surprised her when a series of lights through the downstairs lit up. She didn't know how Jason managed to accomplish some of the things he did, but they seemed to happen in much less time than typical service requests. She wondered if he used a little shifter mental *persuasion.*

Butch measured the spaces where the appliances stood. They were ancient models from decades ago in the deplorable avocado green. "You might lose a cabinet or two to make room for newer appliances."

"Make sure we get Viking appliances," Ari said. "They're made in the United States."

"Do you like the cabinets?" Butch asked Ari. "They're solid wood."

She opened one of the cabinets and nodded. "Yeah, they're good looking and there's a lot of them. Is there enough room for an island, or would it crowd the kitchen?"

"There's more than enough room. Are you considering bar stools along one side?" he asked.

Ari nodded while she thought about it. "Thanks for asking. That would be nice. Also, that kitchen sink has to go. Put in a large-sized farmer's sink along with one of those all-in-one sprayer faucets that lifts."

Joe captured everything on the iPad. "Any preference on the sink size?"

"Yes. I want one that's big enough for a large frying pan to sit flat in the sink. I hate it when the sink won't accommodate a large pan!" Ari winked at Joe. "Good question."

They went through the house room by room, downstairs first, then they took the stairs to the second floor. Butch noted the need for a new water heater.

"We'll remove those old space heaters. Need to see if

there's a propane tank buried somewhere," Butch said. "Probably was removed, but if it's still underground, might need to dig that up and replace it for the gas stove and dryer. Do you want a gas starter for the fireplace?"

"Yes, include a gas starter," Ari said. "How will you find out if there's an old tank on the property?

"They have to be ten to twenty-five feet from the building," Joe said. "We'll start at the kitchen and work our way that distance from the house."

Ari let the men climb the narrow stairs up into the attic.

Butch determined there should be more venting and insulation in the attic to bring the temperature down, which would cool down the house in the blistering Texas summers, and hold the heat in the short winters.

"Ari, the old insulation needs to go," Butch reported.

Then they walked the outside. They added a new air conditioning system to the list, along with a gas-powered whole-house automatic generator. Texas storms had the tendency to shut down power.

"You have a water well. Do you want sprinklers for a portion of the yard?" Joe asked.

Ari looked around. There really wasn't a yard per se. It was all treed around the house with a dirt path. "I'll have Pablo tackle the yard."

She texted Pablo to come pick them up.

"You know, Ari, it might be cheaper to tear this down and rebuild," Butch said.

Ari shook her head. "No, it's a solid house, but no one's attended to it in decades. Pablo didn't even know it was here."

"We'll go talk with Jason to give him an idea about what's needed. I'll work up some numbers," Butch said.

They walked through the trees and met Pablo as he pulled the buggy into the small clearing.

SHERM AND LONNIE met with Acawarman, Eyo, and Sopan. They determined the Indonesians were a good fit for the security business from their background checks. Since half of the guys on Bruce's team stayed behind in Reading, Pennsylvania, where the original Panther Industries was located, the dragons showed up at the right time. Sherm wouldn't have to recruit outsiders and train new people. They would only have to learn Panther Industry rules and regulations, and get outfitted.

The biggest uniform Panther Security had was three sizes too small for the enormous dragons. Lonnie thought it had been a challenge when they outfitted Big Bear Muchisky, but the Indonesians were taller and bulkier. Sherm sent the dragon men and Jason to Mr. Patel, a tailor Marcha had suggested.

When they walked into the shop, the Indian tailor summed up the men in his head before they exchanged a greeting.

Jason plunked an average Panther uniform on the counter. "Hi. I'm Jason Davis with Panther..."

"Oh, yes. Miss Marcha called me," Mr. Patel said. "Let's start with you." He pointed to Warman. "If you could stand over here on the platform—you're very tall. I may need my stepping stool!"

After Mr. Patel finished measuring each of the men, he stepped behind the counter. "How many uniforms do you require?"

"A dozen each," Jason said. "Do you require a purchase order? Bill these to Panther Industries Security Division."

Mr. Patel stared at Jason for a long moment, then he recovered from hearing the number of uniforms. Eyes peeked thru the curtain divider that separated the work area from the customer area. The shifters caught whispers among the employees in the back.

One uniform is going to take several yards of material!

Did Pop measure elbow to wrist?

I hope we get the account for anything else they need. We could really use the money!

Jason noted the whispered conversation. He pulled out his business checkbook. "I'm sure it's going to take a lot of material to make these uniforms. Why don't I write you a check for two thousand dollars to cover the material you need, and you can bill us for the balance and labor?" He grabbed one of the tailor's business cards from the cardholder on the counter and wrote the check.

Mr. Patel stood stock still, stunned, while Jason finished writing the check, then slid it across the counter to the tailor.

"Thank you! When we have the first set completed for each man, I will call you to set up a time for a fitting," Mr. Patel said.

"Great," Jason said. He dug into his pocket and pulled out a business card and handed it to Mr. Patel. He heard a soft squeal from the back room.

He paid Pop for the material up front!

Wow! I wish all our customers were so considerate.

Jason and Mr. Patel shook hands. The dragons nodded to the tailor, then they all left the shop and got in the black Navigator.

Jason pulled his cellphone out and hooked it up to his Bluetooth on the dash. "Call Mom," he said. The car's Siri told him she would *call Mom*. The phone rang a couple of times, then Ari answered.

"Jason, is that you?"

"Hi, Mom, Listen, we just left the tailor's shop that Marcha referred us to. Mr. Patel's workers in the back of the shop—they might be his daughters, because I heard one call him Pop. I overheard them say that they hoped they got our account, because they could really use the money. Maybe you should send a blast out to the community?"

"Why don't we wait until he makes the first set of uniforms so we can see the quality of his work?" Ari said. "When he calls to schedule fittings, I'll go with you so I can see the place."

"Oh, okay. That's a better plan," Jason said. "I advanced the money for the material, because I know it's going to be expensive."

"That was wise. I'll bet it won't take long," Ari said.

Jason disconnected the call.

"You really go out of your way to help people in need," Eyo said.

Jason looked in the rearview mirror to where Eyo sat. "When my brother and I were little kids, we didn't have much. Mom didn't make a lot of money back then before she graduated from college and landed her first decent job. When I know someone is struggling, I try to find ways to help them without it seeming like charity."

NOVI AND INGGIT walked around the house in the woods, their circles widening.

"I like this area," Inggit said. "I will use this for my nest."

Novi nodded. "Yes, it looks like an excellent location." She moved on, intent on finding her perfect nesting place. After several minutes, she nodded, then rejoined Inggit at the front of the house.

"We should build our nests before the workers arrive," Inggit said.

Novi scoped out the nest locations in reference to the house and what she determined to be the extended construction area.

"We should have our mates guard the area while we shift and dig our nests."

Inggit's head bobbed in the Komodo dragon fashion. "That would be wise."

They walked through the woods toward the buildings.

GREG SARANTOPOULOS RANG THE DOORBELL, and didn't have to wait in the Texas heat and humidity very long.

Roman opened the door. "Hi Dr. Sarantopoulos. What brings you our way?" They shook hands.

"Call me Greg, please." He entered the house as Roman stepped aside. "I have some good news!"

Roman guided the doctor to the living room where most of the family relaxed and chatted. Ari and Gage were on their feet immediately. Eddie jumped off the sofa and rushed up to the doctor.

"You came to visit me!" Eddie squealed with glee.

"Hey, Eddie. Guess what?" Greg said.

Eddie shrugged. "I don't know!"

"Your favorite school has accepted your application. School starts in three weeks!" Greg said.

"Oh, that was quick," Ari said. She thought she'd have time to get used to the idea of her four-year-old attending a university.

"They didn't want her to consider any other school," Greg said.

Gage considered that "You're right. Eddie's going to be the youngest genius to attend their program. They would have been stupid not to act fast."

"Come sit down," Roman said.

"To give you a hint of how Eddie ranks in the IQ department, Ainan Celeste Cawley scored 263 back in 1999. William James Sidis scored 250-300 in 1898. Albert Einstein scored 160-190, and Stephen Hawking scored 160-170," Greg said.

"What's my score?" Eddie asked, eyebrows raised.

Greg looked around the room, then settled his eyes back on Eddie. "You, young lady, scored 322!"

Gasps sounded around the room. Ari sank back into the sofa, disbelief etched across her face. "322? Are you sure?"

Greg nodded. "The dean of the McCombs Business School called me. He was practically salivating to have Eddie in his program. He'd like to meet her before she starts her classes."

Ari stared at the psychiatrist a moment. "Should I make an appointment with his office before classes begin, or do we just drop in on her first day?"

"Call and make an appointment," Greg said. He opened contacts on his phone and gave her the dean's name and phone number. "So, Eddie, are you going to wear orange on your first day?"

"Don't be silly," she said. Her face lit up. "I'll wear red and yellow. Those two colors make orange!"

THE HUGE MALE dragon men stood guard, arms crossed at their expansive chests, as Novi and Inggit, in their animal forms, dug their deep nests into the ground. The expressions on the males were enough to warn anyone off, but their physical heft would have anyone backing away, fearful for their lives.

"I'm going to explore." Warman stripped his clothes off, folded them and placed them on the ground on top of his shoes. He shifted from his amazing human form, one of sheer muscles which redefined the term *washboard abs*. The Komodo dragon scented the air, his forked tongue darting out of his mouth. He wanted to explore the area and determine if any threats existed. With the area being heavily treed, other animals could have nests or burrows close by. He wanted to determine if those neighbors were friends or foe.

As the ten-foot-long, three hundred fifty-pound dragon lumbered through the trees and foliage, a curious coyote, nose in the air, stepped out of the trees into Warman's path. The dragon hadn't been quiet by any means on his thick, short legs. He charged forward with no warning. The coyote jumped, startled, then raced through the trees, not even sure what was chasing him.

While Komodo dragons can clock twelve-miles per hour, coyotes are a lot faster hitting thirty-five to over forty-miles per hour. After several minutes of pursuit, Warman ended his chase and returned to the nesting area. He silently sent a message to his dragon brothers and sisters alerting them to the possible danger.

He shifted back to his human form and dressed. "Coyotes are too fast to pursue. All we can do is threaten them."

"That one most likely won't return," Sopan said.

"We need to read up on the wildlife here," Eyo said.

"Sherm can bring us up to speed," Dirdjo said. "He's a good source of information."

"You're right," Warman said. "We'll ask him to educate us about the area, and the State."

Off in the distance, they heard people talking.

"Sounds like the work is about to start on the house," Warman said. He judged the distance between the nests and the house. "The nests seem far enough away that none of those workers will be a threat."

"I'll guard the nests if you need to go to work now," Dirdjo said.

Novi, Inggit, are you deep into the ground? Warman sent through mind-talk.

I have completed my nest with two tunnels, Inggit sent.

Yes, I'm very deep, approximately six feet, Novi sent.

We are safe here. Go. There is no need to hover, Inggit sent.

The males nodded among themselves and walked toward the construction area.

"Let's check in with Sherm and Lonnie," Warman said. "Dirdjo, ask Mr. Butler if he needs help with meal prep."

As they approached their house, workers stopped and stared at the four enormous men. Luckily, Ari was at the site talking with Butch and Joe. She noticed the reaction the construction crew had to the approaching dragon men.

"Listen up, everyone," Ari called out. "This is Warman, Dirdjo, Eyo and Sopan. They work for Panther Security. They walk the area to make sure we remain safe."

She heard some breaths released. Then everyone went about their business.

"We saw a coyote nearby, but we don't think he'll pose any problem," Eyo said.

Ari understood his meaning and nodded.

The dragons walked through the woods toward the office building and the main house.

CHAPTER FOUR

Eddie squirmed near the front door of the house as Gage adjusted her backpack. Roman, Ari, Sherm and Phoebe hovered around the four-year-old as they prepared her for the first day of school. They were still shocked that their imp was heading off to university. She had skipped all traditional schooling: pre-K, kindergarten, elementary, middle, high school and undergraduate.

"Stop it!" Eddie said, wriggling out of Gage's grasp. "You're all acting like I'm going to the White House instead of school!"

"Honey, this IS a big deal," Ari said. "You won't be riding the bus like Jason and Kevin did when they started school. Your fathers and I have a lot of adjusting to do."

"You're not all riding to school with me, are you?" Eddie grilled them with a glare.

Gage opened the front door. Warman stood beside the BMW SUV in one of his new Panther uniforms. A holstered Glock 19 under his jacket at the left shoulder produced a slight bulge. An added deterrent to his immense size.

"No, you and Phoebe are riding with Warman. He'll be in all your classes with you to keep you safe," Ari said.

Eddie eyeballed her, then her dads and Sherm. "Phoebe is a Pitbull. She can take care of me!" She stamped her foot.

"Don't argue with us, Eddie. Warman will accompany you everywhere except to the bathroom," Roman said. "There's a lot of threats on a large campus. Remember, we are very wealthy. That alone makes us targets for bad people."

Sherm kneeled in front of Eddie. "Listen to reason. Phoebe can't shift in public to protect you. Warman doesn't need to shift. No one will threaten you with him around."

Eddie's face relaxed as she thought about what he said. "Oh, okay. That makes sense." With that, she got into the back seat of the SUV and climbed into her child's seat.

Roman wondered how many college students arrived at their university riding in a child's car seat.

Phoebe winked at the group of stressed parents and Sherm, then climbed in after Eddie. Once everyone buckled in, Warman got behind the wheel and the SUV turned down the driveway with GPS directing him.

EDRIS DAVENPORT-DAVIS-STRYKER STOOD on the seat in the packed theater in her first class with Professor Akobar in the accounting regulation and liability class. Phoebe sat beside her, while Warman stood nearby in the shadows at the end of the row of seating.

The Komodo dragon's eyes surveyed the students. He located all exits and studied the stage where the professor stood in front of a wall-sized whiteboard.

The professor blathered on about fraud in the workplace, when Eddie raised her hand during his speech. The man looked irritated that (1) a child interrupted him, and (2) he couldn't believe a student would even consider bringing a child to his lecture.

"Yes, what is it?" he snapped out.

Eddie started to talk, but her little voice didn't project very well in the theater. So, she hopped down from her seat, and with Phoebe leading the way holding her hand, they threaded through the row of seated, snickering students. They quickly shut up as Warman glared at them as he brought up the rear.

They walked down the stairs of the theater seating, then up the stairs to the stage where the professor stood, fuming. His eyes took in the giant hulk of Warman, then settled on Phoebe. He figured she was a trust-fund baby who required security.

"I'm sorry, miss—but couldn't you find a babysitter for your child? I don't allow children in my lectures," he said.

Phoebe tried desperately hard to hide her smile, but just gave up. "I'm her nanny-slash-tutor. She's your student."

The professor stared at Phoebe as if she was crazy. Then he swung his focus down... way down to Eddie. "This little girl?"

"Didn't you read the email from the Dean?" Eddie asked. She harrumphed in irritation, hands on her tiny hips, as she looked up at the professor. She wasted no time at all in jumping to tell him she disagreed with what he said. She quoted the work of someone else.

All the students were on the edge of their seats, stunned with the little brainiac in their class. Lucky for them that the sound system captured the entire conversation of everyone on the stage.

The professor squatted in front of Eddie. "Did you verify the information and the source?"

"You can look it up on corporatefinanceinstitute dot com. Even Warren Buffett mentions it on his website," Eddie said.

The man stared at his pint-sized student. He wondered if there was anything at all he could teach her.

"You may have heard of my mother, Arianna Davis?" Eddie asked. "She's a forensic accountant with the nickname The Sifter."

"The Sifter is your mother?" Professor Akobar asked, shocked. He almost teetered on his butt as he recognized Ari's name. He knew her reputation well, and had studied some of her legendary forensic accounting coups, as she pointed the finger at thieves in corporations and governments. The case studies had been riveting.

"I can introduce you to her," Eddie said. "She'd be most interested in meeting you."

Professor Akobar's eyes widened as if someone presented him with an unexpected award. "That's very generous of you!" He cleared his throat. "I think it's time for me to continue with my lecture, don't you?"

Eddie beamed up a smile to the professor. She grabbed Phoebe's hand and met Warman's eyes; the three of them walked across the stage, down the stairs, then up the theater stage to their seats. Students stared, whispering about the youngest genius they would ever come across in their lifetimes.

At the end of the class, Warman held them back as the students piled out of the theater through the exits. When all was clear, the dragon indicated with a nod that they could leave.

"Let's find a bathroom," Phoebe said.

"There," Warman said, as he pointed at a sign.

They walked to the restroom and Warman stood opposite the door, his eyes alert. When Phoebe and Eddie exited the bathroom, they huddled.

"Your next class isn't until after lunch. Why don't we find a place to eat?" Phoebe said.

"Ask your phone where restaurants are," Eddie said.

Phoebe pulled up a browser and typed in restaurants. The location app found dozens of places close by. It was Austin, after all. "What type of food are you hungry for?"

"Let's have spaghetti and meatballs!" Eddie said.

"Italian it is," Phoebe said. She studied the restaurants listed and picked through the three Italian places. "Let's go to this one, we can walk there."

They headed out on foot and walked three blocks. The restaurant had outdoor seating in a fenced area that was only accessible through an interior door. Warman grabbed the door handle, and they stepped inside.

"Do you want to sit inside or outdoors?" Eddie asked.

"It's a nice day, why don't we sit outside?" Phoebe asked. She turned to Warman. "Is outside okay with you?"

He nodded. "It's very pleasant today."

Phoebe turned to the hostess. "Three for the patio."

The hostess grabbed a booster seat and led them through the restaurant to the door that opened to the patio. Once they were seated at a table by the fence under the colorful umbrella, the help staff brought water and a breadbasket filled with bread sticks. They presented Eddie with a child's placemat and crayons.

They perused the menu and made their choices. The waiter hurried over and took their orders.

Warman stood. "I'll be back in a moment. Be vigilant while I'm away." He went inside.

"Did you like your first class?" Phoebe asked.

"Professor Akobar was mad at first—he didn't like having a little kid in his class, but it turned out okay," Eddie said. "I hope I didn't hurt his feelings when I challenged him. He should have known about the information I found online."

Phoebe studied Eddie across the table from her. "He's probably teaching from the syllabus he created a while back that he hasn't updated."

Three guys ambled down the sidewalk on the other side of the fence, side-by-side. They forced all foot traffic to walk around them on the grass. They boasted loudly among themselves, laughing and jostling each other while making lewd comments to women who passed them by.

As they approached the fenced-in patio of lunch-goers, they spotted Phoebe. They steered over to the fence and ogled the brown-haired beauty.

"What say you get a babysitter and we go have a good time?" one of the guys said. A lit cigarette dangled from his lips and the smoke wafted toward the table.

Phoebe tried to ignore the men.

Eddie coughed, then waved her hand as the smoke was blowing her way. "You do realize that smoking cigarettes will kill you, right?"

One of the guys reached out and slid a stray wave behind Phoebe's ear.

Lightning fast, Phoebe grabbed the guy's hand in a crushing grip and yanked. "Don't you ever touch a woman uninvited!"

"I didn't mean to get you mad, Honey," the creep said. He rubbed his wrist when she let go of him. "Damn, you sure are strong."

Seconds later, the man was snatched up into the air, and his cigarette dropped to the sidewalk. Warman had the man's t-shirt fisted. The dragon hopped over the fence as if it were only a foot high instead of the actual six-foot.

The other two creeps stared up at the giant who had their buddy in his grip.

"Hey, man, no harm done," the guy squeaked out as he dangled in the air, arms flapping.

"You need a class in manners," Warman said. He pointed to Phoebe and Eddie. "Off limits. Understand?"

The guy nodded for several seconds.

"You ever disrespect a woman and I hear about it, your lesson learned will be tough—very tough. Understand that?" Warman warned.

His buddies backed off as Warman dropped the creep to the sidewalk. They rushed in and lifted their friend off the ground, then the three hurried down the sidewalk a bit and crossed the street.

Warman watched them leave, tracking where they disappeared to. He hopped back over the fence and returned to his chair.

The hostess hurried over to their table. "I'm so sorry they disturbed you. Is everything okay?"

"Not to worry," Phoebe said. "We're very good at taking care of ourselves."

The hostess glanced from Phoebe to Warman. "Yes, I saw that."

The door opened, and their waiter approached with their food.

"WE'RE HOME," Eddie called out as she rushed inside the house.

Ari came out of her office and scooped Eddie up into a big hug. Roman and Gage joined in the hug-fest. Aileen and Mr. Butler came out of the kitchen to join them.

"You're smothering me!" Eddie squealed with delight.

"Did you like your first day?" Ari asked.

Roman switched his eyes over to Phoebe. "Any problems?"

"Did you make any friends?" Gage asked.

The front door opened, and Sherm rushed inside. "Hey, munchkin, how'd it go?"

"Warman is like *The Hulk!*" Eddie said.

"Uh-oh, what happened?" Aileen asked.

They all drifted into the living room and the story unfolded.

"Can I go outside and play?" Eddie asked.

"For a little while. Supper will be ready in an hour," Ari said.

Eddie zipped off the sofa and scooted out the door.

All eyes swung over to Phoebe.

"Don't worry, she handled herself well in the classes. Professor Akobar is most likely having a stiff shot right about now, though. He didn't read the dean's memo, and he was rude at first, but Eddie eased him over to her side," Phoebe said.

"The rest of her teachers were okay with her in their class?" Gage asked. He fumed over Professor Akobar's attitude.

"Evidently, the other professors got the memo. I noticed several of them searching the class for her. Not everyone was happy to see Warman close by, but they understood that he was part of the deal," Phoebe said.

"I'm glad we sent him," Roman said. "I would have ripped into those punks a hell of a lot more than he did."

"I made strawberry shortcake for dessert," Mr. Butler said. "I figured Eddie deserved a treat after her first day at university." He shook his head. "Four-years-old and way over my head in the brains department."

"I'm just worried that people will gawk at her and she'll feel uncomfortable," Ari said. "Those college students are more respectful than high school kids, but they could still make her feel like a freak."

"She's going to be okay," Aileen said, as she one-arm hugged her niece. "Remember, while Eddie's small and only four, she's also smart enough to understand her situation and deal with it."

The front door opened and closed. Jason and Kevin tromped into the room.

"We saw Eddie outside playing hopscotch," Jason said. "She doesn't seem phased at her first day at college."

Kevin flopped down onto a sofa. "She's a little kid. They adapt."

Sherm held his arm out to Kevin. "See, Kevin has the right idea." He got up. "Gotta go. Have some coordinating to do."

CHAPTER FIVE

S ometime during the night, Ari got up. She was uncomfortable and couldn't drop off into a deep sleep. She paced around the sitting room, then retrieved her robe and slippers and quietly opened the door. She slipped out of the bedroom and made her way to the kitchen. She opened the refrigerator and perused its contents. Nothing looked appealing.

Ari went through the living room to the French doors that opened to the covered summer kitchen and the pool area. She walked around the pool, flopped down on a lounge chair with her arms and legs akimbo. She felt a twinge in her belly and pressed her hands to her stomach, smiling.

After a minute she got back up again. She just couldn't get comfortable anywhere. She stripped off her robe, slippers and gown, then walked down the stairs into the pool. The water was like a warm bath. She floated on her back for a minute, then swam to the center and back.

Maybe I need more exercise, she thought.

She swam from the middle to the deep end and back again.

Then she held onto the edge of the pool and kicked her legs underwater. She got bored with that, swam some more, then left the pool. She shifted into her liger, walked over to the grass and sprawled out on the ground. She rolled onto her back and wiggled her body, scratching herself.

After several minutes she got up and trotted off, away from the house. She ran where she could, but her size kept her in check. Soon, she found herself at the dragon's future house. It was still a work in progress, but almost ready for them to move in. As she walked around the house and the area, one of the female Komodo dragons charged her.

Ari jumped back. *It's Ari. Are you Novi or Inggit?*

The female dragon stopped and lowered her head. *I'm so sorry, my queen. Please forgive me. Inggit and I have to protect our eggs.*

I understand, Ari sent. *I couldn't sleep. No one knows whether this is a human or an animal pregnancy, so I could go the full nine months, or have a shorter pregnancy.*

Oh no! I hope it's short, Novi said.

I need to run off some of this energy, Ari said. *I'm going to search for an open field.*

That may not be safe. Someone could see you and call the authorities, Novi warned.

Oh! With my pregnant brain, I didn't think about that. I guess I'd better return to the house.

The animals nodded to each other, then Ari disappeared through the trees.

ARI FLOPPED BACK onto the grass by the pool, but didn't stretch out. She perused the area surrounding the house for any abnormalities. Everything was quiet and calm. One of the

French doors off the living room opened and Roman and Gage stumbled outside. They looked around, then spotted Ari's liger.

They headed over to her, waking up as they walked.

"Are you okay?" Gage asked.

Yes, just restless.

"Do you need something to eat?" Roman asked.

I looked in the refrigerator earlier, but nothing called to me.

They dropped to the grass on either side of the largest cat in the world. When Roman shifted to his panther and stood beside Ari in her liger form, he looked like he could be one of her kittens.

"I can make you a hot fudge sundae," Roman said. "Mr. Butler made the fudge sauce from scratch. All I need to do is heat it up a little and pour it over ice cream."

Ari stared at him, thinking about it. *Okay. I'll shift and you can make me a sundae. No skimping on nuts or cherries!* She stood and shifted back to her human form.

Gage snatched up her clothes from the lounge chair and handed them to her, while Roman launched into the house. The kitchen light came on.

Ari dressed swiftly. She and Gage went into the house and watched Roman making three sundaes. He didn't skimp on the ice cream. The microwave dinged the last ingredient. Roman grabbed pot holders and carefully lifted the glass canning jar of hot fudge out of the microwave.

He found the scoop Mr. Butler used for the fudge, then he poured dollops over the ice cream in all three bowls, then topped each off with sprinkled nuts and maraschino cherries. He pulled out spoons and slid the biggest bowl across the counter to Ari. Roman passed Gage his bowl and spoon, then he joined them on the barstool to Ari's left.

It was quiet but for a few moans and groans as everyone enjoyed the sundaes. After spoons clattered into empty bowls,

Gage grabbed up the dishes and rinsed them off and stacked them in the dishwasher.

"Think you can sleep now?" Roman asked.

"Maybe," Ari said. She placed a hand on her belly. "I'm not even showing yet. I don't know why I'm so restless. If this is the way it's going to be, this will be a long pregnancy."

"We'll help you in any way possible. You just have to tell us what you need, no matter how bizarre you think it sounds," Gage said. He wiped his hands on the dishtowel that hung on the cabinet in front of the sink.

"Let's go to bed. There's too much to think about," Ari said.

They left the kitchen. Roman turned off the light, and they went to the master bedroom, grateful for their excellent night vision.

INTO EDDIE'S third week of school, Professor Akobar became ill, and Graham, one of his assistants, took over the class in his absence. After two days, Graham called Eddie aside and showed her an email from the professor. He requested that Eddie assist with one class. He wanted her to present the case her mother solved where she earned her nickname, and to provide the class with Ari's background and her process.

Eddie squealed in delight. "My mother is going to be so excited! My entire family will want to come to class!"

"How about if we record it?" Graham said. "The class is filled to capacity this semester."

"Let's film it," Phoebe said. "Then we can show it in the movie theater at home."

Graham gawked. "You have a movie theater in your house?"

"It's a media room," Eddie said. "Not a real movie theater."

"To me, it's a small theater. Your great uncle thought of everything," Phoebe said, then she turned to Graham. "There's comfortable seating, a popcorn machine, drink machine, and the wall is lined with shelves of DVDs."

"How long do I have to prepare?" Eddie asked.

"Can you take next Tuesday's class?" Graham asked.

"Oh, sure. I'll interview my mother tonight or tomorrow, depending on her schedule," Eddie said.

Graham stared at the four-year-old, trying to control his awe. He couldn't wait to attend her class.

"Let's go get some Tex-Mex food," Phoebe said. "We have two hours until your next class."

EDDIE'S FEET dangled from the chair in Ari's office as she watched her mother gather files and copy them to a memory stick.

"How much of this spreadsheet do you want to use?" Ari asked.

"I'll take it all and set it to scroll so the students can see how enormous your audit was," Eddie said.

"Are you nervous about teaching the class?" Ari asked.

Eddie shook her head. "It'll be a good experience. I don't think I'll have stage fright."

Ari swooped in and crushed Eddie in a hug. "Your birth mother would be so proud of you, honey. Your fathers and I are proud of you. Sherm is over the top happy for you."

"I can't wait for my brother and sister to be born," Eddie said, smushed against Ari.

"I think it's going to be awhile yet," Ari said.

They separated out of the hug.

"I'd better go and prepare for my class," Eddie said, as she slipped out of her chair.

Ari ejected the memory stick out of the USB port and handed it to Eddie.

PHOEBE AND EDDIE sat on the grass drinking milkshakes, while Warman leaned against an old oak tree sucking down a coffee shake. Two young men in their early twenties walked across campus, their eyes focused on them.

Warman became alert as he listened to their low verbal conversation, which no human could have ever made out because of the distance.

"There she is!" one of the men said.

"Someone said they're billionaires," the other one said. "We have to capitalize on this situation."

"We need a good, solid plan," the first one said.

"I don't like what I'm hearing," Phoebe said. She glanced over to the dragon, but he was already sprinting toward the two men. They didn't realize they were targets until he was practically in their faces.

Warman pounded a finger in the first guy's chest, knocking him back a little way. "Don't even think about making any plans regarding that child or the family," Warman jerked his head in Eddie and Phoebe's direction.

The guy stammered. "What are you talking about, man? We were minding our own business..."

"I read lips," Warman said. "I distinctly heard what you said."

Saw! You couldn't have heard anything at that distance, Phoebe sent.

"Excuse me, I meant I saw what you said. Lips don't lie," Warman said. "If I see you two lurking around watching Eddie ever again, you'll deal with me and I can't guarantee your safety."

The two men held up their hands in a surrender gesture, backed away, turned and ran full out as Warman watched their retreat. He returned to where Eddie and Phoebe were. He noticed that Eddie was a bit unsettled.

"Don't worry. Nothing will ever happen to you while I'm on duty," the dragon said.

"My daddies warned me about bad people wanting to hurt us for our money," Eddie said. "I didn't really believe them until now."

Phoebe took Eddie's hand. "Come on, let's go inside and prepare for your presentation. Do you still want to teach this class, or should we go home?"

"Yes! People are counting on me. I can't let Professor Akobar or Graham down," Eddie said.

They walked across the grass to the building and went inside. Warman scrutinized the area every step of the way. About a dozen people were already in the theater classroom. Graham was on the stage at the podium where a laptop sat.

"I've queued up your slide presentation, Eddie," Graham said.

Eddie and Phoebe climbed the stairs to the stage, while Warman walked to the shadows on the right side of the theater-style classroom.

"Here's the remote for the slides," he said. "Why don't you try it out?" He showed her the remote. "You can pause, go back, move forward, or choose something from the thumbnails."

Eddie took the remote and pressed a button. She looked at the screen as she practiced. "Okay, I should be okay. If you notice I'm talking about something that isn't on the screen, let me know so I can get back on track."

"Okay," Graham said.

"I'm going to set up a video camera on the table in this center aisle to record you, but I'm also going to get shots of you from different angles," Phoebe said. She left the stage, walked over to the table and eased out of her backpack. She pulled out a video camera and a mini tripod. She unfolded the tripod and set it up as students piled into the theater.

Once she had the camera mounted on the tripod, she tested the recording function on the camera. "All set up here," she called out to Eddie and Graham on the stage.

Graham checked his watch. Class was scheduled to begin in three minutes. He clipped a microphone to Eddie's shirt. "You can mute yourself by pressing this once. Press it again and you're live. Right now, you're muted. When we start, press the button so you're live."

"Okay," Eddie said.

The assistant looked her square in the eyes. "You nervous?"

Eddie shook her head. "Nah, I'm okay."

Graham's eyes swept over the theater. All available seats were filled, and people were standing against the walls. He noticed several professors in the crowd. "I'll briefly introduce you, then let you take over," he said.

Eddie gave him the thumbs up sign. She walked over to the edge of the stage, sat, and dangled her legs and feet over the threshold.

Graham stood at the podium. "Welcome to Professor Akobar's class. As you know, the professor has been on sick leave for the past several days with a raging case of strep throat. He's asked his youngest student to take his place today. I'm proud to introduce Edris Davenport-Davis-Stryker, who goes by the nickname Eddie."

"She's the youngest genius and has the highest score of any known test results. With an IQ of 322, Eddie skipped all early schooling, including undergraduate work, and is currently working on a PhD. Please hold your comments and questions until the end of the program."

Eddie wasted no time in beginning her talk. She never once glanced at the screen on the wall behind her. She talked and clicked. The theater was so quiet you could hear cellphone cameras clicking pictures throughout the theater seating. When she finished her presentation ninety minutes later, it was still quiet.

"Does anyone have any questions?" she asked.

A college student sprang to his feet. "How did you do that? You never looked at the screen. How did you know you were on the right slide?"

"I timed my talk with the number of screens, so all I had to do was click the slide forward when the subject matter changed," she explained.

The student's friend grabbed his t-shirt and pulled him back to his seat.

"What was your mother's nickname again?" someone else asked.

"The Sifter," Eddie said.

"Why did they call her that?" that student asked.

"Because she sifted through tens of thousands of line-items of information and documents, noticing a pattern that the Feds' top people missed. She succeeded where others failed," Eddie explained.

The questions continued for twenty minutes, then Graham took to the stage and called the end of the class.

Eddie scooted back from the edge of the stage and stood. Graham retrieved the microphone that was clipped to her shirt.

"That went very well, Eddie," he said. "I learned a lot about the process your mother used. She's one smart woman."

Phoebe packed up her camera equipment and Warman stepped out of the shadows. He approached Phoebe.

"There were some government people here. I don't like it, and I'll talk to Roman, Gage and Sherm when we get back to the house," the dragon said.

"Government people? Why would they be interested in Eddie's talk? They know all about Ari," Phoebe said.

The three of them left the building and walked to the SUV and headed home. Warman kept his senses alert until he drove up the long, treed driveway in San Marcos.

They piled out of the car as the front door opened. Ari, Roman and Gage followed by Aileen and Mr. Butler swarmed the trio. Sherm, Lonnie, Kevin and Jason followed by Kenneth and Melly, headed over from the office building.

"Well? How did it go?" Ari asked.

"Were there a lot of interruptions with questions?" Gage asked.

"Did your slide pack work okay?" Roman asked.

"Hey, squirt, did anyone make fun of you?" Kevin asked.

Eddie huffed. "Will you all stop asking silly questions? The theater was packed. Graham asked that questions be held until the end of my presentation. Everyone was extremely interested in your process, Mommy. Warman said there were some government guys there."

All eyes swung over to the large dragon guard.

"Did you pick up on who they were or what they wanted?" Roman asked.

Warman shook his head. "Their thoughts were focused on what they were hearing."

Sherm quirked his head. "I don't recognize any of them from your mind pictures."

"Sure would be nice to know their agenda," Lonnie said.

"Why don't we ask Greg and Amy over for dinner, then we can watch the recording?" Gage asked.

"Oh, good idea," Ari said. "Mr. Butler, I'll let you know if they're available."

They all moved in a group toward the house and the front door, then Lonnie, Kevin, Melly and Jason veered toward the office building.

"See you later, Mom," Kevin yelled.

Warman drove the SUV over to the garage and housed it.

DINNER WAS a lively affair in the big dining room. Greg Sarantopoulos and Amy Sterling didn't hide the fact that they were romantically involved. Kenneth openly flirted with Phoebe, which raised Ari's brows.

Looks like your father and Phoebe are interested in each other, Gage sent privately to Ari and Roman.

I thought he was interested in Marcha, Roman sent. *Maybe's he the type that flirts? We don't know him that well.*

I don't want Phoebe getting hurt, Ari sent.

Honey, we don't have any control over people's emotions and their choices, Gage sent.

Ari harrumphed, which raised a few brows. It was obvious to the shifters around the table that a private conversation was underway. The humans, on the other hand, didn't have a clue.

Mr. Tran was having a lively conversation with Janina and Jason about herbal remedies.

Roman's phone dinged a message. He pulled it out of his pocket and read the screen. "Leander and Trisha just arrived at the Hilton hotel. Should I invite them over, or will they be too tired?"

"Invite them for lunch tomorrow," Ari said. "They've been on the road for two days straight. They're most likely stiff and road weary."

Roman sent a message to Leander. He replied that they

were going to get something to eat, then crash. He'd check in with Roman in the morning.

Dirdjo and Mr. Butler had prepared osso buco, which turned out to be a huge hit with everyone.

"What is this again?" Amy asked.

"It's an Italian dish," Mr. Butler said. "It means bone with hole."

"This is the modern version," Dirdjo said. "The older version did not use tomato paste."

"I love it," Amy said, as she chose another piece of the pork from the platter in the middle of the table. Then she ladled sauce on top of the meat.

"Who's Leander and Trisha?" Aileen asked.

Roman set his fork on his plate. "I can't wait for all of you to meet them. Leander is a king cobra, and Trisha is a cougar."

"A cobra?" Mr. Butler asked, somewhat startled.

"How big is he," Greg asked.

Roman and Sherm shared a guessing look.

"He's got to be eighteen feet long, don't you think, Roman?" Sherm asked. "He's much scarier than Big Bear Muchisky, or Larry, the Kodiak."

Janina was wide-eyed. "I've never seen a king cobra before."

"His human counterpart is a shoe salesman," Roman said.

"He owns a thriving shoe store in Reading, and he's going to open a store in San Marcos," Ari said. "He's much more than a salesperson, but you'd never suspect that this mild-mannered man was a king cobra."

Ari looked over to her son. "Where's your brother?"

"He and Lonnie are doing something," Jason said with a shrug.

"Lonnie's not with Melly tonight? That's surprising," Ari said.

CHAPTER SIX

Phoebe pulled the memory stick out of the camera and inserted it into the USB port on the DVD player in the media room. Eddie sat on Ari's lap. All the seats were filled and everyone waited for the show to begin.

"Who wants the remote?" Phoebe asked. She looked from Roman, Gage, Ari and Eddie.

Gage stood. "Give it here. Everyone ready, or does someone want popcorn?"

"Ooh, popcorn," Amy said.

Greg stood and walked over to the popcorn machine, "How does this work?"

Sherm joined him at the machine and walked him through the process. He turned the heat and light switch on.

"It's going to take three or four minutes for the kettle to heat up," Sherm said.

He turned the kettle motor switch on, then opened an oil pouch and poured it into the kettle. Then he snagged one package of popcorn and added it. He turned to Greg. "This next step is very important. Close the lid. If you don't, oil and popcorn will spray all over the place."

"Sounds like personal experience to me," Greg said with a chuckle.

After a few minutes, the popcorn started popping and the media room filled with the delicious aroma of movie-theater popcorn. Sherm served bags of popcorn to everyone who wanted one, then people settled into their chairs.

"Are we ready to begin?" Gage asked.

"Yes," Jason said. "We've got movie popcorn. Start the show."

Gage pressed Play, then sat. Ari handed him his popcorn, and they watched the presentation. Phoebe had started the recording as soon as she set the camera on the tripod. The clarity was excellent, and the sound was good. They watched Eddie walk to the edge of the stage and sit while students filled the seats, then Graham introduced her.

Everyone sat in stunned silence while Eddie went through her slide pack. She talked about charts, graphs, spreadsheets, even specific line items, and she never looked at the screen in back of her. When the presentation was over, Phoebe removed the camera from the tripod to capture the Q&A. The theater was packed full. Some students sat on the stairs or leaned against the wall. They saw a few professor types among the large group.

"Stop!" Roman said. "Phoebe, where are those government agents you mentioned?"

Phoebe took back the remote and backed up the recording a tiny bit, then pressed pause. "Right there, in that corner."

Roman, Gage, and Sherm stood to get a better look.

Sherm shook his head. "I don't know any of those people."

Everyone sat in stunned silence for a long moment while they thought about what they had watched.

"Honey, that was quite a..." Gage was at a loss for words.

"Performance," Roman picked up. "Did you memorize all that information? You never looked at what was showing on the screen."

"I counted my lines to the slides," Eddie said.

"I'm borrowing your daughter," Greg said. "We're going to Vegas!"

"No kidding," Jason said.

"That pretty much summed up the whole process I went through," Ari said. "You did a great job in translating what we talked about. I'll bet Professor Akobar gets lots of requests for you to speak again."

"Should you send a copy to him?" Phoebe asked.

"Eddie, ask Graham if he'd like to send the presentation to Professor Akobar," Ari said. "I'd bet he'd like to see you in action."

Roman stood. "Everyone ready for a drink?"

They all filed out of the media room to the living room. Sherm and Jason manned the bar while everyone got comfortable.

"I overestimated the time for Eddie to get her PhD," Greg said. He turned to Eddie. "If you look over everything your proctor gave you and organize your schedule, you should be able to cut the time in half."

Eddie sat on the floor near her parents. "I'm almost finished."

"How could you be almost finished? You just started," Sherm said, barely controlling his shocked expression.

Eddie shrugged. "It's easy."

Phoebe shrugged when everyone looked to her for an explanation. "She should be finished with the coursework and her dissertation proposal within the next six to eight weeks."

"Can I go play now?" Eddie asked.

"Yes. You don't have to hang around us old people," Gage said.

"Can I see if Cassie and Kylie can come over?" Eddie asked.

"Sure," Gage said, eyeing Ari and Roman. They nodded their okays.

Eddie hopped off the floor and pulled Phoebe to her feet. "Can you call them?"

"Let's go outside," Phoebe said, as she pulled her phone out of her pocket.

When the front door shut behind them, everyone left in the living room looked at each other.

"You have quite a remarkable child on your hands," Kenneth said.

"We need to find her birth mother's family," Ari said. "I'm pretty sure this intelligence didn't come from her father."

"Maybe we need to haul him in and find out what he knows about Eddie's mother's family," Sherm said. "We're still monitoring all those banished shifters. Travis can get a bead on him."

Mr. Tran cleared his throat. "I am excellent at genealogy. Why don't you give me what you have and I'll see what I can find? The databases that are available now have most of the birth and death records online."

Ari nodded. "That's an excellent idea. I'll send you what information we have about her birth mother and her father, but it isn't much."

CASSIE AND KYLIE both squealed as they got out of Cassie's mother's car and ran over to Eddie, who met them halfway. All three girls grabbed each other's hands and jumped in a circle, squealing in delight at seeing each other.

Cassie's mother waved out the window. "I'll be back in an hour and a half. I'm going to the grocery store."

"No hurry," Phoebe called out.

"Do you want to swing?" Eddie asked.

"Yes!" Kylie said. "We can swing and catch up."

They ran over to the swings hanging from the huge oak branches, and started swinging,

"Did you start school?" Cassie asked Eddie.

"Yes, my school is way up in Austin," Eddie said.

"Wow, that's a long drive. We go to school in San Marcos," Kylie said.

"Do you have show and tell at your school?" Cassie asked.

"Yes! I had show and tell today!" Eddie said.

"What did you talk about?" Cassie asked.

"My mother's work," Eddie said. "Everyone liked my presentation."

"Oh, that's good! Did your teacher give you a prize?" Kylie asked.

"No, my teacher is out sick. We had a substitute," Eddie said.

Phoebe sat on a bench nearby, listening to the conversation. She didn't know how Eddie managed to fit herself into conversations that were, for sure, far beneath her intelligence level. But she did, and it was amazing to hear her responses and questions. She was happy that her young charge still played like a child and was still happy to be with her girlfriends.

After five minutes of swinging, they played hopscotch. Then they ran inside the house to Eddie's room to play with her toys.

The adults in the living room watched the girls thundering down the hallway.

"It's amazing to see your daughter playing with these little girls," Greg said.

"I'm grateful that she's not going to miss out on all of her childhood and being a little girl," Ari said. "Who knows what's going through her head while she plays with her friends."

"Has she had any problems at school?" Amy asked. "I hope people are treating her okay, and not like a celebrity."

Phoebe slipped into a chair. "For the most part, people are in awe of her. They have asked her so many questions and she's so patient explaining her answers. I think sometimes it takes an effort for her to put her thoughts into words and expressions others can understand."

Greg rubbed his chin for a moment, lost in thought. Amy watched him.

"What are you thinking?" Amy asked. She recognized the rubbing of his chin as one of his thought processes.

"It would be an interesting project if I were to document Eddie's progress," Greg said. "I'm so thankful you contacted my office for that first appointment."

"Butch told Ari about you," Roman said.

"Now there's a mess I saved from a big problem!" Greg said. "I really shouldn't say anything, but you probably know his background already from talking with him."

"Butch is a great resource because of what he endured until you helped him through it," Ari said.

"Quite frankly, I'm shocked at what the human medical professionals overlook most of the time," Amy said. "I believe Butch could have been diagnosed correctly years earlier, but there are some lazy doctors out there."

Greg harrumphed. "It's not just the humans. There's plenty of shifter doctors who don't want to diagnose. They only want to push prescriptions. They've lost their way and don't even believe in the code they swore an oath to."

Sherm didn't let the left turn in the conversation steer him off what Greg had said earlier. "What progress would you document? Are you going to write a book about Eddie?"

He could see from everyone's expressions that they switched back over to that dialog.

"You have to admit that she's a conundrum," Greg said. "She's the smartest person walking the Earth, as far as I know, but she's balancing between two worlds. That of a physical four-year-old child, and a walking, talking brainiac. It's a shame Stephen Hawking didn't get a chance to meet her. Think about how that conversation could have gone."

"It would be a good idea to document her progress," Gage said, as he looked at his life partners for a read on their feelings.

"I'd agree to this as long as we got a first look before anything was published," Roman said.

Ari was on the fence. "I don't want people to point fingers at her. She needs to have as much of a normal life as possible. Publishing would mean the media hounding her and us."

Mr. Tran cleared his throat. The Asian man was so quiet most of the time, that when he interjected himself into a conversation, he had something important to contribute. "Your daughter is smart enough to let you know when things are getting too intense. And if she doesn't want to take part in something, she won't. You should realize that when she grows up and enters the puberty cycle, many things will change. How that affects her thinking process is a big question."

Ari, Roman, Gage and practically everyone in the room nodded in agreement with Mr. Tran.

The herbalist and historian glanced at the floor for a minute. "Something else to consider is that she may turn her back on all her intelligence to try to have a normal place in life."

Greg Sarantopoulos stared at the Asian man, considering that statement. "There is that possibility."

"What do you mean?" Kenneth asked—he looked confused.

"There are many people who have walked away from careers, family life—different situations they felt were destroying them," Mr. Tran said. "Eddie is no different. She's learning the ways of the world at an age where any other child would be only interested in cartoons and dolls."

EDDIE AND PHOEBE swung on the swings under the enormous old oak trees.

"Can we get a buggy and go see what they're doing to the dragons' house?" Eddie asked.

Phoebe dragged her foot along the ground to stop the swing. "That's a good idea. I'll bet they're finished with the renovations."

They stopped swinging and walked over to the building where the buggies were stored. The big garage door rolled up where several buggies were charging in their slots. Phoebe looked around, but didn't see anyone. She walked over to a two-passenger buggy and climbed in behind the wheel.

"Ready?" Phoebe asked.

"Yup!" Eddie said.

They rolled out of the garage. Phoebe pressed the fob on the key ring and the door slid down.

"Lead the way. I can't remember which direction the house is located," Phoebe said.

Eddie stuck out a finger. "Go that way, around the office building."

They had a pleasant drive through the woods, then the trail got very bumpy. When they were within walking distance, they heard a large mowing machine nearby. Phoebe parked the buggy, and they scooted out.

They walked through the trees and discovered Bem mowing an area in and around trees to make somewhat of a front yard for the dragons' house. He noticed them and slowed down the mower, then shut it off.

"Hello," Bem called out.

"Hello," Phoebe and Eddie said simultaneously.

"My name's Edris, but you can call me Eddie," she said.

Bem smiled. "Pablo told me about you. I'm Bem wo Taugh."

"This is Phoebe. She's my nanny-slash-tutor," Eddie said.

"Hi, Bem," Phoebe said.

"Is this what you do all day long?" Eddie asked.

"Sometimes. I have other odd jobs all over the county," Bem said. "Do you want to go for a ride on the mower?"

"Can I?" Eddie asked, all excited. She looked to Phoebe for permission.

Phoebe eyeballed the large commercial mower. "I don't know..."

"I'll go real slow," Bem said.

Eddie wailed out a *please*.

"Oh, okay," Phoebe said.

Eddie squealed in delight. She ran toward the mower.

Bem caught up with her. "You can sit beside me—there should be enough room since neither of us is plump."

Eddie giggled.

He lifted Eddie up to the seat, then climbed up after her and made sure she was secure in the big bench seat.

Phoebe watched as he explained all the controls. She chuckled as Eddie asked questions about how the equipment worked. She figured Bem would get an earful from the precocious four-year-old.

He started the mower and drove it very slowly through the trees and continued mowing down the tall grass. Phoebe's shifter hearing wasn't catching all the conversation over the loud noise of the equipment, so she gave up on trying to follow along. Several minutes later, Bem rolled the mower up to within ten feet of Phoebe and stopped.

Eddie climbed down and ran over to Phoebe's side. Bem waved with his hand in the air, then continued his job.

"Was that fun?" Phoebe asked.

"It's very noisy," Eddie said. "Do you think Bem will go deaf from all that noise?"

Phoebe watched the mower make the rounds in and out of the trees. "No, look, he's wearing headphones."

"That's good!" Eddie said. She grabbed Phoebe's hand and guided her to the dragons' house. The first things they noticed, was the brand-new porch, stairs, front door and door frame. All the windows were new as well.

"They're going to love it here!" Eddie said.

CHAPTER SEVEN

Eddie sat in her booster chair and waited patiently for everyone to arrive so she could eat breakfast. Sherm slipped into his chair and dropped his napkin in his lap. He leaned his head toward Eddie and nodded to her place setting.

"You going to use that napkin, or wait until someone mentions it?" Sherm asked.

Eddie huffed out a sigh. "You're mentioning it, Sherm!" She grabbed the napkin and plopped it on her lap.

"Sounds like you may need to go back to bed and get up on the right side," he said.

Gage led Ari and Roman into the kitchen.

"Someone got up on the wrong side of the bed?" Gage asked.

"Don't stand too close or you might get bitten," Phoebe said, as she sat in her chair.

The breakfast attendees had shrunk considerably. Jason and Janina were experimenting in their own kitchen. Everyone in the rooms over the garage decided they would make use of their kitchen. Aileen was also absent. Kenneth entered from the front door.

"Sorry I'm late. Don't laugh, but I was watching a squirrel argument," Kenneth said. He sank into his chair.

"What were they arguing about?" Roman chided.

"Probably a bunch of nuts," Kenneth said.

"Oh, Dad, that's so lame," Ari said.

Mr. Butler brought a tray ladened with bowls of scrambled eggs, sausages with peppers and onions, and toast.

Roman sprang to his feet and grabbed bowls and set them on the table.

Gage went to the refrigerator and brought the orange juice pitcher to the table.

Sherm forked a sausage and dropped it on Eddie's plate, then cut it for her.

"Thank you! I was starving!" Eddie boasted. "Mr. Butler is the best cook!"

"Why thank you, Eddie," he said.

"Do you want any peppers and onions?" Ari asked.

Eddie nodded enthusiastically. "Yes! I want everything!"

They passed bowls around the table. Gage stood, reached across the table and poured juice into glasses. Roman and Mr. Butler brought prepared coffee cups to the table.

Roman looked around at everyone. "Is that it? Anyone need anything else?"

"This is perfect," Ari said. "Sit, let's eat."

It was quiet for several moments while people ate. Eddie hummed and swayed while eating.

"Are you happy, little girl?" Gage asked.

Eddie nodded while chewing a chunk of sausage. After she swallowed, she sipped her juice. "Did you know that Bem wo Taugh was a physicist?"

"The mower?" Roman asked.

"Yes," Eddie said. "He gave me a ride on the mower yesterday. I'm glad he wears headphones because it's very loud."

"Tell us about Bem," Ari said.

"He used to work for a large company a long, long, long time ago," Eddie explained. "He didn't like it because there were a lot of meetings and no time to do the actual work during the work week. He didn't want to spend his weekends catching up."

Gage stared at his daughter. "So, he dropped out? He mows for a living now?"

Eddie nodded again, shoveling eggs into her mouth.

"He's not the first person I've heard of who's left the corporate world," Roman said. "Do you remember Bobby Miller?" He looked to Gage for acknowledgment.

"Bobby Miller?" Then Gage had a moment of recollection. "Oh, I do remember him. He had a nervous breakdown from running that supply company of his. Didn't he walk away and start painting pictures?"

"Yup," Roman said. "His sons took over and suddenly experienced just how stressful it had been for their dad. They hired more help and monitored the people for signs of extreme stress. They didn't want anyone suing them, or dropping dead at their desks."

"Oh, that's awful," Ari said. "I've known people in my profession to change careers. It's difficult auditing a company when there are liars, thieves and hidden records to contend with."

"He loves mowing," Eddie said. "He said it's his Zen."

There was a knock on the front door. Mr. Butler got up and went to see who would come calling that early in the morning. He opened the door to Tommy Littlefield.

"I'm sorry to bother you, but would you have a stick of butter I can borrow?" Tommy asked.

"Of course," Mr. Butler said. "Come in."

Tommy followed Mr. Butler into the kitchen.

"Hi, Tommy," everyone chorused.

Mr. Butler went to the refrigerator and grabbed a stick of butter and handed it to Tommy.

"Looks like a butter emergency," Gage said.

Tommy blushed, as was his typical response. "We need rules for the kitchen and groceries."

"Rules for a bunch of bachelors?" Ari snorted. "Good luck with that."

"Lonnie said he's not chipping in because he spends most of his time at Melly's, but he steals things from the refrigerator and eats our snacks," Tommy complained.

"You guys are going to have to work that out," Sherm said. "I don't envy you. Roommates can be a problem if everyone doesn't pull their weight. Think how bad it might be if you had to pay rent and utilities. That's when you discover there's a deadbeat among you."

Eyes swung over to Sherm. He put down his toast and looked from Roman to Gage. "Remember years ago, when I had an apartment with some guys before I moved into the Panther building?"

Gage nodded. "Oh, yeah. I remember that time you had to borrow money from your mother to have your apartment unlocked. That guy Marlon didn't pay the rent, and the landlord changed the locks."

"He spent our rent money on drugs," Sherm said. "That's when Steve and I threw Marlon out. We split the bills between the two of us. We both wrote a check to the landlord, and we never had problems after that."

Sherm raised his eyebrows to Tommy. "Your fun's just starting, dude."

Tommy groaned. "Not something I needed to hear."

"Go get your breakfast made. Toughen up and tell Lonnie to keep out of the refrigerator and pantry, or you'll get locks for them," Ari said.

That seemed to appeal to Tommy. He left with new enthusiasm.

"Sounds like Lonnie and Melly are getting serious," Kenneth said.

Roman made a little snort noise. "I think they have assignations in the stairwell. Maybe we should get Do Not Disturb signs made for those doors."

Gage threw his head back and laughed. "Oh, that would be good."

Sherm did not join in the joking. "Sounds like I'm going to have to sit down with him..."

"You'll do no such thing," Ari said. "Let them have their fun. What harm is it doing? Is he still doing his work?"

"Yes, but..." Sherm said.

"No buts. Just let it be. We have to see where this is going," Ari said. "Remember, he was worried because he wasn't a shifter. It sounds like they are getting very serious. Give it time."

Eddie followed the conversation in silence. "Will their kids be shifters or humans?"

All eyes swung over to the munchkin, then they darted around the table.

"I'm not sure," Roman said. He looked at his life partners.

Gage shrugged. "Don't look to me for answers. I know less than you do on this subject."

"I would think it depends on who has the dominant genes, don't you think?" Mr. Butler asked.

Kenneth nodded. "That makes sense. I'm not sure how that's determined."

"I don't have any idea," Ari said. She rubbed her barely

rounded belly. "I'm still clueless about what type of delivery I'll be having, and if I'll be carrying these twins for the full nine months or less."

"Seven..." Gage said.

As everyone was finishing up, Mr. Butler started piling empty plates into a stack. "Don't forget that Leander and Trisha will be here for lunch." He glanced over to Eddie and winked. "And we'll have a very special desert to celebrate their arrival."

"I hope they hurry up and get here!" Eddie said.

"You just had breakfast, don't expect desert the minute they show up," Roman said.

She put her tiny hands on her hips. "I know!" She scooted out of her chair and marched out of the room.

"I sure hope her attitude improves," Gage said. He turned to Phoebe. "Does she get this way often?"

"She has her moments. Don't laugh, but I think sometimes she resents her age. She wants to be twenty or thirty years older, because her brain doesn't fit with being in this child's body," Phoebe said. "It's basically what we talked about last night when she was playing with her girlfriends."

Mr. Butler brought the stack of plates to the kitchen sink. He had plenty of help. Gage gathered the silverware, Roman grabbed some empty juice glasses, Kenneth grabbed the remaining glasses, and Sherm just sat there drinking his coffee.

When Sherm finished the last drop of his breakfast blend coffee, he stood and started gathering empty cups. He left Roman and Gage's cups because he figured they'd get seconds. Sherm carried the cups to the counter.

Ari prodded him in the side after he set them on the counter. "Don't forget, do not take any action with Lonnie. If he's being productive, let this—whatever *this* is—play its way out, or through."

"I promise, *Mom*," Sherm said, as he scooted out of her reach.

They heard a car horn toot in the driveway. Everyone wandered to the front door, Mr. Butler pulling up the rear. Roman opened the door just as Cama stepped out of her VW Thing hippy car.

They all stepped out of the house and greeted the human herbalist.

"Hi, Cama!" Roman said.

There was a chorus of hellos.

Cama waved one swipe of her hand at the group.

Ari noticed Cama did not seem her exuberant self. "Are you okay?"

"I came to warn you. Burke Dudley, a human who has a vegetable farm southwest of here, was run down. Not sure he's going to make it," Cama said.

"Is he the one who has the vegetable stands alongside the road?" Ari asked.

Cama nodded. "I can't think of why anyone would want to harm that man. He's the kindest person, always giving away food to people in need."

"What happened?" Sherm asked. He sent a mental call-out to his team. Within a few minutes, Kevin, Tommy, Lonnie, Travis, Big Bear, Bruce, Doug and the OPERA team trotted from the office building, along with the huge dragon males.

Pablo saw everyone rushing toward the house. He put the buggy in high gear and followed them, stopped and got out of the golf cart. "What happened?"

Cama waited for everyone to arrive. She did a doubletake when she saw the dragons, but said nothing. "Someone in a pickup truck ran down Burke Dudley early this morning. He was setting up his vegetable stand, and a truck swerved and plowed through the stands. Knocked Burke into the air. His wife and daughter are traumatized from witnessing it happen."

"What are the cops doing?" Sherm asked.

"They're treating it as a hit and run by possibly a drunk driver," Cama said.

"You have a different opinion?" Roman asked.

Cama nodded. "It was six-thirty in the morning, not much traffic yet, and the Dudley's were stocking their stands with produce. Everyone knows the schedule. Donna said the truck deliberately swerved—it started speeding up, then whoever was driving steered right into the stands, then steered back onto the road."

"Is Donna Burke's wife?" Ari asked.

Cama nodded. "She said she shoved their daughter Teresa back when she saw the trajectory of the truck, but the truck hit Burke full on. She thinks it was deliberate, but couldn't think of anyone who would want to harm them."

Lonnie looked at Sherm. "What do you want us to do? We can go over there and take in the scene." He turned to Kevin, Travis, Tommy and Doug. "I want the four of you to take a look at any available cameras."

"Should we get involved?" Gage asked. "This isn't Reading. These people are humans."

"I've been meaning to drop in the Sheriff's office and the police station," Sherm said. "Sounds like this is a good time to do that. I'll see what they're doing about this, but in the mean-time, check out the cameras."

Aileen walked up to the group. "What's going on?"

Mr. Butler brought her up to speed.

"An Da and I are going to help Donna and Teresa with some herbs to settle their nerves. He wants to go to the hospital and talk to the doctors, but I doubt if they'll pay any attention to him," Cama said, with a sad shake of her head.

"Why don't I call Amy Sterling. She probably knows the surgeon and can talk to Burke's medical team to give them a heads up about Mr. Tran," Ari said.

"If you think it will get him in to help," Cama said.

"I'll tell Amy how Mr. Tran has helped us. She can be pretty persuasive," Ari said. "I'd better reschedule our lunch with Leander and Trisha until tomorrow."

"I need to go. I've got to stop by my place and pick up some supplies, then get back to the hospital. Donna and Teresa are in the waiting room," Cama said.

Roman walked Cama to her car. He opened the door for her, then looked her straight in the eyes. "I know you saw something in our Indonesian employees, Cama. Please do not tell anyone what you saw. They have come to us for asylum."

"They're Komodo dragons, aren't they?" she asked, her voice lowered.

"Are you SURE you're not a shifter?" Roman asked.

"Ha! That'd be something, wouldn't it?" Cama said. "I'm just very fine tuned into your world from my years of experience with Ari's uncle Charles. Don't worry, I won't mention what I saw."

She slipped onto the driver's seat, let Roman close her door, then she drove off.

Sherm headed over to the six-car garage as the group broke up and went about their business.

Roman joined Gage, Ari, Mr. Butler, and Aileen. "I can't imagine why anyone would run down a vegetable farmer."

"Something's not right," Gage said. "I'm not saying Cama didn't give us the full story, but someone's leaving out important details."

"Could it be a rival farmer?" Mr. Butler asked.

"Farmers aren't likely to run down each other over crops,"

Aileen said. "I'm with Gage. I think we're missing some details."

"If this were in the mountains, I'd say there was a woman involved," Kenneth said.

"Sherm's probably going to find out what's going on," Roman said.

Warman drove the BMW SUV up to the house. Phoebe and Eddie came out of the house and the dragon opened the back door for them.

"Bye Mommy! Bye Daddy one and Daddy two!" Eddie yelled.

"Have a good day at school," Ari hollered.

Roman nodded to Warman. They had a new *understanding* about how the dragon was to handle anyone who threatened to harm Eddie or Phoebe. Warman nodded in return.

"Bye, honey!" Roman called out.

"Bye, sweetie," Gage yelled. He waved.

"Did you make sausages?" Aileen asked Mr. Butler.

"I did. Would you like me to fix you a plate?"

"That would be lovely," she said.

They turned, walked arm-in-arm and entered the house.

"Well, that answers that question," Ari said.

"Looks like they're a couple," Gage said.

"I'm glad Aileen lives on the property. I'd hate to see Mr. Butler leave!" Roman said.

"He's not going anywhere," Ari said. "He loves his job."

Roman tugged her close and gave her a kiss. Gage nibbled the side of her neck.

"I don't think we should do this out in front of the house," Ari said.

Roman looked around. "No one's around..."

"There's a big, comfortable bed in an air-conditioned room,

calling to us," Gage said. He cupped his ear toward the house. "Do you hear that? *I'm a big empty bed. Come to me!*"

Ari chuckled. Gage threw an arm across her shoulders. Roman was on the other side with his arm across her lower back. They walked back to the house and entered the cool interior.

CHAPTER EIGHT

Sherm learned that the police department was seven miles down the highway from the sheriff's department. Since he was closest to the sheriff's department, he figured he would start there. As he locked up the Navigator, two deputies spotted him and headed his way. He recognized them from the attempted kidnapping incident. They met at the halfway point in the parking lot.

"Hey, how's it going?" Sherm asked.

The deputies took in the Panther Industries uniform, saw the bulge of the gun under Sherm's jacket and didn't blink an eye at it.

"Hi. Sherm, right?" the taller deputy asked.

"That's me, but I'm sorry, we weren't introduced," Sherm said.

"I'm Quartz Gonzalez," he said as he stuck his hand out. He and Sherm shook.

"Rudy Rodriguez," the other one said.

"Quartz, huh?" Sherm asked. "Who named you, your mom or dad?"

"The story is, my mom was heavy into crystals—still is, but I never understood how my father let her name me with no say so whatsoever," Quartz said.

Sherm stared at the man. "I like it. Sets you apart, but I bet you had a lot of fights in elementary school."

"You don't know the brutality... kids today seem more tolerant, but that's a toss-up," Quartz said.

"What brings you our way?" Rudy asked.

"What can you tell me about that hit and run early this morning?" Sherm asked.

"We're investigating it, so it's not something we can discuss," Quartz said.

Sherm stared hard at the men. "You are fully aware what I do for a living, so don't give me your standard bullshit line. I'm not the general public."

Each man had a private human dialog going through their heads. Sherm read enough off of them to fill in some details. They had a suspect in mind, but couldn't find him. They had motive. Sherm had to remember he was in their heads, and the words did not come out of their mouths, so he waited to see what they'd impart to him.

"Yeah, you Panther people have a reputation for getting the job done," Rudy said. "This guy from town wanted to set up a booth by the Dudley's vegetable stands, which are at the edge of their property. They get a lot of customers and he wanted to cash in on that traffic."

"I take it they shot him down. What was he going to sell?" Sherm asked.

"Crafts and antiques," Quartz said, with a shake of his head. "He has a booth at craft fair weekend events, but he barely makes the rent for the place."

"So, he goes bonkers and decides to run down the family?" Sherm asked. "You can't locate him?"

Quartz and Rudy shook their heads.

"No one has seen him or his truck," Rudy said. "He's not married, so we don't know where he went."

"Want our help?" Sherm asked.

"We don't have the budget to hire your team," Quartz said.

"This is our community. We want to keep it safe," Sherm said. "We won't send you an invoice, but we will find your man. I guarantee it."

"If you bring him in, we'd appreciate it, but I'm not sure how you could find him when we can't," Quartz said.

"We have our ways." Sherm winked, nodded, and headed back to the Navigator. When he was on the road, he called Roman and gave him the lowdown.

"This is over crafts and antiques?" Roman roared. Gage opened the door between their offices and stood in the doorway, waiting for Roman to get off the phone. "Get a team on it. Send someone to that man's place and get his scent."

Roman told Gage what Sherm found out.

"What kind of loser does something like that?" Gage asked. "What do we know about this guy?"

"Let's go over to the building and see what Lonnie can do," Roman said. He and Gage left their home offices and headed across the parking lot, walked around the garage building and entered the office building.

"Hey, Roman, Gage," Big Bear Muchisky said.

"Good morning," Marcha said as she beamed smiles their way.

Roman sent Big Bear a silent message. The bear shifter looked like he was going to shift, he was so angry.

Marcha looked from Roman to Big Bear, wondering what was going on.

Gage and Roman walked to the elevators. They stopped on the third floor. The elevator door opened to the Panther Industries Security Division. The fairly new etched sign with the panther logo in the bullet-proof glass looked good. Roman used his badge to open the door.

Lonnie stood and came around his desk. "What's going on?"

They discussed the hit and run. Sherm didn't get the culprit's name, but he had a solid picture from the deputy's heads.

Lonnie shouted out for his team to come to his office. Kevin, Tommy, Travis and Doug sauntered into Lonnie's glassed-in office.

"What's up?" Kevin asked. "Find out something about that hit and run?"

Lonnie pointed to Kevin and Tommy. "I want you two to do some groundwork." He looked over to Travis and Doug. "Have you found anything on the cameras? We don't have this guy's name or anything. We need that license plate."

Roman shared the picture Sherm plucked from the deputy's heads.

Travis perked up. "Bet I can find that craft fair. Probably be easier to discover him through that instead of the cameras."

Lonnie, Roman, and Gage nodded.

"Makes sense," Gage said. "Find that place, then you two can go trolling for our suspect."

Travis jogged back to his cubicle. His fingers flew over one of his many keyboards. Within moments, he found two places that fit the description of places to search. He buzzed Lonnie. "There's two places that fit the criteria. One's a weekend farmer's market that operates every Saturday downtown. The other place looks more like where he'd set up shop fulltime. It's an antiques mall."

Kevin and Tommy headed out the door. They drove to the antiques mall first because it felt like the most obvious place.

They studied the directory that listed the names of the vendors. Tommy snapped a picture of the directory with his phone. There were several businesses that sold art. Several more that seemed to be strictly antiques. A few different businesses: custom signs, framing, essential oils, cat and dog products, then the craft places. They noted the three craft places and walked around to find them.

Two of the craft's places didn't sell antiques. The third place was closed. It was crafts and antiques. Tommy read the sign beside the door. *Took Manville.* He noted the cellphone number. He sent a message in mind-talk to Travis.

Took? Travis sent back.

Tommy snapped a picture of the sign beside the door and texted it to Lonnie.

Come on back to the office, Lonnie texted. *Travis will find this guy's information and then we'll make a plan.*

TRAVIS WALKED into Lonnie's office as Kevin and Tommy stepped off the elevator. He waited until they were inside the office.

"Ashitook Manville, originally from Duluth, Minnesota. He moved to San Marcos in November of 2000. Single. No education past high school. Sporadic low-paying jobs; no actual career. Leased the space in the antique mall two years ago. Found some apartment eviction notices. He might be living in the antique mall."

Sherm stepped off the elevator and entered the office. "Kevin, get out an electrician's uniform. Set up a camera at this guy's door, and slip a listening device under the door if there's space." He swung his gaze to Tommy. "Go talk to some of these vendors. Buy some stuff to loosen their tongues; put it on your expense report. Find out who stays the latest. I'll bet this *Took* person lies low until everyone's gone, then comes out at nighttime."

Kevin went to the supply cabinet. He looked through some logos, slapped one on the back of an electrician's uniform in his size, found a t-shirt for Tommy, slapped a logo onto it. Then he grabbed a toolkit and slapped an identical logo on the Velcro patch. He searched through magnetic logos for the vehicle and grabbed three identical signs.

He looked at the electronics stacked in boxes on a shelf, then stared into space a moment, visualizing the area where Took Manville's place was located. He wondered if there was a back door to the suspect's interior location. He placed two small, powerful camera kits into the toolkit along with two listening devices.

Kevin met up with Tommy in Lonnie's office and tossed him the t-shirt. Tommy shrugged out of his Panther shirt and put on the one with the fake electrical company logo.

"Got everything?" Lonnie asked.

"Yeah. we'll take the van," Kevin said. He handed the magnetic signs to Tommy.

"Make sure you communicate with us," Roman said.

Gage stood. "I'll walk out with you."

KEVIN, Tommy and Gage left the office building and walked toward the garage. A golf cart headed their way, then abruptly came to a stop abreast of them.

Ari climbed out of the cart and stormed over to her son. "What are you doing in that uniform?" Her eyes blazed as she took in his uniform, the toolkit and the magnetic signs Tommy held.

"Mom, I can't talk right now. I've got work to do," Kevin said.

Ari's angry eyes latched onto Gage. "You condone this?"

"Listen, Honey, Kevin has a job to do. You might not like it, but he's good at his job," Gage said.

"You have him doing illegal things?" Ari practically screamed. "What if he gets caught? Goes to jail?"

Gage stood between Ari and Kevin. "Don't... leave it alone, Ari!"

Roman and Sherm hurried out of the office building and ran over to them.

"Ari, don't interfere," Sherm said, forcefully. "We're a security business. There are things we do to get the results we require."

"Use someone else!" Ari fumed.

"No!" Kevin yelled. "Stay out of my work, Mom!"

For one split second, her liger face showed baring teeth.

Gage grabbed her hair at the back of her head and forced her to focus on him. "Don't even think about it. Don't you dare try to bully anyone using your animal size." He was furious that his mate would pull that card and try to use it.

Roman and Sherm stayed out of it.

Jason and Kenneth ran full speed from the office building. Jason was wide-eyed, taking in the scene.

"Gage! Why are you pulling Mom's hair?" Jason asked in disbelief.

Kenneth patted Jason on the back, walked over to Gage and Ari. "Come with me, Ari. No arguments."

Her stormy eyes flickered over to her father's kind face. She calmed, shook Gage off, then she and Kenneth walked to the house. When the front door closed after them, the group in the parking lot heaved out a sigh of relief.

"We are totally fucked," Roman said as he ran his eyes over Gage.

"Not my fault!" Gage said.

"You knew it would happen eventually," Sherm said. "Now it's in the open, but that's all she's going to know."

Jason faced Gage. "What the fuck?"

Kevin grabbed his brother's arm. "She was going to shift, Jace. Gage was keeping her focused."

"Oh, hell!" Jason said. "We sure as hell don't want to go there!"

"I hope Kenneth can talk some sense into her," Roman said. "If not, we may find ourselves living in our offices for quite a while."

"We don't have any clothes in our offices!" Gage said.

"Guess that's something you two should remedy," Sherm said. He looked over to Kevin. "Still up to the task?"

"Hell, yes! I'm not letting my mother stop me from working," Kevin said. He let out a huff, turned to Tommy. "Ready?"

Tommy shook off his fright from seeing the liger's face. The animal's teeth looked about as long as his fingers. "Yeah. Let's get going."

They walked to the garage and entered by the side door. Kevin stowed the toolkit in the rear of the white van, while Tommy attached the magnetic logos to each side and the rear right door of the vehicle. They climbed into the front.

Kevin keyed up the navigation program, entered the address of the antiques mall, then pressed the button to open the garage door of that bay. He eased the van out of the garage and drove down the long driveway with the overhanging oak trees.

Once they were on the highway, Kevin opened up. "I'm sorry you had to witness that. My mother has a hard time realizing I'm in my forties."

"At least she cares about you. My mother was so wrapped up into worshipping my father, she barely remembered she had kids."

"I'm never going to hear the end of this," Kevin said. "She doesn't have to worry about Jason—he works behind a desk. The most he could get hurt is by getting a paper cut, or stapling himself."

Tommy looked across the front seat to Kevin. "I worked with this guy who got his tie caught in one of those big office paper shredders. He had to wear a neck brace for months. The thing practically choked him to death. Everyone said he was beating the controls trying to turn it off when someone came to his rescue."

"Damn. It's a good thing my brother doesn't wear ties! I'll have to tell him about that," Kevin said.

Stay in the right two lanes, the mapping program announced.

In seven-hundred-feet take the next exit.

Kevin followed the navigator's instructions. They drove under the freeway at the U-turn and pulled into a parking lot that faced the freeway. The antiques mall was a rather large, sprawling, stand-alone, one-story building. The parking lot held a lot of vehicles. Kevin found a place to park the van, grabbed the toolkit, and Tommy grabbed the ladder. Then they went inside.

Tommy set the ladder up where Kevin indicated, then left to mingle with the customers and vendors to see what knowledge he could gain about Took Manville in suite forty-four.

No one paid any attention to Kevin. He climbed the ladder and replaced a lightbulb in the ceiling with one that contained a hidden camera. It didn't make any difference if they turned off the lights or if there was a power failure; the battery-operated camera still functioned as it was supposed to.

Kevin opened a small acrylic case that held state-of-the-art listening devices. He took out a tiny clear plastic case that contained what looked like a short piece of wire. It was no longer than a half inch, and no wider than a piece of thin spaghetti. He glanced over at the floor under the door, rooted around in another case in his toolkit and found a piece of mounting tape that nearly matched the threshold color.

He pressed the bug onto the tape and peeled off the thin backing of the tape. He used long-handled thin tweezers to position the tape in the minute space on the threshold under the door. It was a chore to push the tape far enough into place where it would pick up sound from the room, but the tweezers did the job. He rubbed the tape with the tool so that it would stick to the threshold. He pulled the tweezers out from under the door, stood and gathered up his equipment.

I'm through here. Going to the van. Be right back, he sent to Tommy.

Okay.

Kevin hauled the ladder and his toolkit back out to the van. He climbed in the back, closed the door behind him and pulled up a program on his phone. He activated the listening device and set an alert so he would know there was sound from inside the space. He peeled off the uniform, checked his clothes, then got out of the van. He removed the magnetic logos from both sides and the back of the van, tossed them inside and locked up.

Tommy, where are you?

I'm on the west side of the building. The numbers are screwy. From our original location looking at his door, go to your left. Take the first hallway, go to the end, then make a right. I figure I'm at the backside of our friend's place.

Kevin followed Tommy's directions and caught up with him.

No back doors? Kevin asked.

I'm making my way around to see if there's a back hallway between these shops and his. Almost there.

Kevin patted Tommy on the back, then left him as he walked down that hallway, turned right and discovered the back doors to the shops. He found the rear door for suite forty-four. He studied the paneled wall across the hallway, reached into his pocket and pulled out a nickel-sized bump of a device. He licked the back of the brown bump and affixed it to the old paneling. It blended in perfectly. He pulled out his phone, woke it, then tapped the app and enabled the camera.

This lady said she thinks Took is living in his space here, Tommy sent.

Be right there. I planted a camera opposite the back door.

CHAPTER NINE

Kevin joined Tommy at the shop that was across the back alley from Took's place. They greeted each other with a fist bump.

"I told this lady that Took was holding something for us until we got paid," Tommy said.

Priory Jones stood with a hand on her ample hips. "He didn't open up yesterday, and he's not opening today." She shook her head. "I don't know how he makes rent."

"You think he's living in his space?" Kevin asked.

Priory nodded. "I've seen a light under his door when I've locked up at night."

Kevin glanced at Tommy. "Let's go knock on his door."

Priory shook her head. "Won't do you any good. He won't open up. I've tried."

Tommy made himself look disappointed. "Guess we'll have to wait until he opens back up. Don't spend your half of the money!"

"Thank you, Ms. Jones," Kevin said. He and Tommy walked away.

When they were at the front again, Kevin stopped and looked around. "Wonder if there're any shifters here?"

Tommy shrugged. "Give a call-out."

Any shifters here at the Antiques Mall?

Seconds quietly passed.

Who is that?

Where are you?

Kevin and Tommy shared a thumbs up to each other.

It's Kevin Davis and Tommy Littlefield from Panther Security. We're close to the front doors.

Be there in a minute, one man said.

On my way, a woman sent.

A few minutes later, a guy in jeans and a long-sleeved, button-up plaid shirt arrived at the front, followed by a woman with a toddler on her hip.

"Hi, I'm Kevin and this is Tommy," Kevin said.

They shook hands.

"What do you need?" Roland asked.

"Do either of you know this guy in number forty-four?" Tommy asked.

"Took?" Berniece asked. "He's a worthless piece of mankind, if you ask me."

Roland shook his head. "Don't know him, but I've seen him around. What's going on?"

"We want to question him about something," Kevin said. "Can you let us know if you see him?"

"Priory Jones, the lady whose store shares the back alley with his place, said she thinks he's living there," Tommy said.

"I know Priory," Roland said. "My place is two doors down from hers."

Kevin dug two business cards out of his pocket. "Can you let me know if you see him? You can call or text me, or call out to me."

"Sure thing," Roland said. "Glad to help."

The toddler on Berniece's hip wanted to get down and started fussing. "Guess I'd better get her back to her playpen. If anything comes up, I'll let you know."

"Thanks. I appreciate both of your help," Kevin said.

ARI AND KENNETH were shut inside her office. She was still riled up about discovering what her youngest son was involved in.

Kenneth stared her down. "I realize you have only recently come into your shifter heritage, but you need to understand that you cannot threaten someone with your animal. If you suspect they are going to do you or someone else harm, by all means threaten them."

"He's gone from installing cable to... this... I don't know what," Ari ranted.

"Seems like he loves his job," Kenneth said.

"That's not the point! What he's doing is illegal." Ari continued her rant.

"Cops and investigators play dress-up all the time," Kenneth said. "To catch a criminal takes resources that don't always equate to money. It's not like he was carrying weapons. Did you see guns or knives?"

Ari scowled. She didn't want to admit anything to the positive side to her father. "That's beside the point."

"Is it? He's installing electronic devices to catch a bad person. What's so terrible about that?" he drilled into her.

"Whose side are you on?" Ari asked.

"I'm not on anyone's side, Ari. I'm trying to make you see your youngest son as a grown man who has a career he loves," Kenneth said. "Would you rather he went back to his former job and had to sleep on the sofa in the living room again?"

She scoffed. "He wouldn't have to..."

"You're missing the point!" Kenneth didn't know how to get across to his daughter that she needed to butt out of Kevin's life. She couldn't hold him under her thumb like a teenage boy. She risked alienating him.

There was a tap on the door.

"Go away!" Ari called out, none too polite.

"Mom! Come on, unlock the door," Jason called out.

Ari huffed out an angry breath. Kenneth got up and went to the door and let Jason in.

Jason walked up to his mother and tried to hug her. She wasn't having any part of that, and shrugged away from him.

"Mom, for Christ' sake, I realize you're emotional because you're pregnant, but get over it. Kevin isn't a little boy anymore," Jason said, with a little force.

She glared at him.

"So, what? You're going to pretend you didn't know what Panther Security was all about all these years? It was okay for Roman and Gage to tear apart the man who abducted and tortured you? And it was okay for you to kill a rival Tothar king, but your little boy can't do his job?" Jason didn't give her any leeway in the throwback to his mother.

Kenneth could see that Ari wasn't relenting. He softly gripped Jason's shoulder and walked him to the door. They both left the office and went outside.

"I'm glad you said what you did—it will give her something to think about," Kenneth said.

"It's a good thing I have the job that I do, otherwise I'd be under the bus with my brother," Jason said.

"We need to let her work things out on her own," Kenneth said. They walked back to the office building in silence.

THE AFTERNOON SLID BY, then the BMW SUV drove up to the house and stopped. Phoebe and Eddie got out of the car and waved to Warman as he drove over to the garage.

Eddie opened the front door and hollered out. "We're home!"

The house was silent. Mr. Butler stuck his head out of the butler's pantry and waved them over. He put a finger to his lips.

"Where's Mommy and my Daddies?" Eddie whispered.

"Did something happen?" Phoebe asked.

"Your mother is in her office cooling down," Mr. Butler whispered.

"What happened?" Eddie prodded.

"She's very upset. She found out what Kevin's work entailed, and she's not happy about it. I guess she threatened him, and everyone got all worked up," Mr. Butler said.

Eddie huffed out a loud sigh. "Is that all?" She stomped out of the kitchen and down the hall. She stood outside her mother's office and let out a crying jag as if she had seriously hurt herself.

Ari's office door flew open. "Eddie? What happened? Are you hurt?" Ari went down to her knees and searched for blood.

Eddie sniffled. She took Ari's hand, yanked her to stand, and led her back into her office. "No, I'm not hurt. Why are you mad at everyone just because Kevin is all grown up?"

Ari stared at her daughter with wide eyes. The cunning child had bamboozled her.

"This isn't anything I want to discuss," Ari said.

"Well, if you ask me, you're the one acting like a child," Eddie said, looking Ari squarely in the eyes. "Panther Securities keeps people safe. You should be proud of Kevin. He's learned skills to help protect people, and catch bad people and get them off the street so they can't hurt anyone anymore."

Ari stared dumbly at the little person in front of her. She finally nodded. "You're right. I've acted very badly today. Very, very badly—to everyone."

"Sometimes it's hard to say *I'm sorry*, Mommy, but you won't die from admitting you were wrong," Eddie said.

Ari threw her arms around Eddie. "Thank you for being my little girl. I love you so much."

Eddie hugged her mother's neck. "I love you too."

THE WHITE VAN pulled into the yard. The garage door creaked up and Kevin drove into the garage bay. The door lowered, and Kevin and Tommy got out of the van and left the six-car garage by the side door, toolkit and magnetic signs in hand.

Lonnie greeted them as they stepped off the elevator and entered the Panther Securities Division offices.

"Any luck?" Lonnie asked.

"Somewhat," Kevin said.

Tommy related what they had found out.

"Looks like we'll have to wait and see if he's really in there," Lonnie said.

"Nothing from my tiny mic so far," Kevin said. "He's either really quiet, sleeping, or he's not there. If he were moving around, I'd hear something."

"Travis and Doug got the license plate for the truck, and we sent the image to the sheriff's department," Lonnie said. "They've put out an APB."

Kevin and Tommy walked back to the supply closet and stashed their gear.

"If this guy is as broke as everyone seems to think he is, he won't be riding around," Tommy said. "Either that, or maybe he'll use someone else's vehicle if he thinks his truck is hot."

"Let's go get something to eat," Kevin said.

"We need to go grocery shopping—again," Tommy said, not making eye contact with Lonnie. It was an awkward situation since Lonnie was their boss.

Lonnie appeared embarrassed. "I replaced the food I've been eating like a pig."

"That's good," Kevin said. "What'd you contribute?"

"Chips, crackers, cookies, nuts, some ground meat, steaks, and chicken legs," he said. "Oh, and potatoes. Melly has made me see the error of my way."

"Great! I'll throw some potatoes in the oven, and we can grill steaks," Tommy said. "You eating with us?"

"No, thanks. Melly and I are going out," Lonnie said.

Travis and Doug joined them. "Are we invited to your bar-b-que?" Travis asked.

"How many potatoes and steaks did you buy?" Kevin asked.

"There's enough for all of you," Lonnie said.

Travis and Doug high-fived. They walked out of the office with Kevin and Tommy.

THE POLICE FOUND Took Manville's F150 pickup in the parking lot of the antiques mall. Their suspect had taken black electrician's tape and changed two of the letters on the license plate. The cops took pictures of his wonky try to conceal his truck and had it towed to the police forensics department. The guy wasn't very smart; he hadn't thought to wash away evidence on the front bumper linking him to the hit and run.

Mr. Tran and Cama pulled up to the parking area of Ari's house and got out of the VW Thing. Mr. Tran rang the doorbell.

Mr. Butler answered the door. "Come in. Please join us for dinner. We're just getting ready to sit down."

Cama and An Da entered the house and followed the butler to the kitchen. Ari stood by the table, and it looked like she had just delivered a speech to everyone.

Roman stood. He approached the herbalists. "Welcome! Are you hungry? We're just getting ready to eat."

"Thank you," An Da said. "We're sorry for barging in at dinner time—but we haven't eaten all day."

Cama shook her head. "We have some bad news."

"Oh, no. Don't tell me the farmer died!" Ari said.

Cama nodded, sadly. "He didn't make it through the surgery."

"That changes the charge to murder," Sherm said. "At the very least, vehicular homicide."

"Those poor people," Aileen said.

THE FOUR GUYS were waiting for their steaks to finish grilling. Travis manned the grill. Tommy trotted down the stairs from the apartments over the garage with a stack of plates with hot baked potatoes on the top plate. Doug carried chips and a new container of dip. Kevin carried a cooler of ice with beers and soda.

They gathered around the picnic table at the rear of the garage and unloaded their dinner fixings.

"Just in time," Travis said. "Everyone want their steaks medium rare? Speak now or you'll get medium well."

Tommy plopped a potato on each plate and held his out to Travis. "Medium rare for me."

Travis dished out the steaks, and they sat and dug in.

Kevin raised his beer in the air. "To Melly for making Lonnie a better man, and roommate!"

They all raised their drinks. "To Melly!"

All was quiet while they engaged in chewing. Kevin's phone sounded an alert. He swiped at the screen. "We've got sound from inside that shop."

"Better ask Sherm how he wants to go about this," Travis said.

Kevin texted Sherm. Within less than a blink, Kevin's phone rang. He put it on speakerphone,

"Let's go get our man and deliver him to the sheriff's office," Sherm said.

"Why wouldn't the sheriff's office, or the police for that matter, have the building owner open his shop?" Doug asked.

"Good question," Sherm said. "They've got the truck with the evidence. Now the case is elevated because the man died in surgery." Sherm paused, thinking through scenarios. "Let me call one of the deputies I met. Hold off on any plans. Maybe it would be best for them to take over. We don't have to prove ourselves to anyone."

Sherm disconnected the call.

Kevin picked up his fork and steak knife and dug into his now cold meal.

SHERM CALLED Quartz Gonzalez as he walked across the parking lot to the picnic area behind the garage. The deputy answered on the third ring. "Gonzalez."

"Quartz, it's Sherman Foo with Panther. We know where your man is hiding."

"You found him?" Quartz asked, astonished.

"It's what we do," Sherm said, as he put his phone on speaker and nodded to his young teammates. "Do you want to take over, or have us bring him in, or work with you? Your choice."

"You found him; why don't we work together on this," Quartz said. "Where is he?"

"He's been living in his shop at that antiques mall," Sherm said. "Why haven't you had the place opened so you could search it?"

There was a slight pause. Sherm raised his eyebrows.

"It's political," Quartz said.

"How so?" Sherm asked.

"This dickwad is the sheriff's cousin," Quartz said.

There was a groan from everyone at the picnic table.

"Okay. It's your call. How do you want to handle this? Do you have to check in with the sheriff first?" Sherm asked.

"Let me talk to the captain. I'll call you back shortly," the deputy said.

"Even if this dude is the sheriff's cousin, he still killed someone," Tommy said. "And it sounds deliberate to me."

"I want you two to get over there and retrieve your spyware. I don't want anything letting this guy off the hook," Sherm said.

"Why don't we leave the camera at the back-door alley. We could say the camera picked up light, which it probably did, and we can turn that in as evidence," Kevin said.

Sherm nodded. "Grab that wire from the front door. I'm not worried about the other camera right now, but the wire could let this guy walk free."

"Save my food!" Tommy said, as he and Kevin ran to the garage, got Tommy's pickup and headed out.

Sherm turned to Travis. "Check that camera and see if there's any light from that back alley between those shops."

Travis pulled what he called his *super phone* out of his pocket and poked through several menus. He found the device he was looking for and played it, backed up to the approximate time Kevin's alert sounded, and watched. "There's light under the door at the same time Kevin's wire heard sound."

"Okay. We're all set for whatever the sheriff's department wants to do," Sherm said.

KEVIN AND TOMMY entered the antiques mall. Things were winding down. They made their way over to door forty-four. Kevin pulled a powerful micro flashlight out of his pocket and Tommy handed him a pair of long tweezers from his pack.

Both of the neighboring shops were closed, so Kevin wasted no time kneeling at Took Manville's door. He grabbed hold of the tape with the tweezers and pulled. As luck would have it, the adhesive on the tape stuck to the threshold. He tugged several times to no avail.

Tommy glanced toward the front door of the mall and saw several sheriff's cars parking. "They're here!"

Kevin cussed in his head as he used the tweezers like a scraper trying to get the tape unstuck.

"They're getting out of their cars!" Tommy whispered, frantic.

Kevin gave one last yank. The tape with the wire attached came free. He quickly stood, and they hurried away. "Damn, we're going to be stuck in here and that might look suspicious."

His phone rang. Sherm was calling. "Did you get it? The

sheriff's department is on the way. I told them you'd meet them there to show them that back camera. Travis said there's light under the door at the time you received the alert."

"Yeah, I barely had enough time to get it," Kevin said. "We'll go to the front door and meet them."

As they walked toward the front doors of the mall, Kevin brought Tommy up to speed about what they needed to do.

"That was a close call," Tommy said.

Four deputies and their captain marched to the door. They spotted the Panther logo on Tommy and Kevin's shirts.

"Been waiting long?" Quartz asked. He introduced himself and his coworkers.

"We just got here," Tommy said.

"Would you like to see where we planted our camera?" Kevin asked. "I've got an evidence bag."

Tommy pulled an evidence bag out of his pack and handed it to Quartz. The deputy walked with Tommy and Kevin to the back alley between the shops, and Kevin pointed out the camera.

"That's a neat little device," Quartz said. He took several pictures of the tiny camera, the angle towards the door on the opposite side of the hall. He measured the distance with an app on his phone from the wall to the door opposite. "I bet you guys have all kinds of neat toys."

Kevin pulled a plastic glove out of his pocket, slipped it on, then plucked the little bump off the wall and dropped it into the evidence bag. "You should fill in the details since you're taking possession." He handed the bag to Quartz.

CHAPTER TEN

K evin and Tommy hung around to see how this capture would go down. Four men stood in front of the door to Took Manville's antique and craft shop. The captain knocked on the door.

"Took, open up. It's Captain Tovar. No point hiding out. We know you're in there. We've impounded your truck."

There was a scuffle around the corner. Deputy Quartz tried to restrain the fleeing criminal. Took Manville slipped through his grip and raced for the mall doors.

Kevin and Tommy controlled their animal speed, but still got to the mall doors faster than humanly possible. They captured the guy and brought him down to the floor.

The captain and deputies rushed over to take possession of their hit-and-run driver.

"Where d'you think you were going, Took?" the captain asked. "I just told you we had your truck. Do you think you can outrun our cars?"

"It was an accident! I didn't mean to run down that guy," Took whined.

"Well, you're in deep trouble. Burke died this morning in surgery, and your cousin's hands are tied." The captain grabbed one of Took's arms and dragged him to his feet. Quartz secured the other arm and slapped the handcuffs on one wrist, ready to cuff the wrist his captain held in a grip.

Quartz released the man into the custody of the other two deputies once Took was completely handcuffed.

The captain looked over at Kevin and Tommy. "Appreciate your help. You Panther people know how to get the job done."

"We wanted to make sure this guy was off the streets," Tommy said.

"Glad to be of help," Kevin said. He shook the captain's hand, then Quartz's hand.

They all walked out through the mall doors to their respective vehicles.

Kevin and Tommy faced front, then turned to look at each other.

"That was something else. I didn't think I'd be able to get that wire free in time!" Kevin said.

"Well, it's done and they've got him—all because of our technology," Tommy said. "Let's go home. I want to finish my steak!"

ARI HAD ANOTHER RESTLESS NIGHT. She wasn't sure what was going on and decided to call the doctor in the morning. She wandered the house, went outside and without warning, shifted into her liger. Her enormous animal stood there and blinked at the unexpected change. She looked down at her shredded nightclothes in consternation. She tried to shift back to no avail. Her cat let out a huff of exasperation. She walked over to the grass and laid down. Within a few moments, she dozed off.

Patting on her shoulder woke her. She opened an eye and saw Roman, Gage, and Eddie. Ari rolled to her stomach.

I can't shift back. I planned to call the doctor today about this restlessness. I don't know what's going on.

"I'll call Dr. Rosas," Gage said. "You'll have to tell me exactly what you feel when you try to shift. He may make a house call, along with Duke Cavendish, the vet."

"Do you want us to make you a pallet on our bedroom floor so you can sleep in air conditioning?" Roman asked.

Ari's liger yawned widely, showing all her massive, sharp, pointy teeth. *Yes, that might make me feel better.*

"You're awesome, Mommy!" Eddie said. "Can I ride you?"

Maybe some other time. I'm very tired right now... and hungry. You eat your breakfast and get going to school.

"Okay," Eddie said. "I hope you feel better soon."

"I'll ask Mr. Butler to thaw out some steaks for you," Gage said.

Sherm came wandering out the French doors. "What's going on?"

"Ari's stuck. Must have something to do with her pregnancy," Roman said.

Until I can shift back, someone's going to have to open and close doors for me. I won't be able to talk to Mr. Butler.

"Do you want to come inside now? The rest of us need to eat breakfast and get to work... and school," Roman said, as he nodded to Eddie.

Yes, air conditioning, please.

Sherm held the door open. Everyone followed Ari inside. She stood in the doorway to the kitchen while the others squeezed around her.

Mr. Butler startled, almost losing a dozen eggs.

"Don't worry, everything is okay on the emotional front," Sherm said. "She's stuck in her liger form and can't shift."

Mr. Butler took the opportunity to study the liger. Ari sat on her haunches with only an inch between her head and the ceiling. "Ari, your liger is beautiful!"

She yawned.

"Mr. Butler, you're going to have to thaw out some steaks for her until she can shift back," Gage said. "Also, what could we use to make a pallet for her in our bedroom?"

Mr. Butler thought for a moment. "I don't think there's enough room for king-size mattresses on the floor. Why don't we use one of the garage stalls? It's climate-controlled, and we could place four king-sized mattresses on the concrete. That should be large enough for her to sprawl out, don't you think?"

The guys thought about it, then nodded.

"Good idea," Gage said. He turned to Ari. "What do you think? Will you be okay in the garage?"

As long as there's air conditioning!

"She said that would work."

"I'll have to order the mattresses, but I think they could be delivered today," Mr. Butler said.

"I'll get Jason on it. He has a way with getting things done," Roman said, as he worked his phone.

Can you open our bedroom door? I'll go lie down.

"Of course, honey," Gage said. He squeezed around her and went down the hallway to their bedroom as Ari lumbered behind him.

She gazed longingly at the giant bed. Gage noticed.

"I don't think your uncle's bed would support your liger weight."

I know. I just want to get some sleep and not be so hot.

"We'll check in on you after breakfast. I'll let you know when the doctor can make a house call," Gage said.

Thanks. Ari flopped down on the floor.

Gage left the bedroom and left the door cracked a few inches so Ari could exit if she wanted to. He returned to the kitchen and sat in his usual place.

Eddie and Phoebe ate their breakfast. When they heard the SUV horn toot, they grabbed their backpacks that were against the wall, said their goodbyes, and left.

"How many steaks do we have on hand, Mr. Butler?" Gage asked.

"We're getting low. I put in a meat order with the farm yesterday," Mr. Butler said.

"Maybe it would be a good idea to get some whole chickens, legs of lamb, and larger cuts of beef for Ari," Gage said. "We can get a chest freezer. I think there's enough room in the pantry for one, don't you think?"

Gage got up and he and Mr. Butler walked into the large pantry with Roman following. There was a portion of shelves that weren't stocked.

"Let's get some measurements for different size chest freezers. I think a medium-sized one would fit here," Gage said.

"How long would it take to defrost a larger cut of meat? Should we get a large refrigerator as well?" Roman asked. "If Ari's liger is hungry, she's going to want to eat right away. It's not safe to wait several hours for something to defrost."

"When I placed this last order, I was talking to Bob, the man who takes the phone orders. He said they keep a lot of fresh cuts in their cold storage locker that keeps the meat cold, but doesn't freeze it," Mr. Butler said. "We should be able to call and go pick up something in a pinch."

"That's a much better solution. I think we should get the chest freezer, but we won't require a spare refrigerator," Roman said.

AS LUNCH ROLLED AROUND, a mattress truck pulled up to the garage area, followed by a car with Pennsylvania license plates. Jason waited at the open garage bay and instructed the delivery people where to place the mattresses.

Leander and Trisha got out of their vehicle and waved.

"Leander!" Jason said. "Hi, Trisha! You made it." He frowned slightly as he remembered his mother's situation. "Mom's a little indisposed right now." *Mom's stuck in her liger form. We're waiting for the doctor and the vet to arrive.*

He silently called out to Roman, Gage and Sherm to let them know their guests had arrived

"Is she okay?" Trisha asked.

Jason shrugged. "Hard to say." *Her liger looks healthy. I only know she's been very restless and hasn't been able to sleep well. We bought these king-sized mattresses to put in the garage —it's climate controlled, so she'll be able to sleep in comfort until she can shift back.*

Oh, no. What a mess, Leander sent. "Where's Eddie?"

"You just missed her," Jason said. "She's off to college." He shook his head. "Hard to believe she's in such advanced classes."

Roman, Gage, and Sherm rounded the corner from the office building.

"You made it!" Gage said. He and Leander thumped each other on the back in a man hug. "Hi, Trisha! I see you're none the worse for wear."

"That was a long drive," Trisha said.

"Come on over to the house," Roman said. "Ari will be so happy to see you."

"At least we hope she'll be happy," Sherm said with a wink.

Roman jostled him.

The mattress company truck backed up and drove off. Jason lowered the garage door, then jogged to catch up to the group. "We're going to have to remove the plastic. I had the delivery people leave the mattresses on the floor. It would have been too weird to have them remove the plastic."

"Maybe we should do that before we go inside," Gage said.

"You go inside," Sherm said. "Jason and I can tackle this."

Jason and Sherm trotted back to the garage.

Two vehicles pulled into the driveway. Roman saw someone waving, then realized it was Dotty, Dr. Rosas' nurse. She and the doctor got out of the car at the same time Duke got out of his car.

"You're just in time to meet our friends who just moved from Reading, our old stomping grounds," Gage said. "Leander, Trisha, this is Dr. Humberto Rosas, a shifter OBGYN, his nurse Dotty, and Dr. Duke Cavendish, a shifter veterinarian."

"Human," Dotty said, with a wink and a smile as she shook their hands.

"What're your animals?" Duke asked.

"King cobra," Leander said.

"Cougar," Trisha said.

"Oh, my!" Dotty said. "I've never seen a cobra before."

"He's something to see in action, Dotty," Roman said.

Roman opened the front door, and they all went inside. Gage eased around them and headed to the kitchen to let Mr. Butler know there were more guests than expected.

Roman settled everyone in the living room, then he slipped down the hallway to see if Ari was awake. She lifted her head off the floor as he entered the bedroom.

"You have company," he said, as he squatted beside her.

Is the doctor here?

"Humberto and Dotty are here, along with Duke Cavendish, Leander and Trisha," Roman said.

We have a houseful! Does Mr. Butler need help?

"I'll find out. He can have Dirdjo lend a hand. That dragon knows his way around a kitchen," Roman said. "Do you want people to come back here, or do you want to come out to the living room?"

I'll go out there. She hauled herself to her feet and ducked her head to exit through the bedroom door.

Roman followed her to the living room.

"There she is," Leander said. He jumped to his feet and approached the gigantic cat.

Gage grabbed the coffee table and dragged it over to the wall so there would be enough room for Ari to lie on the floor.

The doctors swarmed the liger. Dotty gawked at the enormous size of her patient.

"Do you have any discomfort?" Duke asked.

No, just this restlessness that won't let me sleep.

"Have you felt flutters in your abdomen?" Dr. Rosas asked.

Yes.

"I may have miscalculated then," Dr. Rosas said.

Dotty opened the chart on her iPad. "You determined she was at the end of her first trimester."

"Can you make any determination, Duke?" Humberto asked. "I may have been four or five weeks off."

Duke kneaded Ari's belly. He listened with a stethoscope. "Strong heartbeats. Going to have to bring portable equipment to get a scan. At this point, I can't make a determination."

The shifters in the room were suddenly aware of someone approaching who was running hard. Roman led the group to the front door.

"Something's wrong with someone," Humberto told Dotty.

It was tough being a human around so many shifters. Dotty never heard the silent conversations. She and Mr. Butler exchanged wide-eyed looks.

The group flocked outside as Sopan ran toward them, full out. "Inggit's in trouble!"

"What's wrong?" Roman asked.

Sopan bent over and took a deep breath. "I went over to the nests to see how Inggit and Novi were doing, and Novi said she hadn't heard Inggit all day, which was unusual. I went to her nest and crawled inside. She's naked, in her human form!"

Humberto and Duke moved to the front of the group.

"Species?" Duke asked.

"Komodo dragon," Sopan said.

"Let's go to the nest," Duke said.

"I'll grab the big cart," Roman said. "Gage, get one of the smaller ones."

They ran toward the garage, and two golf buggies sped toward the group. Everyone piled into the 10-seater cart that Roman drove. Gage followed in a four-seater. They sped through the property all the way to the house, thanks to the clearing and ground leveling that Bem did.

"The nests are around this way," Sopan said, as he sped off around the house.

The doctors rushed after the dragon. Dotty ran with the rest of the people.

When they arrived at the area where the nests were located, Sopan ran his hands through his hair. His face was in full panic mode.

"Try to calm down," Dotty told him. She grabbed his wrist and checked his pulse. "Breathe in and out, slowly. There're two doctors here. One a human OBGYN, and the other a veterinarian. Your lady will be in expert hands."

Duke dropped to his knees and lowered his body so he could crawl into the nest. "Humberto, I'll let you know if there's enough room for you in there."

Novi came out of her nest in her dragon form, highly agitated.

Eyo and Kartodirdjo approached on foot in a hard run. Eyo ran up to Novi and spoke to her through mind-talk. He sunk to the grass and stroked her head and back.

It's okay. Everything's going to be okay.

"Should I call Warman home?" Eyo called out.

"Yes. He should be here," Roman said.

Muffled sound came from deep in the nest. "Humberto, there's enough room. Better come in."

The OBGYN dropped to his knees and belly-crawled into the nest.

"Tell us what's going on, okay?" Gage hollered.

She's unconscious, Duke sent.

PHOEBE AND EDDIE were among the throng of students in the theater classroom. Warman leaned against a column in the shadows, as was typical for him. Suddenly, he lurched up straight as he received a mind-message from Eyo. His phone dinged an incoming message at the same time.

He rushed to the end of the row where Eddie and her tutor-slash-nanny sat. They grabbed their packs and apologized as they made their way around slouched students' knees to the end of the row. The trio rushed up the stairs to an exit.

"What happened?" Eddie asked, tamping down panic.

"Inggit is sick. Two doctors are there with her in the nest," Warman said in a very low voice.

They exited the building and rushed over to the car.

Phoebe stuck her hand out. "Keys."

"I can drive," Warman said.

"You're upset. Keys," Phoebe said, as she wiggled her fingers.

"Give her the keys, Warman. You don't want to make the Pitbull mad," Eddie said.

He reluctantly dropped the keys in Phoebe's hand, and they all got inside the car. As soon as Eddie strapped herself into her seat, Phoebe hit the gas pedal.

"Don't speed," Warman said. "You can get a ticket on campus."

"You just let me drive and we'll be fine," Phoebe said. "I have excellent reflexes and my peripheral vision is fine tuned."

DUKE AND HUMBERTO were on either side of Inggit in the dark nest. Luckily, their shifter vision didn't need to adjust to the pitch-black cavern. The Komodo dragon was still unconscious, stretched out, prone in her human form, facing the entrance of the nest. Her eggs lay undisturbed about four feet deeper into the nest.

"Looks like she tried to leave the nest," Duke said. "She must have realized she was sick. I don't know if she shifted before or after. Could have shifted due to a reflex of whatever made her sick."

"Her pulse is erratic," Humberto said. His fingers were at the carotid artery on her neck. "We need to get her out of here."

"I'll see if we can get a sheet to slip under her so we don't hurt her while we pull her out of here," Duke said.

We need a sheet or something to put under Inggit so we can drag her out of here.

A long moment passed.

Okay, give us a few minutes.

"Let me try to turn around so I can get the sheet,"

Humberto said. He crawled toward the eggs and managed to turn around. Then he crawled back to where he had been on the opposite side of Duke, and continued toward the nest entrance.

He made it to the front of the nest. Hands pulled him the rest of the way out and helped him to his feet.

Humberto faced Roman and Sopan. "Thanks. It's a tight squeeze in there."

"Do you know what's wrong with her?" Sopan asked. Eyo and Kartodirdjo hovered close by.

"We're not sure at this point. When we get her out of the nest and have more room and light to make a better assessment, we'll be able to help her," Humberto said.

"I'm calling Mr. Tran and Cama," Gage said.

Roman nodded. "Good idea. The more experts that can diagnose and help, the better."

Sherm ran up to the group with the folded sheet in hand. "Why don't I bring the sheet? I'm used to crawling through tight places in my line of work."

"Sure," Humberto said.

"Low roof?" Sherm asked.

"There's headroom further in," Dr. Rosas said.

Sherm handed him the sheet. "Drop this on my back."

Dr. Rosas dropped the sheet on Sherm's back as soon as he was flat on the ground at the nest opening.

Fifteen minutes later, Sherm's legs appeared in the opening. He squirmed backwards with the sheet gripped in his hands. Roman and Leander relieved Sherm of the sheet. Sherm stood, stretched his back out and moved to the side. Roman and Gage gently pulled Inggit out of the nest, while Duke pushed at her feet.

The vet crawled out of the nest and stood with help, then dusted himself off.

"Is there furniture in the house?" Duke asked.

"Only one bed, a kitchen table and a sofa," Eyo said. "We're ordering more furniture."

A golf cart pulled up. Pablo parked the cart, and Mr. Tran and Cama rushed over to the group with bags of herbal supplies.

Humberto and Duke were examining Inggit. The herbalists joined them on the ground.

Cama looked over the woman. She felt her skin, lifted one of her eyelids, then lifted her hands and examined the fingertips and fingernails.

"Castor bean! She's eaten a poisonous plant that can be fatal," Cama said.

"How can you tell?" Duke asked.

"The red stains under her nails," she said.

Mr. Tran got close, and she showed him the telltale signs. He lifted one hand and sniffed. "I see. There's no smell."

"Let's get her inside the house," Cama said. She turned to Mr. Tran. "Do you have any activated charcoal?"

An Da dug through his bag. He pulled out a jar that was half full. "Not enough to treat her, I don't think."

"That's a start." Cama turned to the hovering crowd. "We need activated charcoal. We're going to have to get as much into her stomach as possible to draw up the ricin poison from the plant."

Thunderous stomping feet approached fast. Warman broke out of the trees and stumbled to a halt. "Inggit?"

"She's alive," Sopan said. He brought Warman up to date.

"Someone needs to go to a vitamin store and buy some activated charcoal," Gage said.

Sherm was on his phone. "I'm sending Tommy."

Warman, Sopan, Eyo and Kartodirdjo carefully gripped the corners of the sheet and carried Inggit to the house. They set her on the porch because there wasn't enough room for the large men to get through the doorway two at a time. Warman gently picked up the woman and carried her into the house and up the stairs to the only bed they'd set up.

Cama flicked her head at Mr. Butler. He rushed over to her. She counted down on her fingers. "We're going to need a jug of water, a bucket for the heaves, and a funnel."

Mr. Tran approached. "Also, some plastic tubing. We're going to have to get the water and charcoal into her stomach."

"Thin tubing," Dr. Rosas said.

"We might have that on hand," Sherm said. He texted Travis, who texted back in a few minutes. "We have two feet of three-eights-inch tubing. Will that work?"

The doctors and herbalists concurred.

"Yes, that will work," Duke said.

CHAPTER ELEVEN

They mixed Mr. Tran 's activated charcoal with water. Cama was the only one with experience in getting the tubing down to the stomach, so she had the tough job. The doctors discussed the two methods: through the nose or down the throat. They decided to go down the nasal passage.

"We're going to need some pillows to position Inggit properly," Cama said.

"We can get pillows from the garage apartments," Gage said.

Pablo and Mr. Butler took off in the golf cart. They raided the first bedroom and grabbed both pillows off the queen bed. Mr. Butler grabbed another pillow from the next room just to be on the safe side. They ran down the stairs, jumped back in the buggy, and Pablo drove them back to the dragon's house in the woods.

Ten minutes later, Tommy returned with a sack bulging with bottles of activated charcoal.

"Add two bottles to the water and stir it until it's dissolved," Cama said.

THEY FINISHED THE PROCEDURE. All they could do was wait to see if Inggit survived. The charcoal would absorb the poison. They just hoped it hadn't done irreparable damage to her internal organs.

Duke spoke with the dragons. "I'll write a prescription for an antibiotic so she doesn't get an infection from the procedure."

Three hours later, she stirred on the bed.

The dragons lurched toward the bed amid a chorus of "Inggit!"

She slowly lifted her eyelids. She was drained of all energy. "Where am I?" She pressed fingers on her nostrils, then slid her hand to her throat. "Am I sick? My nose and throat are very sore."

Mr. Tran came forward. "You should keep your throat moist. We had to run a tube up your nose and down your throat to your stomach. You accidentally poisoned yourself when you ingested a castor bean plant. The charcoal neutralized the poison in your stomach."

Inggit blinked slowly. "I was poisoned?"

Warman came forward and positioned his face within inches of her face. "You ate a poisonous plant and almost died."

"My eggs?"

"Your eggs are okay. Don't worry about them," Eyo said.

"Novi is keeping watch over your nest," Sopan said.

Inggit closed her eyes. Exhaustion overtook her, and she fell back to sleep.

Cama waved everyone out of the room. "The worst is over. She will sleep, then she will recover."

GAGE, Roman, Sherm, the doctors and Dotty, along with the herbalists, headed back to the house. They found Ari in the living room with Leander and Trisha. After everyone took turns washing up in the various bathrooms, Roman and Gage helped Mr. Butler prepare food to feed their guests and themselves.

After lunch, everyone returned to the living room.

"Ari, all I can say for now is to get more exercise during the day," Duke said. "I'm not picking up any dire problems with your liger. Humberto and I can coordinate bringing out some portable scanning equipment within the next few days."

Okay. Thanks, Ari sent.

"If you can't shift back, get out there and run," Dr. Rosas said. "You need to wear yourself out."

After everyone left, Gage, and Roman walked Ari's liger to the garage. Roman pressed the fob and the first stall opened. The four mattresses sat on top of a tarp on the floor, with another very large canvass tarp across the top. Gage placed folded clothes on the corner of one mattress, just in case she shifted.

Roman dropped her shoes on the concrete at the edge of the mattress.

"You're going to have to call out to us, or anyone you hear close by when you want to leave," Gage said.

I will. Right now, I only want to sleep, then I'll go for a run. She climbed onto the mattresses and gently flopped down diagonally. Her liger didn't leave much room for anyone else.

Roman scooted onto the mattress and rubbed Ari's animal face. He pressed tiny kisses on her face.

Gage had her back. He flung a leg over her side and snuggled into her, stroking her fur. After a few minutes, she dropped off to sleep. The men carefully got off the bed and left the garage by the side door.

The next morning, Ari silently called out to someone who was walking near the garage. One of the OPERA people entered the garage through the side door and pressed the button to lift the garage door for stall one. He lowered the door when Ari trotted out of the garage and around the corner to find a place to relieve herself. She headed to the house and stopped on the porch. She considered her dilemma.

Can someone open the front door?

After a few minutes, the liger huffed out in exasperation. She bonked the doorbell with her large nose and was rewarded with the sound of the bell ringing inside the house.

Mr. Butler hurried to the door. It startled him when he saw the enormous animal. "How did you do that?" He opened the door wide and stepped back out of the way.

Ari sauntered inside and headed to the kitchen. She parked herself by the refrigerator to let Mr. Butler know what she wanted.

He went into the butler's pantry and opened the spare refrigerator.

"Do you want a roast, or would you like this leg quarter?" He held the offerings in his hands.

Ari carefully grabbed ahold of the leg quarter from the timid butler. She gauged the room to see if there was enough space in the pantry to turn around so she could go outside and eat.

Mr. Butler shoved the roast back inside the refrigerator, then got out of the cat's way. He scooted around her and hurried to the kitchen door and opened it.

Ari's animal lumbered outside, crunching the leg quarter clenched in her jaws. Mr. Butler shut the door and leaned against it. He was getting used to the liger, but he understood that one wrong move and he'd be the leg quarter.

Sherm entered the kitchen, still in a sleepy fog from his

bedroom, and headed to the coffee machine. He made himself a cup of breakfast blend, added half a spoon of sugar and one shake of creamer. After he took a sip, made a deep sigh of satisfaction, he then focused on the lack of activity in the kitchen.

He noticed Mr. Butler at the kitchen door. "You okay?"

"I gave Ari a leg quarter," Mr. Butler said.

Sherm smiled. "Getting used to this shifter world, Mr. Butler?"

"Your world is definitely more interesting than the dull human one," he said. Mr. Butler moved away from the kitchen door and got busy with pulling plates, napkins and silverware together. He placed them on the table and headed to the refrigerator where he carefully pulled a flat of eggs out and set it on the counter. He grabbed a bowl of mushrooms, a large canning jar of chopped onions, another jar of colorful chopped bell peppers.

Gage and Roman wandered into the room, headed to the coffee and tea bar and started their brew.

Mr. Butler pulled out two packages of tortillas, a bag of shredded cheddar cheese, and a package of bacon.

Gage slurped his coffee and approached the counter where all the preparations for breakfast were laid out. "What do you need help with?"

"Do you want to make the cheese quesadillas, or the bacon?" Mr. Butler said.

Roman joined them. "I'm the bacon man."

Everyone set about with their tasks. Mr. Butler made the eggs. Gage tackled the quesadillas and Roman heated the frying pan to cook the bacon.

Sherm set the table, pulled glasses out of the cabinet for juice and poured it.

When Eddie and Phoebe entered the kitchen, everything was under control.

"I'll drive you to Austin today," Sherm said. "Warman's taking care of his people."

"Is Inggit going to be okay?" Phoebe asked.

"Yeah. It may take her a few days to recover fully," Sherm said. "The men are guarding the nest."

"What are we going to do about the castor bean plants?" Mr. Butler asked.

"We'll educate people," Roman said. "Pablo said there are too many plants all over the property, and the entire area to consider pulling them up."

"It's like fire ants," Gage said. "It's not like we can get rid of them. We have to be aware of them."

Aileen entered from the kitchen door. "You can get rid of fire ants, but you'd be poisoning the ground. So, it's best to be careful where you plant your feet."

Kenneth joined everyone. "Can I do anything to help?"

Mr. Butler did a quick inventory. "I believe everything is under control, thank you."

After a while, everyone settled at the kitchen table and dug into the food.

"Roman, I'd like you to look over some paperwork that my wife left behind," Kenneth said.

Roman quirked an eyebrow. "What is it regarding?"

"Property over in Ireland," Kenneth said.

"Did she have a will?" Roman asked.

"I don't know," Kenneth said. "I still have several boxes to go through."

"Since you were never divorced, you would be the first person in line to inherit, then Ari—if Alannah didn't specify people in a will. You might want to contact her people over in Ireland to see if anyone contacted them," Roman said.

Aileen laid a hand on Kenneth's arm. "I'll help. The clan is pretty easy to talk to. You and Ari need to be introduced to the family. A lot of them Zoom with me." She tipped her fork in Roman's direction. "No one back home knew she died until Charles and I informed them. I don't think Alannah would have created a will. Her entire focus was keeping under the radar so no one could find her."

"Oh, good. I appreciate your help," Kenneth said. "Ari and I spoke briefly about it, but I need to finish going through the boxes." His jaw tightened. "I don't know how she could have denied me my daughter!"

"Charles and I should have stepped in," Aileen said. "We argued about it, but we should have taken action. I know he regretted his decision, but he was the elder brother."

A loud raking of claws on the kitchen door made people jump. The liger's face took up the entire window as she glanced at the people seated at the table.

Can I come in? I'd like some company.

"You still can't shift?" Gage asked.

Ari hissed at him. *Don't you think I would have shifted already?*

There were grimaces among the shifters at the table.

"What's going on?" Mr. Butler asked. He felt left out.

Aileen leaned into him. "She's in a *mood*."

Mr. Butler quickly glanced at the door with trepidation.

Gage went to the door and stood back as he opened it. Ari hissed at him as she entered the kitchen. He swatted her rump as she passed by on her way to the living room.

"Does she need anything else to eat?" Mr. Butler asked.

Tell Mr. Butler I'm okay for now, Ari said.

Eddie finished up her breakfast and went over to Ari. "I love you, Mommy. Don't worry, it will be okay."

Ari gently licked her daughter on the cheek. *Have a good day at your school today, honey.*

Eddie squealed as she wiped her cheek. "Mommy!" She

ran over to the table, grabbed her napkin and scrubbed her cheek dry. "Gross!"

Phoebe snickered. "Ready to go?"

"Yes!" Eddie grabbed her backpack from against the wall.

Sherm drained his coffee cup, stood and dug keys out of his pants pocket. He and Roman nodded to each other. "You know where I'll be. Let me know if anything comes up."

Kenneth joined Ari in the living room. "Why don't I bring your mother's boxes over here and we can go through them... I'll go through them and show you what we're dealing with."

Okay, that will be great. We need to get this over with.

"I'll be back in a little while," Kenneth said.

Aileen and Mr. Butler began the kitchen cleanup and shooed Roman and Gage to the other room.

"I think I'm going to shift and go for a perimeter run of the property," Roman said.

"I'll join you," Gage said. "It's been quite a while since we've let our animals run loose, and we've never really explored any further than the dragon's house."

"Let's leave our clothes at the pool," Roman suggested.

See you later, Ari sent.

"Have Kenneth put aside anything he wants us to look at," Gage said. He ruffled Ari's hair, stood and walked to the French doors to the covered summer kitchen and the pool.

GAGE'S EAGLE soared over the trees. He spied Roman's panther on the ground as the cat wove through trees on the vast property. About an hour later, Gage noticed that he lost track of Roman. It brought up irrational fear from when Roman was kidnapped by the old Tothar king.

Roman? Where are you? I can't see you from the sky.

Get down here. Roman appeared in a small clearing in his human form and looked to the sky.

Gage spiraled down to the ground. *What's up? Did you find something?*

Yes. Not sure what, though.

Gage landed, then shifted. "Where is it?"

Roman led the way into the forest. He approached a huge old oak tree. There were three strands of rotted rope dangling from the thick branches.

"I think this was a hanging tree," Roman said.

Gage spied the rope and branches from different angles. "Geeze. Wonder when, who and why."

They searched the grounds with their keen shifter eyes. Roman tripped over some groundcover and caught himself before he face-planted. He stared at three old wooden crosses, cockeyed in the ground.

"Gage!" he called out.

Within moments, Gage trotted over to him. "Find something?" His eyes followed Roman's direction. "Are those grave markers?"

"That's what I'm thinking," Roman said.

"Do you think Ari's uncle hung these people?" Gage asked, shocked.

"His property. Wonder who might know about this," Roman said. "Do you think any of the OPERA people were around this long ago?"

"If I remember correctly, rope can last up to ten years outside," Gage said. "When Pablo was installing the rope swings, we looked it up online to see when we'd have to replace it."

Roman nodded while thinking. "The OPERA team has been there longer than that, so someone should know something about what happened here."

"We really need to discuss this with Ari before we poke our nose in the bee's nest," Gage said.

"Yeah, you're right," Roman admitted. "Let's head back."

They shifted and headed back to the house.

Gage beat Roman back to the house. He landed at poolside, shifted and dressed. He was sitting on a lounge chair putting his socks on when the panther arrived.

"Took you long enough," Gage said, ribbing Roman.

Roman shifted. "Yeah, well, you don't have to run across the ground around trees and brush." He made quick time of dressing, then they went inside.

CHAPTER TWELVE

They found Kenneth pulling papers out of a box, silently reading, then holding the paper up for Ari.

Aileen carefully went through the second box. She had several papers off to the side of a stack.

Roman and Gage joined Kenneth on the sofa.

"Anything of interest?" Roman asked.

"Most of this has to do with the various properties," Kenneth said.

Suddenly, Aileen gasped. She held what looked like a small notebook. She dropped it to the floor and dug into the box again and pulled out a second one and opened it. She scooted over to Ari.

"Your mother set up bank accounts for your sons!" Aileen said.

What are you talking about? She passed away before they were born!

"While that may be so, evidently she must have had a prescient moment and knew you would have two children, because she set up two bank accounts," Aileen stated.

She handed the bank books over to Roman. He, Gage, and Kenneth looked at one bank book, then the other. It appeared Jason and Kevin were quite wealthy.

"Did this money come from her family trusts?" Kenneth asked.

"It must have," Aileen said. "I can't imagine where else she would have accumulated millions of dollars."

Kenneth dug through one of his piles of papers and pulled out several stapled pages. "I found this brokerage information. She was quite gifted when it came to investing. This money may have been separate from the family trust."

How will the boys be able to claim these bank accounts? Ari asked.

"That may be tricky," Roman said. "These accounts are for *Grandchild #1,* and *Grandchild #2.* We'll have to find other documentation to determine how they can claim their accounts." He thought a moment. "This will be very tricky. She didn't use her given name, remember? She went by Susan Murphy."

Kenneth studied the brokerage paperwork. "These accounts are in her actual name—Alannah O'Briain." He flipped through pages. "There's paperwork in Susan Murphy's name as well. It may be a mess to sort out."

"We're going to have to establish a paper trail from Ireland to America," Roman said. "Then we can determine what names she used where, within the banking and investing businesses here."

"Maybe there's more money sitting in the brokerage accounts?" Kenneth looked at the remaining ten-inch stack of papers and folders in the box in front of him and the nearly full box in front of Aileen.

My poor boys! All the years they struggled when they could have been living in comfort, Ari said.

"While that may be so, look at their growth just over the years we have been together as a family," Gage said. "They wouldn't have been ready to handle the responsibilities of that wealth."

Let's call them here. They can help go through these files.

"Hold off a minute... I almost forgot. We discovered something in the woods that we need to find out about, and I'm pretty sure you're not going to like it," Roman said.

What? Ari asked.

"We think your uncle hung three people," Gage said.

WHAT? Ari looked from Roman to Gage. If a liger could express disbelief, it was what her face showed at that moment.

They shared the mind pictures of the old oak tree with the rotted ropes hanging down, then the three graves Roman stumbled onto.

"Maybe Pablo knows something about this," Gage said. He pulled out his cellphone and texted the groundskeeper to come to the house. Several minutes later there was a tap at the kitchen door, then Pablo let himself in.

"We're in the living room," Gage called out.

Pablo walked into the living room, hat in hand. His eyes landed on the huge liger. He grinned. "Do I need to make a run for meat?"

"No, we're fine for now," Roman said. "Pablo, this may be a touchy question, but do you know if Charles ever hung someone in the woods?"

The groundskeeper nodded. "You must have come across the tree."

So, my uncle hung someone? Ari asked.

Roman held his hand out to Ari. "Just hold on, Ari." He turned to Pablo. "What were the circumstances, and who were they—humans or shifters?"

"They were shifters. They raped a woman from town, and she killed herself," Pablo said.

The liger hissed. *I wish I could shift!*

Gage ran his hand through Ari's fur. *It will be okay.*

Pablo stared at the floor for a moment. "It was justified as far as I was concerned. Rosa felt the same way. Not all shifters are as civilized as you are, or how Charles was. He said there were some wild ones who barely kept their true identities a secret." Pablo nodded to Roman and Gage, then Ari. "You have brought about good changes for your kind."

"That reminds me, we never had a jail built," Gage said. "We should get ahold of Butch and fly him to Reading so he can see what we had built there. He can meet Wendell Smith, the ironworker."

"Okay, one thing at a time," Roman said. "Pablo, do you know the names of the three men?"

Pablo shook his head. "That happened a long time ago. Chewie probably knows more about it than I do."

"Okay, thanks," Roman said.

You could probably find out who the woman was by checking the newspaper archives. Surely, they'd have something about the rape and suicide? Ari asked.

Gage patted Ari. "Let's check with Chewie first. He may be able to provide details."

"Thanks, Pablo," Roman said.

The groundskeeper plopped his hat on his head and left by the front door just as Mr. Butler carried the mail to the house. The butler shuffled through the mail as he came into the house and set a piece of mail on the small table by the front door. There were times when mail that should have gone to the business post office box ended up in the mailbox for the house. Whoever headed to the office building could drop it by the front desk for Marcha to handle.

Mr. Butler noticed the tension from his bosses in the living room, along with Aileen and Kenneth. "Can I get anyone some tea, hot chocolate or coffee?"

"We may be drinking the hard stuff early today," Gage said.

"Is there anything I can do to help?" Mr. Butler asked.

"We have a sticky situation, Mr. Butler," Roman said. He and Gage reiterated the details. "Let me get Chewie over here since Ari can't go to the office building." He pulled out his cellphone and sent a text. An immediate reply sounded.

Be there in a few, Chewie responded.

There was a tap at the front door, then Chewie let himself in. He headed to the living room where Roman had said they would be.

"What's up?" Chewie said. He smiled widely at Ari in her liger form. "Hi, Ari. I hope you're doing okay."

I'm holding up as well as I can, she sent to Chewie.

He sat on the edge of a chair, wondering what was going on. He didn't have to wait long.

"Chewie, what do you know about the old oak tree in the woods with the three ropes?" Roman said. He purposely evaded the knowledge Pablo had given on the off chance that Chewie didn't know about the hangings.

"I knew we should have removed those ropes," Chewie said. "Charles wanted to leave them as a reminder to everyone that he would not tolerate any bullshit."

"Roman literally stumbled over the graves," Gage said. "What happened?"

Kenneth and Aileen quit digging into the boxes. Everyone focused on Chewie.

"There was this little gang that kept getting into everything. Mostly petty stuff, but there were a few times they were on the edge of serving time," Chewie said. "Bob Pettigrew, Steve Sawyer, Boo-Bear Anderson and Johnny Trevathan. There was another guy, but he got his act together and left the gang before that happened."

"We only saw three ropes and three graves," Roman said.

"Johnny saved himself from swinging on the tree when he turned in his pals to Charles," Chewie said. "Trust me, he didn't get away with much. Charles whipped him to within an inch of his life for a long list of shifter discretions. But in his defense, he didn't rape the woman. He tried to get his buddies to leave the woman alone."

Aileen patted Ari's shoulder. "My brother had little tolerance for anyone who was not up to his standards."

Chewie shook his head. "It was a tough time. Charles could barely keep his human form, he was so furious. Then when that poor woman killed herself, he came unglued. That's when he had us round up the guys, and he dealt them their just punishments."

"Didn't anyone miss those three men?" Gage asked.

"They probably assumed they moved on to another town," Roman said.

"The entire shifter community from here to Austin and San Antonio knew what happened," Chewie said. "Believe me when I say that they were glad to be done with those bastards. They caused so many problems for us."

Where's this Johnny Trevathan now? Ari asked.

"He lives in New Braunfels," Chewie said. "Turned his life around. He's married with a couple of kids."

Gage looked at Mr. Butler. "I'm ready for that whiskey now."

"Make that two," Roman said.

Kenneth, Aileen and Chewie raised their hands.

I wish I could drink! Ari said.

AFTER CHEWIE LEFT THE HOUSE, they returned to the business at hand.

"Why don't we wait until we have everything worked out before we drag the boys into this mess?" Roman said. "Right now, we don't know if they could access this wealth. I'd hate to get their hopes up, only to find out that it would be a lengthy process to stake their claims."

"Let's keep digging into the boxes and see what else we can find," Kenneth said. "I may have to backtrack through some of this information I set aside, now that we know what to look for."

"Hand me a stack," Gage said.

Roman held his hand out to Aileen.

Ari yawned.

TWO AND A HALF HOURS LATER, a bigger picture was taking place. There were three stacks of documents. One was for the bank accounts, and the other two were for two investment accounts.

They discovered Susan Murphy had opened the bank accounts in Philadelphia in the 1960s. She had used that name when she opened one of the investment accounts and used her birth name when she opened the second investment account.

"There's a good chance that this bank has gone through several mergers and acquisitions over the past fifty-plus years," Roman said. "It may take a while to hunt down the actual accounts."

"They should be collecting interest, shouldn't they," Aileen asked. "I don't know what happens to accounts if no one claims them."

"The investments will be a little easier to track because the company is still in business," Gage said.

"I can start the ball rolling," Kenneth said.

Roman shook his head, emphatically. "That won't work. You do not look old enough to have been her husband, even with an ID. Ari is in her middle seventies, so you would have to be in your late nineties or low one-hundreds. See what I mean?"

"While I enjoy my fountain of youth look, it presents a problem every once in a while," Kenneth said. "That's why I moved to the mountains."

"Don't worry about it. I'll handle all of this. I am still an attorney, after all," Roman said. "We're going to need supporting documents for the banks and the brokerage firms. They'll want proof of her identity, residency, rental or home ownership—we're going to have to build a big picture from the dates of last transactions to her death."

I have her death certificate, and other bits and pieces, in my closet in a box back in Reading, Ari said.

"Maybe you have most of the proof we need," Roman said.

"Why don't I ask one of Sherm's people to go upstairs and get whatever you think we'd need? They could overnight it," Gage said.

The front door opened. Thundering feet sounded, coming through the door.

"Hi, Mommy! Hi Daddy Roman and Daddy Gage!" Eddie all but yelled.

Phoebe followed Eddie into the room, then Sherm.

"What are we shipping overnight from Reading?" Sherm asked.

"Man, do we have a lot to tell you," Gage said.

ARI SHOWED Sherm the boxes through her mind pictures. "Miller, go to the third hallway and enter the door at the far end on the left side." He waited. "Okay, the walk-in closet in the bathroom—it's immense. You'll see the shelves on the right where some boxes are." He waited while Miller got into place. "The third shelf up from the floor is where three boxes are. Ari said they have Mom written on them."

Sherm looked to Ari for confirmation.

Mom in black marker.

"Find them?" Sherm asked. "Okay, secure them and ship them overnight." He shoved his phone back into his pocket and stood. "I'll be at the office. Holler if you need me." He headed out the front door.

"Can I go play outside?" Eddie asked.

"I think Phoebe needs a break, honey. You just got home," Gage said.

The nanny-slash-tutor's eyes flipped over to Kenneth, then quickly moved away again. "It's been a long day, and I didn't sleep well last night."

Kenneth looked guilty. He manned up and confessed. "It's my fault. We were talking until late."

All eyes bounced from Kenneth to Phoebe.

"It's okay," Eddie said. She looked at the others in the room. "They like each other. I'm going to change my clothes." She rushed toward the hallway where her room was.

Phoebe's face was crimson. She implored Roman and Gage with her eyes. "If you forbid this, I'll step back."

Kenneth reached out and grasped her hand. He shook his head. "Why would you think what we're heading toward is forbidden? I don't think my daughter would condemn us." He turned to Roman and Gage. "What about you two?"

"Knits the family closer," Gage said.

Phoebe visibly relaxed.

Eddie rushed back toward the front door. "I'll be right outside playing hopscotch."

"Have fun. Watch out for fire ants," Aileen said, as the front door slammed shut.

"Let's build a timeline," Roman said. "No matter how frivolous this paperwork is, start getting it into order, from the earliest to the latest date." He turned to Ari. "I feel bad that we'll be going through those boxes instead of you."

There's nothing personal in them—no secrets. However, I have things my mother didn't know I snuck from her—utility bills, which might help with the timeline. I even swiped a department store bill once. Everything was such a secret as I was growing up, and we moved so often. It was difficult for me as a kid to understand why I couldn't stay at one school, make friends.

Kenneth reached across the stacks and rubbed the side of Ari's face. The liger leaned into his hand. "If I knew you existed, I would have fought for you!"

"Those things could also help establish credibility," Gage said.

Aileen appeared thoughtful. "I had a thought. What if I pretended to be Ari, and she pretended to be my assistant— can't say granddaughter because of those bank accounts. That way we could go with you to meetings, and Ari could provide information, if it would be helpful."

Roman thought about it. "You have all the knowledge of the clan over in Ireland, and when Alannah came to the states. Let's see how my phone calls go. I'll use your suggestion as a backup plan."

Everyone nodded at the plan.

EDDIE TOSSED her rock piece that had her first name initial painted on its surface, onto the hopscotch layout. Her brothers had drawn it in chalk at the side of the parking area alongside the old oak trees. She leapt over two squares, precariously landed on her feet, rocking from heels to toes until she steadied herself. She looked over her shoulder to see if she missed stepping on the lines. Happy that she landed fully in the squares, she hopped through the rest of the layout: one foot, two feet, one foot, one foot, two feet.

BIG BEAR MUCHISKY had his eyes on the security monitors at his station at the front desk of OPERA and Panther Industries. He quirked a smile as he watched Eddie playing hopscotch.

Just as she hopped and turned around to go back to the home square, three black SUVs pulled up into the driveway.

Big Bear was on his feet sounding the alarm mentally to all shifters on the property as he ran for the front door. *UNIDENTIFIED INCOMING VEHICLES!* He sent a mind-picture of the black SUVs that were now parking in the parking area between the house and garages.

Eddie stared at the vehicles, wondering who they were.

Six men in black suits with earpieces in their ears got out of the cars. Their eyes darted all over the place, taking in the environment.

Eddie eyed the men with mounting fear. She didn't recognize any of them from all the people she had met in San Marcos, or back in Reading. Thoughts of her attempted kidnapping rushed through her head.

One of the men walked up to her, smiling. "Hi. What's your name?" He rested his hand on her shoulder.

"Daddy!" Eddie screeched, totally freaking out. She mentally screamed for all it was worth.

Big Bear Muchisky was running toward Eddie like a runaway train. Security shifters stepped out of the woods ready to engage in protective action.

"Identify yourselves!" one of the shifters said as he listened to the mind chatter of the strangers.

"No one's going to hurt you," the strange man said to Eddie. He patted her shoulder, trying to reassure her.

The other agents' eyes darted from their associate to the Panther employees on the sidelines.

Big Bear yelled as he approached. "STEP AWAY FROM THE CHILD!"

The agents had their guns trained on the enormous man that approached.

The front door flung open with force and bounced against the entry wall, creating a dent in the wall as Roman and Gage rushed outside. Roman took one look at the stranger with his hand on Eddie's shoulder and sprinted over to her, barely controlling his shifter speed.

Big Bear joined the shifters on the sidelines as he watched the big boss deal with the situation.

Roman grabbed the agent's hand, wrenched it behind the guy's back, then applied immense pressure and crushed it.

"Aiii!" the man howled as his bones crunched.

"Don't you ever lay a hand on my daughter again, or you will pay the consequence," Roman warned.

Sherm! Get out here. There're some government agents here, Gage sent. *I don't know how much longer Roman will hold his shit together!*

"It's okay, honey. You're safe." Gage grabbed up Eddie and swiftly moved away from Roman. Gage saw that his life partner was barely controlling himself, and he prayed Roman wouldn't accidentally shift into his panther.

A roar sounded from inside the house.

"Turn down the TV!" Gage yelled toward the house, trying to cover up for Ari's furious liger. *Ari, Roman and I have it under control. Quiet down!*

Kenneth, Aileen, Phoebe, and Mr. Butler tried to steer Ari away from the front door toward the master bedroom. Her enormous size, which was six foot at her shoulders, and approximately twelve feet long, made it nearly impossible to even push her in that direction.

"Ari, if those are government agents, you have to get out of the living room!" Aileen said. "Please try to focus. Roman and Gage will take care of whatever is going on outside."

I swear, if one of them so much as puts a finger on Eddie, I'll shred him! Her upper lip lifted in a snarl.

Suddenly, she shifted to her human form. "Ooof! Finally!" She stumbled and grabbed onto one of the chairs, which prevented her from tumbling to the floor. She straightened up, but was slightly unstable on her human feet as she headed to the front door.

"Ari!" Kenneth and Aileen called out at the same time.

"I need to get out there!" Ari said.

"You'd better get dressed first," Kenneth said, as he raised an eyebrow.

Ari looked down. "Oh!" She covered herself with her hands. She was a little out of whack from being stuck in her liger form for several days. She rushed from the room toward the master bedroom.

Only a few minutes later, she dashed down the hallway and into the living room. It was apparent that she grabbed clothes and dressed hastily because her clothes were mismatched. Her hair was a mess, as if she had napped and didn't bother to brush it.

Ari flung the front door open with force, and emerged outside, somewhat unsteadily followed by Phoebe, Mr. Butler, Kenneth and Aileen.

Gage rushed over to her with Eddie in his arms.

"Mommy!" Eddie wailed and flung herself into Ari's outstretched arms.

They caught the terror running through Eddie's mind as she relived the kidnapper grabbing her and pulling her into the woods.

"It's okay, Eddie. Mommy's here," Ari said, as she stroked Eddie's hair.

The agents pulled badges out of their jackets. The Feds postured aggression, with guns drawn.

"Release Agent Jones, or we'll use force," one of the Feds said.

Roman tightened his grip on the agent. "You come on our property, uninvited, accost a minor child, then threaten us? This guy may not leave here with this arm."

"I didn't accost your daughter! All I did was pat her on the shoulder, I swear," Jones wailed.

Sherm, in full commando gear, ran full speed from around the garage building with Lonnie, Kevin, Jason and two of the huge male dragons thundering toward the hostile government intruders.

"What the hell's going on here?" Sherm asked, as he slowed and took in the obvious agents who were dressed in the typical government uniforms: black suits.

The agents were spread out. They all had their weapons drawn. Guns swung in different directions to the ever-changing dynamics of the situation.

Everyone from the house was gathered in a protective circle around Eddie, still in Ari's arms.

Sherm recognized the danger of Roman's position. The agent he had more or less captured, was in pain with broken bones. Rage was mucking around in Roman's head, and he had a tight hold on his panther who wanted to shred these people.

Four of the agents attempted to stop Sherm from approaching his people. Within a matter of minutes, three were down on the ground writhing in agony.

"You government drones better stand down or you may leave in an ambulance," Sherm warned.

The two standing agents had their weapons pointed at him.

Sherm's eyes widened as he recognized one of them. "Johnson? What the hell?"

CHAPTER THIRTEEN

"Sherm?" Johnson asked, surprised. He holstered his gun, started to approach, then thought better of it. "Jesus Christ, don't kill us man!" He focused on his teammates. "Listen carefully. I can personally attest that this guy is a deadly walking weapon. You've heard of Panther Industries, right? They do *special* projects for us sometimes. Stand down if you want to be able to walk to the cars."

The other agent standing with Johnson reluctantly holstered his gun. The agents on the ground got up and brushed themselves off. They all took in Sherm's backup, including the huge dragon men.

"What the hell are you doing here, Johnson? No one gave us a heads up," Sherm said. He turned to Roman. "Let him go, Roman. It's contained."

Roman's face and posture softened, slightly. He nodded to Sherm, then released Jones. Roman joined Gage, Ari and their people from the house.

Agent Jones cradled his broken arm and stumbled toward Johnson and his team. He didn't look or act like a hotshot anymore. "You take lead," he gasped out to Johnson, trying to dial back the agony in his voice. Jones managed to dig into his jacket breast pocket and pulled out a folded piece of paper and jabbed it at Johnson.

Johnson smoothed out the paper and held it out to Sherm.

Sherm snatched the paper Then he and his team walked around the agents and joined their people. He unfolded the sheet of paper and held it out to Gage.

"We want to borrow your daughter for an assignment," Johnson said.

They all thought Ari would shift right then and there. Kenneth threw an arm across her shoulders and whispered in her ear. "Stay calm. Listen to what they have to say. You **cannot** shift."

Roman and Gage were visibly furious at the request.

"You want to *borrow* our daughter?" Gage asked.

For a moment, Sherm thought he saw feathers sprouting on Gage's head, but they disappeared.

Johnson looked from Roman to Gage. He addressed Roman. "I thought she was your daughter?"

"We share custody," Roman said.

"This is a low-risk assignment," Johnson said. "She would be in a conference room with a bunch of foreign dignitaries. She can color or play with toys. The big wigs want her to listen to all conversations and report what she hears from whom. That's it."

Roman stared down Johnson with steely eyes. "You want to use a four-year-old child as a spy instead of your spyware? Seriously?"

Jones cut Johnson off. "Look, we know about her skills. I've seen her in action at Texas A&M with my own eyes. She has the highest IQ ever recorded, and we know this would be child's play for her brilliant mind. The Pentagon will pay top dollar for her services."

Roman, Gage, and Sherm were dead against this. Ari was beside herself with the *request*.

"No way in hell," Roman said. He icily stared at Jones. "There've been too many times when your *simple* assignments turned into mortal combat. If you think you're going to put our daughter in danger, you're crazy."

"Call your contact at the Pentagon," Ari insisted.

Roman pulled up a chart on his phone and placed the call. "General Dickinson, please." He listened. "Tell him it's Roman Davenport with Panther Industries. Believe me, he'll want to talk with me." He placed the call on speaker.

"Roman? I'm kind of tied up right now..." General Dickinson said.

"Toby, if you want your boys returned in one piece, you'd better find the time to stay on the line," Roman stated.

The government agents controlled their faces. They couldn't believe someone would talk to a four-star general that way.

"What the hell's going on? Where are you?" General Dickinson asked.

"I'm in San Marcos, Texas at our new place." Roman reiterated what Jones and Johnson presented to them.

They could all hear General Dickinson inquire to whoever was in the room with him. There was a muffled conversation that the shifters couldn't quite make out.

"Okay," General Dickinson said to someone in the room. "Roman, you there?"

"Still here, waiting for an explanation," Roman said.

"There's a meeting with some Russians tomorrow afternoon, and I'm told you have a brilliant daughter who might be able to lend a hand in obtaining some intel," the general said.

"My daughter isn't flying to Russia. Not for you, the President, or God for that matter," Roman said.

"DC, Roman, not Russia," the general said.

They heard someone in the room talking to the general.

"Roman, it's in your best interest to agree to this meeting," General Dickinson said.

Roman, Gage, and Sherm became even more livid. Ari caught up, and her face flared into rage.

"Toby, are you suggesting that the United States government would seize my daughter—a four-year-old child—for this *assignment?*" Roman asked with disbelief.

The government agents tensed as the conversation on the phone heated.

"No one's going to *seize* your daughter, Roman! Calm the hell down," the general said. "It's one time."

Roman, Gage, Ari and Sherm eyed each other.

"One time, Toby. Do I have your word?" Roman asked.

"You have my word," General Dickinson said.

"You will never ask for this kind of favor ever again. Sherm and I will accompany her," Roman said.

"Hand the phone over to the agents," the general said.

ARI PACKED pajamas and two sets of clothes into Eddie's backpack, along with a toothbrush and a hairbrush.

"Why can't you come with me, Mommy?" Eddie asked, whiny.

"Mommy's too unstable right now, honey. I don't know when I'll shift to my liger," Ari explained. "Your sister and brother are growing stronger in my tummy, and my animal wants to protect them."

"I'll be the best big sister ever!" Eddie said.

Roman and Gage came into Eddie's bedroom.

"All set?" Gage asked. He tried to hide his nerves, but failed as he ran his fingers through his hair.

Ari zipped up the backpack as Sherm entered Eddie's room.

"You make sure you don't let her out of your sight," Ari said with force.

"They're not going to whisk her off to a secret place," Gage snapped.

"How do you know? It's the government, after all," she hissed.

"Look, we need to go; they're waiting for us," Sherm said.

Ari's eyes filled with tears as she clutched Eddie to her. "You be a good girl for Daddy and Sherm... and the government people, okay?"

Eddie clung to Ari. "I promise, Mommy."

THE NEXT DAY, a limo brought Roman, Sherm and Eddie to the Pentagon. An aide met them outside and escorted them inside the building through security, then to a conference room. Several men and women sat around a table in high-backed, comfortable, leather padded rolling chairs, including General Dickinson. They stood as Roman, carrying Eddie, and Sherm entered the room.

The general shook Roman's hand. "Good to see you again, Roman. Sorry for the misunderstanding." He fluffed Eddie's mop of blonde hair. "So, this is the smartest human being on the planet? Do you speak Russian?"

"конечно, я делаю," Eddie said, in flawless Russian.

"What did she say?" Sherm asked, looking from Roman to the General, then Eddie.

"I said, of course I do," Eddie said. She beamed a smile at the general.

The general shook Sherm's hand. "I hear you're still causing trouble, Mr. Foo."

"Only when it's called for," Sherm said. He smiled wickedly, then winked. He loved jerking the government's bells when he could.

"I think you should train our people. Johnson told me you had the drop on three of the team before they knew what happened," General Dickinson said. He shook his head. He moved toward the table. "Come sit down so we can talk about this meeting."

The general patted a chair next to him. "Eddie, why don't you sit here."

Roman deposited Eddie on the chair. "We're all curious to find out what you want Eddie to do."

One woman in a colonel's uniform couldn't conceal her surprise. "This is a little child. I thought you said..."

Eddie looked a little steamed. "I'm working on my first PhD at Texas A&M university. Maybe you should ask me something you consider difficult, as a test."

The woman stared at Eddie. "A PhD? In what? Coloring?" She tittered at her own joke. Then she noticed the hostile looks from the other side of the table, including the general.

"Colonel Jenkins, did you not take the time to look over the dossier I sent to everyone around this table regarding Edris Davenport-Davis-Stryker?" the General asked.

"Well, of course I did, but I don't recall reading that this genius was such a young child," Colonel Jenkins said, somewhat offended at the general's tone. She focused her attention on Eddie. "What do you know about The Pentagon?"

Eddie snickered. "It's where the Department of Defense is located. They started building it in 1941. It's considered the world's largest office building with six million five hundred thousand square feet of office space, with five floors above ground and two floors underground. This is boring. I thought you were going to ask me something difficult. I can explain nuclear fusion if you don't understand how it works."

Roman frowned at his daughter. "Eddie, that's not nice. Apologize to the colonel."

Colonel Jenkins shrunk back in her chair, fully aware she had been bested by a four-year-old kid.

Eddie rocked from side to side while chewing on her finger after Roman's scolding. "Sorry, Colonel Jenkins."

"If you don't mind, Colonel Jenkins, time's passing," General Dickinson said rather gruffly. He turned to Eddie. "We're expecting some Russian delegates in a little while. We would like you to sit in the conference room with them—you'll be in there before they arrive—and just listen to their conversations. You can color, or read, or play with your toys. If you can learn all of their names so you can identify who is talking, that would be good."

Eddie looked the general in the eye. "Do you want me to pretend I don't know Russian?"

"Yes! Don't let on you understand them at all. Can you keep a straight face, no matter what you hear?" the general asked.

"Sure," Eddie said.

The General turned to Roman. "I'd like you to go into the conference room after our people join the Russians. Act surprised someone's in there, apologize, but explain that you had to bring your daughter to work, your wife's expecting twins—just blather on like you're sorry for the inconvenience."

Roman glanced at Sherm, then back to the general. "You want me to play a part in your game? No one mentioned that."

"I thought it would be an explanation, of sorts," the general said.

"Okay, I can do that," Roman asked.

"Don't worry, Eddie. These are all nice people. They won't do anything to scare you," the general said. "Ready?"

"Okay," Eddie said.

The general rose to his feet, and they all walked out of the room.

They travelled down a long corridor and the general guided them into a conference room with a long conference table and black padded rolling chairs.

"Why don't you sit at the end of the table, over there?" he suggested to Eddie as he pointed to the chair opposite where they stood.

Eddie trotted around the long table and climbed onto the chair. She stayed on her knees with her back to the wall.

Roman removed Eddie's backpack and placed it on the table. "Do you need anything to snack on?"

Eddie shook her head. "No, I'm okay."

Everyone marched out of the room; the last person out closed the door softly.

Eddie looked around the light gray room. There were no embellishments on the walls. Not even a white board. She dug in her backpack and pulled out a box of crayons, some copy paper, one of her books, her little stuffed tiger, and a juice box. She drew a picture with the crayons.

Around ten minutes later, the door opened. A man in a suit escorted a group of seven Russians into the room.

Eddie looked up from her coloring.

"What is this?" one of the Russians asked, his hand waved out toward Eddie.

"Hi," she said, shyly.

"Oh! I'm so sorry. This is the daughter of someone who's

here for meetings. She won't bother you... I don't have anywhere else to put her right now. Her father will come and get her when his meeting ends," the man said.

The man left the room; the Russians crowded together at the other end of the room. They whispered in Russian as they stared at Eddie suspiciously. They were a little irritated and had heated discussions in Russian.

They probably put bugs in her crayons and things.

How do you think that tiny child is going to spy on us?

I seriously doubt that a four-year-old is fluent in Russian, so let's discuss our agenda. We're wasting valuable time.

We should scan her before we say anything else. Did you bring the scanner, Max?

Yes.

Max opened his briefcase and removed what looked like an iPod. He turned it on and set it on the table. He held up his hand to make everyone understand he wanted them to be quiet. After only a few minutes, the device emitted a soft beep. The man nodded, picked up the device and walked down to the other end of the table. An older man followed him.

The older, grandfatherly man sat in a chair by Eddie. "Hello. What is your name? I am Sacha, and this is Max." Eddie reminded him of his granddaughter.

"My name is Edris, but you can call me Eddie," she said. "Where are you from?"

"We're from Moscow, which is the capital of Russia," Sacha said.

"Is that a long way from here?" Eddie asked. She knew full well where Russia was. She had memorized the map of the world and was familiar with every country, their capitals, demographics and other tidbits of information.

"Yes, it's across the big ocean," Sacha said.

Max waved the iPod scanner around Eddie as she knelt on the chair.

"What's he doing?" Eddie asked, as she squirmed around trying to watch him.

"Oh, he's just scanning you and everything on the table," Sacha said.

"Why?" Eddie asked.

"To see if there are any bugs on you or in your things," Sacha said.

"Bugs?" Eddie giggled. "I don't have bugs!"

"Well, we have to make sure, because we don't want to catch your bugs, or bring any home with us," Sacha said.

Eddie looked very serious. "We moved to Texas and they have fire ants there!"

"Fire ants? What are those?" Sacha asked.

"My daddy stepped on their nest and they crawled all over his feet and legs and bit him all over the place!" Eddie said. "Uncle Sherm turned on the hose and got them off him. We had to go see this lady who put medicine on the bites. Daddy almost cried."

"That's terrible!" Sacha said.

"We have these big mosquitos too. They make you itch when they bite you. Do you have mosquitos in Russia?" Eddie asked.

"Not all parts of Russia, but there are some in the city where I live," Sacha said.

"Have you had mosquito bites?" Eddie asked.

"Yes, they are quite unpleasant," Sacha said.

Max picked up Eddie's tiger and scanned it.

"My tiger doesn't have bugs! Mommy won't put up with fleas in the house," Eddie said. "A lot of cats live at our house."

"What are their names?" Sacha asked.

"Ari, Roman, Aunt Aileen, Jason, Kevin, and a bunch more," Eddie said.

"You have a cat named Aunt Aileen?" Sacha asked.

Eddie nodded. "Yes, she's a very old cat."

Sacha looked at Eddie's drawing. "What are you drawing?"

"This is where I live. See, this is our house, and there's the garage. I have a hopscotch game on the ground that my big brothers made for me," Eddie said as she pointed everything out.

All set, Max said in Russian. *I didn't find anything.*

Let's get started before the others get here, Sacha said.

"I have to go talk to my associates now," Sacha said.

"Okay," Eddie said. "I'll draw a picture of you so I won't forget you!"

Sacha kissed Eddie's forehead. He joined his people around the table.

THE RUSSIANS TALKED among themselves for a half an hour when a tap sounded on the door before it opened. Four men and a woman entered the room. Everyone seemed acquainted with each other as they all shook hands, exchanged pleasantries and sat.

A few minutes later, the door opened, and Roman entered. He faked startled when he saw the room full of people.

"Oh! I'm so sorry for disturbing your meeting. I'll just gather up my daughter," he said.

Sacha stood. "You have a precious little girl." He shook Roman's hand.

"We're expecting twins and my wife is having a difficult time, so I bring Eddie along when I can," Roman said. He helped Eddie pack her backpack.

"She was no bother. So much like my little granddaughter, Irina," Sacha said.

Roman picked up Eddie.

Eddie waved to everyone. "Bye! Bye Sacha!"

"Bye, Eddie," the Russians and the other people said.

ROMAN AND EDDIE were escorted down a long hallway to another room where Sherm, General Dickinson, Colonel Jenkins and the others waited. Roman settled Eddie in a chair next to Sherm, and he sat in the chair on the other side of her.

"We're going to record everything you say here, Eddie. How did the meeting go? Was everyone nice to you?" General Dickinson asked.

"I like Sacha very much. I hope I get to see him again," Eddie said.

"That may not be possible because he lives a long way away," General Dickinson said. "But I'm glad he was nice to you. Shall we get started? Can you tell us what happened in the room before the American's arrived?"

"First, Max scanned me and all my stuff with something that looked like an iPod," Eddie said.

"How did a scanning device get through security?" Colonel Jenkins asked, alarmed.

"If it looked and functioned like an iPod when it was scanned by security, it stands to reason someone would think it was one," one of the people said.

"Sacha talked with me while Max scanned everything. Then he told Sacha in Russian that there were no bugs. Sacha said they needed to get started with their agenda before the others showed up," Eddie explained. She pointed to chairs around the table to identify who was in the other room. "Max,

Sacha, Dimitri, Oleg, Adrian, Leo and Viktor. No one mentioned their last names."

She told them verbatim what was said in the room and by whom, even mimicking voices.

When she finished. Everyone stared at her in awe, including Roman and Sherm, but especially Colonel Jenkins.

"Please forgive me for acting like a jerk before," the colonel said, directly to Eddie. "I feel privileged meeting you, Eddie. Now, tell me about that PhD you're working on."

The general eased an envelope out of his pocket and slid it across the table to Roman. "Why don't you and I spend a minute catching up." He stood, then Roman stood.

"Don't let her out of your sight," Roman told Sherm. "I'll be back shortly."

"They'd have to go through me to take her from this room," Sherm said, with a nod of confidence and a wink. It would take more than the governmental officials in the room to subdue him, regardless of their training.

Roman followed the general out the door. They walked across the hall to a secured office. As soon as the door closed, the general bowed low and stayed there longer than a blink.

"I'm sorry, King Roman. There wasn't any way I could give you a heads-up," General Dickinson said.

"Toby, this better never happen again," Roman said. He was furious. "I'm grateful that everything turned out okay, but Eddie needs protection now. We didn't think things through when her scores were uploaded to the gifted children's website. Her intelligence puts a huge target on her back."

"Christ, if anyone can get through Sherm and his team, that would be a miracle," the general said. He looked thoughtful for a minute. "Did Sherm shift? I thought he was one-hundred percent human?"

"Man, you should have been there," Roman said. "He was a

mess. Had no clue he was a wolverine until his mother and grandmother showed up."

"Sherm's a wolverine? Damn!" General Dickinson said. He looked thoughtful. "Makes sense now that I think of it. As a human, he had some of those traits."

"I'd better get going. Ari is having a hard time, and shifts into her liger at the drop of a hat," Roman said.

"Tell her *thank you* from me," the general said.

They returned to the room where they found Colonel Jenkins and Eddie in a deep conversation with Sherm listening in. The others had left the room.

"Ready to go home, Eddie?" Roman said.

Sherm and the colonel stood.

The colonel shook Roman's hand. "You are one lucky man. I've just had the most remarkable conversation with your daughter and let me tell you. She taught me a few things."

Roman nodded. "She amazes us on a daily basis."

Sherm swung Eddie up on his hip. "Ready to go back to hot Texas?"

"Yes! But, you know, we really should get mommy a present before we get on the plane," Eddie said in an all-knowing voice.

CHAPTER FOURTEEN

Roman declined the government's jet to return home, fearing they would be monitored closely. He and Sherm didn't worry about the trip to DC since it had been late in the day, and they either rested or slept on the government's dime.

Sherm arranged for one of Bruce's team back in Reading, Pennsylvania to fly to DC and bring Sherm some weapons, and a device that could scan for bugs. They kept their conversations generic while they waited for Russ to arrive.

Roman booked them into a different hotel for the night, since Lonnie wouldn't arrive in their own private jet to fetch them until the next day. Roman and Sherm were certain that the agents had planted bugs in the pre-arranged hotel room. They wouldn't be surprised if the clothes they were wearing at the Pentagon had picked up tiny listening devices.

Sherm told Eddie in shifter mind-talk not to say anything about what happened at the Pentagon until Russ scanned them and all their possessions when he arrived.

In the meantime, Roman and Sherm entertained Eddie with a trip to a jewelry store to pick out something for Ari.

Then they went to a store and found souvenirs for everyone else back at their house in San Marcos. By the time they finished lunch at a seafood restaurant, Russ called to tell them he had arrived.

They met in the lobby at the new hotel and went up to the rooms Roman had reserved. Russ pulled a queen-size, white bedsheet out of his pack. They moved the coffee table and spread the sheet on the floor, all without talking verbally.

Eddie said the Russians scanned her and all of her things, but she still could have picked something up in the final conference room, Sherm told Russ.

Okay, let's start with each of you standing in the middle of the sheet, one at a time, and let me scan you, Russ said. *You're still wearing the same clothes from the meeting, right?*

Yes. I figured we wouldn't change until you scanned everything. If we have to buy new clothes, I can have something delivered for each of us, Roman said.

Eddie, let's start with you, since you're the most obvious to be bugged. They're probably hoping that you'll bring the bug back to Texas so they can collect intel, Russ said.

Eddie walked to the middle of the sheet and stood with her arms at her sides, then outstretched while Russ ran the scanner over her. Sure enough, the device alerted them that there was a listening device on the back of her t-shirt.

Take your shoes off, Eddie, Russ said.

He dug into his pack and removed a high-powered magnifying glass, a pair of long tweezers, and an evidence bag. He and Sherm took turns searching for the device. Sherm found it on his second try. He wiggled his fingers for the tweezers, then plucked the tiny bug off Eddie's shirt and put it in the bag. He filled in the information so they could determine who planted the device, the government, or the Russians.

They scanned the bottoms of Eddie's shoes, but didn't find

any other bugs on her, so they moved on to her backpack and all of her items. They found another different type of bug on her tiger.

I'll bet Max put that there because he scanned my tiger, she said.

Roman and Sherm each had a bug attached to their clothing. Roman carried his rolling bag to the middle of the sheet. Russ scanned the exterior of the bag, then Roman unzipped the suitcase and lifted the lid.

The first thing he noticed was two black hairs on top of his clothes.

These aren't my hairs. Same color, but too short.

Russ examined them, then Sherm looked.

Clever, but too obvious. Should have hidden them, Sherm said. He opened another evidence bag, grabbed the tweezers and put the spyware into the bag and sealed it.

Russ scanned every item, then the interior of the bag. Next up was Sherm's bag. They uncovered three bugs. Two attached to different pieces of clothing, and the third attached to the bottom of his bag, which looked like a metal grommet.

Sherm shrugged. *They must think I run a sloppy ship or something.*

Russ took all the evidence bags and put them into a metal case that would contain them so they could speak freely. He scanned the sheet to make sure an overlooked piece of spyware hadn't fallen to the floor. Satisfied that all was safe, he rolled up the sheet and stuffed it back into his pack, along with his tweezers and magnifying glass.

"Well, that was fun," Russ said.

"When you get back to Reading, I want you to identify these bugs and see if there's any intel we can use," Sherm said.

"You don't want to bring those back to Texas so Travis can do his thing?" Roman asked.

Sherm shook his head. "Better to let Reading handle them. Once we have the facts, you can let the general know we're on to him and his little game."

"I'm pretty sure Toby wasn't involved," Roman said. "I might want to have a conversation with him to let him know he's out of one of the loops."

"That's not good," Sherm said. "Maybe he should think about retirement."

Russ gathered up his pack. "I'm going to head back home. I really want to get into these devices, especially those wires that looked like hairs."

"Thanks for the quick trip," Roman said.

THE NEXT DAY, Lonnie fetched them in the jet. Roman, Sherm and Eddie took a cab to the airport, and they were happy they were back on trusted ground once again, so to speak. Their private jets were swept for spyware before and after each flight. They settled into their seats and prepared for takeoff.

"You know what, Daddy?" Eddie started. "I think we should try to find an island so Inggit and Novi's eggs can go back to where all those other Komodo dragons live."

"Honey, they came to Texas for sanctuary, so I'm pretty sure they wouldn't want their eggs to go back there," Roman said.

"Think about it, Daddy," Eddie said. "Texas can't have forty to sixty Komodo dragons running around—not all of them will be shifters. People would come from all over the place to see them, then they'd be in danger all over again."

Roman and Sherm sat quietly in thought.

"I hadn't thought about that," Roman said. "Do you think

you can find an island near their original home where their eggs would be safe?"

"I'll try," Eddie said. She yawned.

"Why don't you take a nap? It's going to be a few hours until we get home," Roman said. He stood, retrieved a blanket and a pillow and put Eddie's seat in a sleep position, then he covered her up and kissed her cheek. "Have a nice nap."

He and Sherm moved to the back of the cabin so they could talk without disturbing Eddie.

"I don't like anything about this trip," Sherm said. "We're going to have to step up security when we get back home. I want cameras all the way out to the front and back roads. Something tells me there's a bigger agenda than Eddie spying on the Russians."

"Ari and Gage are going to go ballistic about this," Roman said. "We're all going to have to be extra vigilant about our conversations in town, or anywhere else we go. That includes the OPERA people. Better set up a meeting as soon as we know what Russ discovers."

Sherm worked his phone. "I'm having Travis start on the cameras. He'll let Jason know how many we need to order."

"I'd better call Gage. I don't know if Ari shifted back or not," Roman said. He pulled out his phone and placed the call. "Hey, is Ari doing okay?"

She's shifted a couple of times. Doesn't seem like its anything she can control. I had to do a little damage control, Gage said.

"Damage control? What happened?" Roman asked, tensely.

Sherm stopped texting and focused on Roman.

She stole a cow from the farm and hauled it back here. Mr. Butler about freaked out when he found it on the side of the house... or rather, pieces of it, Gage said.

"Oh, shit," Roman said.

"A cow?" Sherm squawked out. "A whole cow... on the hoof?"

Roman nodded. Then he shook his head at the dire circumstances it put them in. "That's not good. Why didn't she tell you or someone she needed more meat?"

Who knows? She's pregnant, and everything's changed. She's all whacked out and her thought processing has flown out the window. How'd it go on your end? Is Eddie okay? Gage asked.

Roman put the call on speaker and he and Sherm quietly outlined what happened in DC.

If those fuckers come after Eddie, they're going to be in for quite a surprise. We may have to expand the cemetery in the woods. I'll speak to Mr. Butler, Pablo, Phoebe, Kenneth and Aileen. The boys as well. I'll let you handle the OPERA people and our people in the office. Ari's going to go off her rocker when she hears this, Gage said.

"We'll be home in a couple of hours." Roman disconnected the call. He ran his hands down his face.

"Comes with the territory," Sherm said. "Going to have to step up Eddie's security for school. May have to recruit shifters from San Marcos to cover all the detail we need between the house and property, and the university."

"Let's see what state Ari's in when we get home. She has that spreadsheet and knows who's employed and who's not," Roman said. "We may be able to put people to work."

"They're going to need training," Sherm said.

Roman nodded. "That too. The list grows."

ROMAN, Sherm, Gage, Lonnie and his team sat in the largest conference room in the office building. The OPERA team leaders, the dragons, and all the Panther people who worked onsite attended.

Sherm started off by detailing the DC trip, the spyware, and the government's interest in Eddie.

"Everyone needs to be extremely vigilant about what they say out in public places and while on cellphones. It's also important to pay attention to the people around you. I don't think the government would actually kidnap Eddie, but it's the government, after all," Roman said. "One more thing. If you're talking with someone at work—either in a conference room or on the office phone, and they start asking questions about Eddie or us, alert someone at Panther immediately. I would not be surprised if they infiltrated your clients for information."

"Jesus!" Melly said. "I'll call a meeting with all the OPERA people immediately."

"If anyone here knows any shifters who need a job, we're stepping up security and we're hiring," Gage said. "Ari's looking over her spreadsheet and she'll send out an email, but we would appreciate referrals."

Roman! There's someone in the woods, Kenneth sent.

Roman startled. "Kenneth said someone's in the woods!"

Everyone stood.

Sherm motioned for people to keep their seats. "Stay put until you hear from me." He turned to Roman and Gage. "Let's go to his apartment and see if we can get a bead on who it is and where they are." Next, Sherm eyeballed Lonnie. "You keep everyone here. I don't want anyone giving away anything prematurely."

Sherm led Roman and Gage to the elevator, and they rode up to the fifth floor. They didn't bother knocking on the door.

"Where are you?" Sherm called out.

"In here," Kenneth said.

They walked into the bedroom. Kenneth stood to the side of the window, using his finger to hold back the darkening drape enough to be able to see outside. Sherm, Roman and Gage hugged the wall so no one would see them from outside.

"I've caught a flash of something two or three times. Nothing should be there, unless one of the squirrels suddenly bought a camera," Kenneth said.

"Let me see," Sherm said.

"Look between four and five on a clock," Kenneth said.

Sherm took his place at the side of the window and barely moved the drape. He studied the entire area for a moment, then focused on the area Kenneth mentioned. A flash of light caught his attention.

He backed away from the window, pulled out his cellphone and placed a call. "Big Bear, I want you to go to the conference room and relieve Lonnie for a few minutes." He disconnected, then placed another call.

"Lonnie, when Big Bear gets there, I want you, Chewie and the dragons to come up to Kenneth's apartment on the fifth floor to get a visual. Then we'll all-out capture us a spy, or as Kenneth said, a squirrel with a new camera."

They heard feet stomping up the stairs at the same time the elevator dinged.

Gage met everyone in the living room. "One at a time, then we'll gather here and make a plan."

After everyone saw the location, the group met in the living room.

"Warman, Chewie and Gage—go toward the house, then veer around through the woods until you're within a visual range. Kenneth, Lonnie and Eyo—get a buggy and make like you're going to the house in the woods. Don't be quiet until you're out of hearing range, then backtrack on foot until you're behind who's out there. Dirdjo, Sopan, Roman and I will take this side," Sherm said. "Make sure you stay in place until I tell you how to proceed."

They broke up into groups and left the building.

Warman, Chewie and Gage walked casually toward the house, joking and laughing.

Kenneth, Lonnie and Eyo walked over to the garage and got a buggy and took off on their venture.

Sherm led Dirdjo, Sopan and Roman to the lobby. "Wait for me." He went to the conference room. "Everyone hang tight until I tell you to leave. Big Bear, head back up to the front. Be on the lookout for someone who may run through the parking lot in a little while," Sherm said.

Sherm walked back to the lobby. He filled in the bear shifter and Marcha at the front desk.

"Don't let whoever it is get away. We'll be circling around to try to apprehend whoever's spying on the building," Roman said.

Big Bear stood at the counter and huffed. "Want me to stay inside, or outside under the overhang?"

"Outside, but make sure you stay out of sight," Sherm said. "I don't want you to be trying to sneak a peek at what's going on."

"Honestly, you'd think I just started this type of work?" Big Bear asked. "You flush him out and I'll tackle him."

Sherm gave a playful jab to the huge shifter's shoulder. "Atta boy." He turned to Marcha. "Stay in here where you're safe. Remember... bulletproof glass is there for a reason."

"I'm not going anywhere!" Marcha said.

Sherm turned to his team. "Okay, Kenneth's bedroom is that way, so we have the protection of the building working for us."

"Let's follow the side of the building, then get into the

woods without being heard. Make sure you're light on your feet," Roman said.

The four of them left the building. The three teams quietly got into place. They discovered a man dressed in camouflage with a pair of binoculars and a camera, taking pictures.

Human, Sherm sent to the teams. *Could be military, or the government, so don't use your animal speed. We'll have to play this carefully.*

Big Bear, he's human, Roman sent. *Use caution if he comes your way. You might be able to get away with your animal speed, but only if he has his back to you.*

Okay, Big Bear sent.

The three teams quietly closed in, then rushed the man. He took off running, as Sherm expected. The man made a mad dash across the parking lot. The bear shifter tackled him to the ground.

"Got him," Big Bear Muchisky called out verbally and in mind-talk. He secured the man's wrists together with zip tie cuffs. Then he dragged the guy to his feet as the three teams arrived, and everyone from the conference room came outside.

Roman patted the guy down and relieved him of his wallet and everything that was in his pockets, which included a keyring.

Sherm instructed a large group. "Search the perimeter, all the way back to the front and back roads. There's a vehicle somewhere. Could be others out there. Use stealth. Kenneth, you and Jason find those binoculars and the camera. See if there's anything else lying around."

"Dirdjo, Sopan and Eyo," Roman said. "Go to your house and check the surrounding area. Alert Inggit and Novi. Kev, you and Tommy go with them."

"Warman and Big Bear, get this spy into the smaller conference room. I want one of you inside the room, one outside the door," Sherm said.

The large men each grabbed one of the man's arms and hauled him inside the building.

Sherm opened the guy's wallet. A Texas driver's license was in the window compartment. He pulled it out. "Robert Fuller." He pulled out a military ID that was in back of the license.

Roman and Gage read the ID over Sherm's shoulders.

"How are we going to handle this?" Roman asked. "Do I contact the general, or what?"

"My gut tells me he's not aware of this little scheme," Sherm said. "I could be wrong, but I think someone else is in charge of this little game."

"That colonel?" Roman asked.

"Doubt it," Sherm said. "Probably someone else who was in the room that wants more decorations on their uniform. Let's go inside and see what Mr. Fuller wants to tell us."

CHAPTER FIFTEEN

Lonnie used hand signals and texting to direct the group through the woods. They were soundless as they crept through the trees.

Someone's down on the ground digging or doing something, Tommy texted.

Stand down. Keep him in view. Wait until I get there, Lonnie texted. He texted Chewie and Kevin to join him so they could nab the guy. He texted the rest of the team to keep searching to see if there were others on the property.

Lonnie, Chewie, and Kevin quietly approached Tommy's location. Chewie called out to Tommy in mind talk to alert him they were approaching. They gathered where the young shifter crouched between a tree and some ground-cover.

They watched the guy on the ground who was dressed in camo, with what looked like military-issued boots.

What's he doing? Kevin texted.

Chewie studied the guy's activity. *I bet he found some mushrooms.*

Psilocybin mushrooms? Lonnie texted.

What are those? Tommy and Kevin both texted.

Magic mushrooms that can get you stoned, Chewie texted.

"Chewie, you go around to the opposite of our position here. Tommy, go to the right, Kevin, go to the left. I'll take the front. Let me know when you're in position, Lonnie whispered. He texted Sherm. *Found someone in the woods digging up mushrooms. May be a civilian, but he's wearing camo. Will know in a while.*

Approach with extreme caution, Sherm texted back.

When everyone was in place, they charged the guy. He got to his feet and attempted sprinting away, but Chewie tackled him to the ground.

"Where do you think you're going?" Chewie asked. He dragged the guy back to where he had been foraging.

Lonnie dug some zip tie handcuffs out of his pocket and secured the guy's wrists together behind his back.

Kevin and Tommy searched the ground where their captive had been diligently digging around. Sure enough, there were mushrooms. Chewie looked at the ground.

"You didn't eat any of these, did you?" he asked the guy.

"I just took a small bite to make sure they were edible," the guy said.

"I hate to tell you, but these are Destroying Angels, a death cap mushroom of the genus *Amanita*," Chewie said. "You may have to get your stomach pumped."

"What were you doing out here?" Lonnie asked.

"Just looking for mushrooms," the guy said.

"On private property? In camouflage?" Lonnie asked. He nodded to Chewie. "Get him back to the building. Tommy, you go with him. Kevin, let's keep looking."

He's escaping! Eyo blasted out in shifter mind-talk.

Human on the run from close to our house. Heading through the woods to the back road, Sopan announced.

"Eyo and Sopan said someone's escaping," Kevin announced for Lonnie.

Kevin and other shifters in the woods took off running at shifter speed. Lonnie held his own in pursuit. He was fast, but not quite shifter fast. Sherm and Roman joined in the chase.

Goddamn infiltrators, Sherm belted out. He didn't care who picked up on his thoughts at that moment.

Dirdjo power-ran in shifter mode for all he was worth. He smashed into the fleeing spy within twenty feet of an extended cab pickup truck. They both crashed to the ground.

Got him! Dirdjo sent. His animal talk didn't give away that he was panting from the exertion.

Eyo and Sopan soon joined him. Others arrived on the scene, all panting.

Lonnie retrieved his phone and shot a picture of the license plate and sent it to Travis, along with a picture of their captive.

Roman was beyond steamed. He got in the guy's face. "How many in your team?"

"I don't know what you're talking about," the guy said.

Roman had a moment where it looked like he'd lose it.

Gage pulled Roman back from the spy. *Remember what we're dealing with. You need to stay on task.*

Roman stared at his partner, his eyes spiked with anger. Then he exhaled and nodded. *Thanks. I'm okay now.*

"If this is the only vehicle, there may be more people out in the woods," Sherm said. He patted the guy down. No keys. "Guess we already have the keys. Everyone, keep searching. If you don't find any other vehicles, we'll have to assume this is it."

The dragons hauled their prisoner through the woods back to the office building. Big Bear stood by the outer door and opened it as the group approached. Dirdjo and Sopan held their captive in the lobby until Sherm, Roman and Gage entered the building.

"Where do you want him?" the dragon asked.

"Need to keep them separated," Sherm said. He looked at Big Bear. "Where's the last guy they brought in?"

"Across the hall in that little room," the bear shifter said.

"Okay, we'll put this guy in the other small room," Sherm said. He directed Dirdjo and Sopan. "I want one of you on the inside of the room, the other on the outside, at the door. Empty his pockets and check his boots."

The dragons hauled the guy through the coded door.

"Let's go upstairs," Roman said.

SHERM, Roman, Gage, and Lonnie slumped into chairs on the third floor in the Panther Securities offices.

Jason stopped working and turned to the group. "What the hell is going on? Are those guys military?"

"Private vehicle belonging to one Robert Fuller," Travis said.

Kevin came through the door and dropped into his chair. He slowly spun his chair from side to side.

"Kevin, go downstairs and get everything that came out of their wallets. Do we have paper lunch sacks to put them in?" Sherm asked.

Travis opened his desk drawer and pulled out plastic grocery store throwaway bags. "How many bags do you need?"

"Three," Gage said.

Kevin got up, grabbed the bags and took the elevator downstairs.

"It was a big mistake to go to DC," Roman said. "And an even bigger mistake to post Eddie's scores. Ari's going to kill me!"

"She's not going to kill you. We all are equally guilty of not thinking things through," Gage said. "We were all agog over Eddie's intelligence and the fact she'd skip the entire standard education of a normal child. I don't think the trip to DC could have been avoided."

The elevator dinged Kevin's return. He carried three plastic grocery bags with names in fat black marker on them, and a pair of boots. He placed them on Sherm's desk. "This is Robert Fuller's, this is Dwayne Johnson's, and this is the last guy, Jack Johnson—no relation to Dwayne. Those dragons said they had to tackle him to get his boots off."

Sherm and Lonnie eyed the boots. They each grabbed one.

Lonnie ripped the inside lining out of the boot. It wasn't hiding anything. He turned the boot upside down and twisted the heel. It slid away to the side. "What do we have here?"

Sherm stopped what he was doing. "Looks like a little kit of spyware, but way too easy to discover." He checked the heel on his boot and made a similar discovery.

"Just received a message from Russ," Travis said. "The spyware on Eddie and her tiger were from the Russians. The rest was USDA grade A-American."

Roman cursed under his breath.

Sherm and Lonnie set the boots aside and dug into the bags. They spread everything out. There were only Fuller's keys, so they assumed only one vehicle. They all had military ID cards, and plastic from the same credit union that catered to the military in San Antonio.

After the group studied all the contents of the bags, they prepared to go downstairs and debrief the three men.

"Hey, why don't I swap out their spyware for ours?" Travis said. "If you put that lining back inside the boot in a sloppy way, they might not think you found anything."

"Let's see if we have something that they won't suspect isn't theirs," Sherm said.

Travis took the tiny cases, opened them and studied the two small pieces inside each. He went to the Panther supply cabinet, unlocked it with his badge, then perused the boxes and bins. He held something out. "I think these will do."

He grabbed an evidence bag and dumped the four from the heel kits inside, then labeled the bag. Then he removed a small soft cloth from the cabinet. He used a long pair of tweezers and chose four almost identical pieces of spyware from the Panther supply cabinet and dropped them on the cloth. He rubbed them all over to make sure they were free of any partial fingerprints. When Travis was satisfied with the results, he used the tweezers and dropped them into the tiny heel cases.

Then he rubbed the cases with the cloth, walked over to where the boots were, and dropped the cases into the heel compartments. Lonnie closed the heels. Travis took the boots and rubbed the cloth all over the heels. He left the top part of the boots as is. The military would expect to see their fingerprints on the top and the inside of the boots.

"If they don't talk, can we use truth serum on them?" Lonnie asked—a little too enthusiastically.

Sherm pondered, making weird faces as he thought of all the different scenarios. "Not such a good idea."

Lonnie thumped his knee with his thumb. "The guy who was foraging for mushrooms said he took a small bite of one. Chewie told him they were poisonous. Maybe we could drug him with a drink. He'd think he was hallucinating, or something."

"That sounds like a pretty good idea!" Gage said. He looked over to Sherm, then Roman to see if they were onboard.

Sherm nodded. "Yeah. Let's try it. Only that one guy, though. The others would know we drugged them, and we'd be walking a fine line with the military."

Lonnie got into a different cabinet and pulled out a brown vial. "What are we going to mix it with?"

"Either iced tea or soda," Sherm said. "Whatever we have downstairs."

They all went downstairs and went to the breakroom where a free drinks machine was located. Roman chose a can of root beer. Kevin retrieved two glasses from a cabinet and put ice in them. One sported a football logo, the other *thanks for donating blood* slogan.

Lonnie squeezed two drops from the vial into the blood donor glass. "Make sure you don't get these glasses mixed up."

Kevin put the glasses on a small tray and carried them out of the breakroom and out to where the conference rooms were. Tommy stood outside the door of the mushroom hostage. He opened the door for Kevin.

Kevin mind-talked to Chewie. *Take the glass with the sports logo. The other one is a special treat for our guest.*

"Thanks, man," Chewie said. He took a big gulp. "Oh, root beer. I haven't that in a long time."

Kevin approached the guy zip tied to the chair. "Here's some root beer if you're thirsty." He set the glass on the table and left the room.

Let us know if he drinks it, Kevin sent to Chewie.

"I'll cut one of your hands loose," Chewie told the guy. "If you don't want that root beer, I'll take it."

"I want it—I'm real thirsty," the guy said.

"Probably from that mushroom you ate. You could feel dehydrated and spacey," Chewie said. He took his knife out of his pocket and cut one of the guy's hands free.

The guy grabbed the glass and chugged almost the entire contents in one long drink. He stopped for a breath, then drank the remaining soda. He swiped his lips with his arm.

He drank the entire drink, Chewie sent.

We'll give it ten minutes, Sherm sent.

Within a few minutes, the guy swayed in his chair. He belched loudly, rested his head on his loose arm on the table.

"Hey, you okay?" Chewie asked.

"I don't feel so hot," he said.

The door opened and Sherm, Lonnie, Gage and Roman entered. Sherm pulled a chair out opposite the guy and sat.

"What's your name?" Sherm asked.

"Dawwayne Johnnnson," he said, stretching out his words as the drug settled in.

"How many of you came out to this property?" Sherm asked.

"Me, Jack, Bobby and Truman," Dwayne slurred.

Lonnie was out the door running down the hall to the front. "Big Bear, call out to the search teams!"

The bear shifter called out to everyone in mind talk. *There's one more guy out there somewhere! Name's Truman. Everyone use speed.*

Boots on stairs thundered down to the lobby and out the door. Other shifters plowed through the inner doors and joined in the search.

Lonnie instructed the bear shifter to pass along the messages.

Someone get to the truck immediately! He could hotwire the truck unless he knows about a hidden key! Big Bear Muchisky sent.

Roman, Gage, Lonnie and Chewie contained their anger at having missed one of the infiltrators.

"Who sent you?" Sherm asked.

"Peterson," Dwayne said.

Sherm glanced over to Roman.

Roman shrugged. He couldn't remember meeting anyone in DC named Peterson.

Maybe that's his commander in San Antonio? Gage sent.

Roman nodded. *Possibly.*

"Is that your commander?" Sherm asked.

"Nah, never met him before today," Dwayne said.

"What were you supposed to do here?" Sherm asked.

"Get intel, schedules. Take pictures of everyone," Dwayne said.

"Was today your first day out here?" Sherm asked.

"Uh huh," Dwayne said.

"Do you work with this Peterson on similar missions?" Sherm asked.

"No, he chose us for this project—sort of random," Dwayne said. He pantomimed pointing to various directions, as if he were making choices from a large group.

"Do you know a General Dickinson?" Sherm asked.

Roman stiffened, waiting for the answer.

"No," Dwayne said.

"Do you know Colonel Jenkins?" Sherm asked.

"Never heard of him," Dwayne said.

Roman let out a silent breath he had been holding.

I don't think we're going to get anything else from him, Sherm sent.

I need to call the general, Roman sent.

Sherm stood. He, Roman, and Gage headed toward the door.

He may sleep for a while, he sent to Chewie. *If he looks like he's going to be sick, we may have to*—suddenly he had a thought. He turned to Gage. *Can you get Mr. Tran down here? Maybe he'll know what to give him for that mushroom he ate.*

Good idea, Gage sent.

They left, leaving Chewie on the inside of the room, and Tommy outside the door.

LONNIE and his searchers combed the woods. He had a thought. He stopped, pulled out his phone and texted Pablo. *Can you take a car and drive the roads around the property and see if you spot a guy in camouflage? Don't use a buggy. That would spook him. Stop and offer him a ride. Let me know if you get him. Maybe take Aileen with you so she can mind-talk with a shifter.*

Pablo texted back, *Okay. I'll go get Aileen and we'll head out.*

Thanks, Lonnie texted. He picked up where he left off on the search.

ROMAN, Gage, and Sherm went upstairs to Sherm's office.

"Travis, see if you can find out who someone by the name of Peterson is," Roman said. "He's military, but I don't know if he's someone from San Antonio, or DC."

Gage pulled out his phone. "Mr. Tran? We've got a situation." He explained about the guy eating the Destroying Angels death cap mushroom, and that they used truth serum on him. They worried about the poisoned mushroom more than anything else. "He's in a small room on the ground floor. Chewie's with him, and Tommy's outside the door. Okay. Thanks." Gage looked over to Roman. "He's on it."

Travis' fingers clacked on one keyboard, then another one. "Okay, there was someone named Peterson with you in the meeting in DC, but there's also a high-ranking Peterson in San Antonio."

"Fuck it," Roman said. "I'm calling Toby." He pulled out his phone, went to his contacts and placed the call. "Can you talk?" He listened. "Are you alone? Call me back from a secured line. You're not going to want anyone else to hear this." He disconnected the call.

They all waited quietly, their thoughts going in a million directions.

Roman's phone rang. He quickly glanced at the screen, then answered on speaker. "Toby, I'm warning you that as your king, if I find out you're lying to me, I will seek revenge, and it will be lethal."

What in the world are you talking about, King Roman? Toby asked.

Roman and Sherm outlined about the spyware they discovered on their clothing and in their luggage in DC, and the current situation in San Marcos.

"You are no longer in the loop, Toby," Roman said. "Someone has taken command and we are all in imminent danger here."

Let me check into what Colonel Peterson has been up to. I swear if that bastard has gone around me, he may suddenly have an unfortunate animal attack.

Roman disconnected the call. "I'm going over to the house and see what Ari's up to. She's going to flip! They'd better find that guy before her liger does!"

Gage stood. "I'll go with you."

"I'll come with you. I want to be around when the general calls back," Sherm said.

They left the building, walked across the parking lot to the house and went inside the house.

"Anyone home?" Gage called out. "Seems awfully quiet."

"In here," Ari yelled back.

Mr. Butler came out of the pantry. "Aileen and Pablo are driving around the property in one of the cars, looking for one of the invaders. Can I get you some iced tea or berry water?"

"That sounds good," Sherm said. He looked to the others. Then he twirled his fingers to show they all wanted tea.

They continued on to Ari's office. She was staring at her spreadsheet and highlighting line items; her back to them.

"We have some local shifters who have responded to my message for security positions," she said. "They'll need training, but we can evaluate them when they show up for the appointment."

"How many?" Sherm asked.

"Eight so far," Ari said. "They are either unemployed, or in low-paying jobs and would jump at the chance to have a career in security. I thought it would be better to have them all in a room at the same time, so you didn't have to go over the details multiple times."

"Honey, you've most likely heard a commotion around here outside," Gage said.

Ari slowly turned in her chair and stared at her men. "What's going on? Something happened on that trip, didn't it? What aren't you telling me?"

Sherm slipped out of the office and returned with a kitchen chair. They all sat in front of the desk to face the music that they knew would surely come.

Mr. Butler chose that moment to enter with a tray of drinks and coasters. He placed the coasters on the desk, set glasses of iced tea down, including a fresh glass for Ari. He snatched up Ari's half glass of now warm tea and left the room.

"I now realize we should have had this conversation as soon as we returned," Roman said. "But I wanted to get everyone in the building on alert. I figured Eddie would have filled you in."

"She came in, kissed me and went to take a nap," Ari said. She glared at Roman and Sherm, then swept her eyes over Gage. He flinched.

They took turns laying out everything that took place as

soon as the DC meeting was over, and all about the spy activity on the property.

She was furious. Ari was so mad, Gage noticed whiskers blooming on her face.

"Ari, you can't shift in here! You'd wreck your office," he warned.

She took a deep breath, picked up her glass and rolled the icy surface across her face. Then she took a sip.

We have your guy, Truman, Aileen sent.

"Who's Truman?" Ari asked.

"He's the fourth infiltrator," Sherm said. *Get him over to the building. Have Lonnie put him in a room by himself.*

Roman's phone rang. "It's the general."

Sherm stood and closed the office door.

"What did you find out, Toby?" Roman asked.

King Roman, the bastard's in San Antonio. I'm having him detained. What intel did his men access?

"Not much," Sherm said. "It was a very loose detail. We just rounded up the fourth guy. I'm not releasing their phones —they contain photos of the property and people here."

"Oh, and one of them ate what he thought was a magic mushroom, but turned out to be poisonous," Roman said. "Our herbalist should be able to help him, otherwise he's going to need his stomach pumped."

Colonel Jenkins and I are flying into San Antonio this after-noon. I'll call you tomorrow when I have the full details.

Roman raised his eyebrow in question to Ari. She nodded at his silent question. "Why don't you and the colonel come to dinner tomorrow evening? We could put you up overnight."

I'd love to come to your home! I look forward to meeting King Gage and Queen Ari in person. But you realize that the colonel isn't a shifter.

"We know. Ari may not be available for the entire visit.

She's having a difficult pregnancy and can't control her shifting," Roman said. "We definitely don't want the colonel to stumble over our little secret."

I'll see you tomorrow evening. Could you text me the time, address and any particular directions I may need to find your place?

"Will do," Roman said. He disconnected the call. "What are we going to do with these guys?"

"Should have followed up with having a jail built," Sherm said. "We could shove them in Leo's old apartment."

"Has it been cleaned out? We sure don't want them finding any weapons or electronics," Gage said.

"I'll ask Tommy and Doug to go through it again," Sherm said. He worked his phone.

"So, this Colonel Peterson was responsible for the spyware you discovered on you on the east coast?" Ari asked. "And the Russians bugged Eddie, right?"

"That's about what we know at this point," Roman said. "We don't know what this Colonel Peterson's agenda is, but Toby will find out and he'll let us know tomorrow night."

CHAPTER SIXTEEN

Mr. Tran knocked on the door. Mr. Butler opened the door and welcomed the herbalist inside.

"Come into the kitchen," Mr. Butler said. "Would you like some iced tea?"

"That would be wonderful!" Mr. Tran said. "Is Roman, Sherm, and Gage here?"

"They're in a closed-door meeting with Ari. There's only been a little bit of yelling, so I guess things are moderately okay," Mr. Butler said.

They both smiled. The royals were known to sound off and even take a swing at each other upon occasion.

Ari's office door opened. Gage came out carrying empty glasses.

"Hi, Mr. Tran," Gage said.

"Is it okay if I report in to Roman and Sherm, or are you continuing with your meeting?" Mr. Tran asked.

"Go... catch them while they're quiet," Gage said, with a little chuckle.

Mr. Tran left the kitchen and headed over to Ari's office. He tapped on the doorframe. "Hello."

"Hi, Mr. Tran," Ari said.

"How's the guy who ate the mushroom doing?" Roman asked.

"He will be purging for the next hour or so," Mr. Tran said. "Too much time lapsed to give him activated charcoal, so I had to treat him with purging herbs."

"Oh, poor Chewie," Ari said.

"We found a large metal wastebasket," Mr. Tran said. "It was fortunate you had administered truth serum, because I used it to convince him to take the herbs."

"Let's hope he doesn't miss the wastebasket," Gage said, returning to the room. "The cleaning people may not appreciate that mess."

Ari's face screwed up in thought. "Let me get this straight. One of these spies was going to deviate from his orders to get stoned on magic mushrooms, but accidentally poisoned himself?"

"That about sums it up," Roman said.

"I sometimes wonder about humanity," Ari said.

"I wanted to also let you know that Janina and I will be going to Italy next week," Mr. Tran said. "Alan and Mr. Benston will return to Reading, and we wanted to have one or two days with them to discuss the progress in the library."

"Are any of the residents of the Palazzo helping with the translations?" Ari asked. "A lot of those shifters are hundreds of years old, and I'll bet they speak several languages."

Mr. Tran nodded. "There are three men and two women helping us. It's a chore just labeling the shelves, but at least a timeline is becoming much clearer in that room."

"How is Alan doing?" Gage asked.

"He's coming out of his shell," Mr. Tran said. "When he's

at the palazzo, he's around people all the time, and it forces him to communicate. I think his family will notice a significant difference in him."

"He's a nice young man," Ari said. "I have a feeling his father is overprotective to the point of smothering him, so these trips are good for him. Maybe he'll show some independence and want to get his own apartment someday soon."

"We should invite him here for a few days," Gage said. He looked over to Mr. Tran. "Why don't you arrange for him to come here and work on the big books when you return?"

"Very good idea!" the herbalist said. "We will discuss it when I see him next week. Well, I best be going. Cama and I are going to swap some herbs."

"I'll bet that's interesting," Ari said. "We like Cama."

Mr. Tran nodded and left the room.

Ari leaned over her desk and whispered. "I think they like each other!"

A BLACK CAR pulled up to the parking area at the house. General Dickinson and Colonel Jenkins, both still in their Army uniforms, got out of the car and approached the house. The front door opened and Roman greeted them before the general reached for the doorbell.

"Welcome to our home, Toby, Colonel Jenkins," he said. "Come in and join us."

Roman guided them to the living room where most of the household inhabitants gathered.

Eddie got off the sofa and ran up to the colonel. "Colonel Jenkins! Are you going to stay for supper?"

The colonel laughed, then scooped Eddie up in her arms

for a quick hug. "Yes, your family invited me to dinner, along with the general." She set Eddie back on the floor.

The front door opened and Jason, Janina and Kevin entered.

There's a human among us who knows nothing about shifters, so everyone be careful, Ari sent.

"Let me make some introductions," Roman said as he guided their guests around the room. "General Dickinson and Colonel Jenkins, this is my partner, Gage Stryker, and Ari Davis, our life partner."

My King! My Queen! The shifters in the room noticed the slight bows Toby made when he was introduced to Gage and Ari.

"You know Sherm and Eddie. This is Kenneth, Phoebe, Eddie's tutor and nanny, Ari's aunt Aileen, my stepson's Kevin and Jason, and Janina, Jason's fiancé. Soon, you'll meet Mr. Butler. Did I forget anyone?"

"Please call me Toby," the general said.

"And I'm Sheila," Colonel Jenkins said.

"Come, get comfortable. Would you like a cocktail?" Gage asked.

"I could use a good stiff drink after the day we've had," Toby said.

"I'll take a glass of white wine," Sheila said.

Gage headed to the bar.

"So, what did you find out in San Antonio?" Roman asked.

"Colonel Peterson is being detained," Toby said. "He faces some serious charges when we return to Washington. He used government resources for this little mission of his, which no one ordered him to carry out. I could be mistaken, but the people I spoke with said he carried this out on his own, thinking he would be promoted. I have ears on the walls trying to find out if I am out of an important loop, as you suggested."

Gage passed a rocks glass to the general and a wineglass to the colonel.

Toby took a drink and let out a swoosh of a breath.

"What about these men he sent on this mission?" Ari asked. "They seem to be innocent victims. Are they going to be demoted or charged with anything?"

"No, they were following orders," Sheila said. "We should question them before they're released."

"We can walk over to the building after supper," Roman said.

"I met with my superiors about your daughter before we flew out here, and everyone has agreed that unless there's a national emergency, we will never call upon her again," Toby said. "That whole scenario was not thought out very well either."

"We don't know what Colonel Peterson thought he was going to gain by having bugs planted in your hotel rooms and on your clothing," Sheila said.

"It's bad enough we have targets on our backs for our wealth, but now with a brilliant child—everyone's going to want to get their hands on her," Ari said. She stood suddenly. "I'm sorry... I have..." She fled the room.

Gage and Roman were on their feet in no time and dashed after her.

"They'll be back," Aileen said. "Ari is having a difficult pregnancy with the twins. She may feel sick, or have to lie down."

"Oh, no," Sheila said. "Is she okay?"

"She'll be fine after a while," Kenneth said. "The slightest things upset her, and with all the problems of late, she's been super sensitive."

Roman and Gage returned to the room.

"Ari's going to lie down for a little while. She may join us a little later," Gage said.

Mr. Butler entered the room. "Dinner is ready."

Everyone stood and followed the butler to the dining room. Once everyone settled around the table, Mr. Butler and Dirdjo served the meal.

Mr. Butler took his place at the table, but Dirdjo bowed and left.

Sheila raised her eyebrows after the impressive man left the room. "Did he just bow?"

"He's very respectful," Sherm said. "He's only been in the States a short time, and it will take a while for him and his group to realize they don't have to bow down to Americans."

They were quiet while everyone ate.

"Looks like you have a wonderful spread here," Toby said. "I want the grand tour. I should look for a place for when I retire."

"Do you have any plans to retire anytime soon?" Roman asked.

Toby glanced at Sheila. "I'm seriously considering it."

Sheila nodded. "We've had private discussions. We don't like the current leadership."

Sherm, Roman and Gage conducted a private, silent conversation.

"We could use someone like you on board at Panther," Sherm said. He eyed the colonel. "You too, Sheila."

Toby stared across the table at the kings and their head of security. "I will take that into consideration. What would that entail?"

"We have teams across the globe. Most of the organization is conducted here. Lots of strategizing between San Marcos and Reading, lots of online meetings with the teams and clients, some of which are government contracts, as you well know," Roman said.

"We run a tight ship," Gage said. "As you already know, Sherm doesn't take any chances, and we hire only the best that his people train to our standards, which are pretty high."

Toby chuckled. "Yes, we know all about Mr. Foo's tight ship." He turned to Sheila. "If you saw Sherm in action, you'd wonder about some of our *highly trained* people."

"Why don't we go over to the building so you can question the soldiers while you're in uniform, then you can change, relax and we'll show you around the property," Roman said.

"Good idea," Toby said.

"The guy who ate the mushroom may not be in great shape," Gage said. "Mr. Tran, our herbalist, administered purging herbs, so your guy may look a little green."

"We're going to have to think about how we're going to address that. He was on a mission, even though it wasn't authorized," Sheila said.

"It's grounds for a writeup," Toby said. "Can't have someone who won't follow orders. Must have a drug problem."

"We'll let you deal with that," Sherm said. "I will tell you they are not well-trained spies from what we observed, depending on their actual functions in the military."

Napkins were left on the table. Chairs scraped back. They all stood and filed out of the kitchen with Sherm in the lead. They walked over to the office building.

Toby and Sheila looked around at the property.

"This is a nice setup," Toby said.

"We love it here," Roman said. "When Ari inherited the property and her uncle's business, we flew out and couldn't believe what we were missing. We thought we had it all in Reading."

They approached the office building and entered through

the bulletproof glass doors. Two very large shifters were on duty for the night shift.

"Good evening, Mr. Davenport, Mr. Stryker, Mr. Foo," a guard said. "Need badges?"

"Evening, Sanderstonn," Roman said. "This is General Toby Dickinson and Colonel Sheila Jenkins. Get them badged up."

"Will do. General, Colonel, I'll need your drivers' licenses or another form of ID, such as your military IDs." Sanderstonn passed an index-type card across the counter to each of them, along with a pen. "And if you could fill out this basic information for me. Then I'll take your pictures and get you each a badge."

Toby glanced at Roman, Gage and Sherm, then fished his wallet out of his inside breast pocket, slid it across the counter and filled in the info on the card. The colonel followed suit.

"Good setup for information gathering," Toby said.

The general moved to stand in front of the camera.

"Don't look so grim, general," Sanderstonn said.

Toby chuckled and loosened his expression for the camera.

Sanderstonn printed the badge, affixed a clip, and handed it to the general.

Sheila smiled for the camera.

Once they had their badges, they all took the elevator upstairs to Leo's old apartment, now the temporary jail. A shifter in a commando uniform by the locked door jumped from his chair, hand going for a weapon as they approached. He relaxed when he recognized his kings and Sherm.

"Everything okay with the prisoners?" Sherm asked.

"No problems other than complaints about their sick pal," the shifter said. He pulled a set of keys out of his pocket, unlocked and opened the door for them.

Roman texted a message for Tommy to bring the bags that contained the prisoners' belongings, minus their phones.

Sherm let the general and colonel enter the apartment first. He followed Roman and Gage inside, and the guard pulled the door shut behind them.

Three soldiers jumped to their feet and saluted. They stood at attention with their bare feet together and their shoulders back. Everyone heard vomiting coming from the bathroom.

The colonel and general walked that way and shared the doorway. The sick soldier noticed them and attempted to salute. The general shook his head at the sorry sight. They returned to the living room.

"Does someone want to explain what you were doing here?" the general asked.

Truman saluted. "Sir, Yes Sir! Colonel Peterson picked us out for this assignment. He didn't explain why we were being sent on this mission. He told us to get intel regarding people's comings and goings, and to take pictures."

The general and colonel looked at the other two for corroboration.

"Do any of you have anything to add to that?" the colonel asked.

"No, ma'am!" the other two detainees said.

The door opened and Tommy entered with the grocery plastic bags in each hand. He set them on the coffee table, then exited.

"We won't detain you here any longer. You're going to have to help that sick soldier out to the truck and get him back to the base," the colonel said.

"Yes, Colonel!" Truman said.

The general turned a stern face to the soldiers. "You are never to speak of this classified mission to anyone, do you understand?"

The three soldiers stood ramrod straight. "Yes, Sir!"

"You will have to replace your phones as they are being withheld," the colonel said. "Panther Industries doesn't fool around when it comes to their privacy."

There were some rather sour faces staring back at her.

"Take three days R & R, then return to work," Colonel Jenkins said.

The general headed to the door, followed by Sheila, Roman, Gage and Sherm. They heard the rustle of plastic bags as the door shut behind them.

"Let's head back to the house so you can change, then we'll give you the tour of the place," Roman said.

They made a stop at the car and retrieved the general and colonel's luggage, then headed to the house.

ARI WAS in her office when she heard the front door open. She stepped out of her office and greeted their guests in the living room. "I'm so sorry for my quick departure earlier. I can't promise I'll be a good hostess until after the twins make their appearance."

"Are you sure we're not imposing?" Sheila asked.

"We invited you, so let's get you settled," Ari said. She walked them down the guest hallway. "You can have your pick of these three bedrooms. Each has its own bathroom."

Ari opened each of the doors. Two were on the same side of the hallway, the third opposite.

"Oh! They're beautiful rooms, fully contained with desks and a TV," Sheila said.

"Ari's uncle went all out for comfort," Gage said. "Roman and I had two of the bedrooms converted for our home offices."

They let the general and colonel have some privacy to get

changed. Ari, Gage and Roman headed back to the living room where Sherm was sprawled on a sofa.

"Sherm, there's fourteen people coming out for the security jobs," Ari said. "Should I cut it off at that, or how many do you want to hire and train?"

He sat up while looking thoughtful. "There may be some rejects among the group. I'd like at least a dozen people on board. We need people patrolling the property in shifts, even when the cameras are installed. I'd like to have four additional people with Eddie at the university. Two or three can be invisible in a second vehicle. One more in the building."

"Need to send Butch up to Reading so we can plan on building a jail," Roman said. "If there're no shifters here who have the same type of setup as Wendell, we could have him come down and supervise. That man knows how to weld."

"Yeah, we've put that off too long," Gage said.

"I'll contact Butch," Ari said. "Roman, you or Gage can contact Wendell."

"Where are we going to build it so it's not obvious?" Sherm asked.

Toby walked down the hall into the living room. "What are you going to build?"

"A jail," Sherm said.

"A jail?" Sheila asked, as she followed behind the general. "Why would you need a jail?"

"Sometimes the Panther Security division detains people, such as your soldiers, and we don't want them in the apartments or conference rooms," Sherm said.

"Seems like a huge expense for what little use you might have for it," Sheila said.

"You'd be surprised," Roman said.

Gage took the opportunity to move the conversation away from an accidental reference to shifters. "Ready for the tour of the house and property? You'll want to retire and move here when you see what we enjoy every day."

He showed them the library, gym, game room, media room, Ari's office, the kitchen and butler's pantry. Then he brought them through the French doors to the outdoor summer kitchen and pool area. He avoided the master bedroom because there was no way to explain that bed and living situation to the colonel.

"Wow! This place has just about anything you could ever want. I'd never leave!" Sheila said.

"Wait until you see the property," Roman said. They walked over to the garage. "There's five or six bedrooms above the garage, what we call the bachelor pads." Roman took count and chose a golf cart that had a canvass cover to help block out the scorching sun. "All aboard!"

He drove over to the orchard, then the vegetable arbor. He explained about the livestock farm that was on another property.

"The world could shut down, and you people would not have to worry," Toby said. "This is a smart setup."

"My uncle was a very wise man," Ari said.

They drove over to where Pablo and Aileen's houses were located, then made the big loop around the office building and returned to the garage.

"Maybe we should talk about that job offer," Toby said.

CHAPTER SEVENTEEN

Dinner was a lively affair with the two extra leaves in the already immense dining table to fit everyone around its circumference. The immediate family and the usual diners were enough for one sports team. The additional people included the general, colonel, Leander and Trisha, Lonnie and Melly, Travis, Tommy, Doug, Warman, Mr. Tran and Cama. Eddie sat at her little table in the corner with Phoebe close by at the big table.

"You certainly have a wonderful household, and your meals are restaurant quality," Sheila said. "I'm ready to make my room here permanent."

"We have Mr. Butler and Dirdjo to thank for the meals," Ari said. "Mr. Butler trained in Europe, and Dirdjo had a restaurant in Indonesia."

"I'm so disillusioned with my job," Sheila said. "It's not fulfilling anymore. Every morning I have to argue with myself to get out of bed and put on my uniform."

"She's definitely not a morning person until I hand her a cup of coffee," Toby said, then realized his gaffe.

Sheila blushed crimson and elbowed him in the ribs as every eye was on them.

"Oh, alright! We've been keeping our relationship secret in DC, but that's been more and more difficult this past year," Toby said.

"I hate it!" Sheila said. "Another reason to consider early retirement." She faced him. "And this big secret you never want to talk about! We've been together long enough to have complete trust in each other. Five years is plenty of time to fully examine every embarrassing moment in our pasts, along with all the other family dynamics, dysfunctions and shortfalls."

"It's not something I can discuss openly," Toby said, with a sidelong glance to Roman, Gage and Ari.

Roman sighed. "If you must know, Sheila, Toby's secret is shared with most of us around the table. We're shape-shifters."

There was a loud silence in the room as the colonel stared across the table. She waited for the punch line. When one wasn't forthcoming, she gaged their faces. Everyone was serious.

"Shape-shifters." She said the words, flat. A million things flashed through her head. "Like the wolves in the Twilight books and movies? Or werewolves?"

"The wolves on Twilight would be the closest example," Jason said. He showed his tiger face.

Sheila's chair jumped back several inches from the table as she let loose a blood-curdling scream. All the shifters around the table showed their faces. Her wild eyes darted from one face to the next.

Lonnie raised his hand. "Human."

Mr. Butler, Mr. Tran, and Cama raised their hands.

Toby faced Sheila and showed his lion's face.

Her mouth hung open with her hand on her chest. After a

minute, she reached out and touched Toby's face. "You're a lion?"

"Yes. Roman and Gage are the kings of the shifter world, and Ari is our queen," Toby said.

Sheila sat in stunned silence. She looked across the table to Ari. "Your animal seemed quite large. What type of cat are you?"

"I'm a liger, the largest of all cats. When I had to run out of the room earlier, it was because with my pregnancy, I've recently been shifting with no warning, and I felt a twinge," Ari said.

"That would have freaked you out," Gage chuckled. "Her animal is enormous. Roman's panther looks like a kitten beside her, and the boys, well, they look like newborns."

Sheila's face turned to Toby. "How have you managed to get through the military and all the bullshit in DC with no one finding out?"

"There are a lot of shifters in the military. Look for or think about people who have such keen abilities in their roles that no one else can seem to outsmart," Toby said.

Her mouth formed a silent O as she let that settle in her mind. Then she turned to Sherm. "No wonder you're so good at your job. Panther Securities always gets the job done. Flawlessly, I might add."

"Well, I hate to spoil your line of thinking, but I'm a relatively new shifter," Sherm said. "While I may have had the attributes of our kind, and have worked among shifters for years, I was just a human with skills. Then my mother and grandmother showed up last year for an intervention to get me to shift finally."

"Yeah, Sherm's a late bloomer just like Ari, Jason and Kevin," Gage said.

"Now that the cat's out of the bag, your lives will be a lot easier," Ari said. "When I met Roman and Gage, I was like you —I had no clue that there was this hidden society all around me. The thoughts I had going through my head the day they told me they were shape-shifters ranged from bizarre to pure sarcasm. Like oh yeah? Prove it—and they did. They shifted. I expected to hear all sorts of stupid reasons like, oh the circumstances aren't right for a shift."

"It was a well-kept secret for the first five years they were together, until Mom was kidnapped," Kevin said. "I'll never forget when I saw Roman and Gage shift for the first time."

"So, do you two live together?" Gage asked.

"We might as well, but we're both paying mortgages," Toby said. "I bet if we sold both our places we could find our own paradise down here."

"What about family?" Ari asked. She firmly believed in close-knit families.

"We both have siblings, but everyone's so busy with their careers and kids, we don't have time to socialize with each other," Sheila said. "If Toby and I retired and moved here, they'd have to find the time to visit. I'm sick of the pace of DC, the cold, and not having much of a life other than the military."

"If you moved here, you'd both be very welcome in our organizations. Toby would be great for the international security side of our business. Sheila, you'd be very welcome to assist in the local security business, or helping Ari with the running and organization of the shifters, world-wide," Gage said.

"In the shifter world, many shifters are in low-paying jobs, like laborers, or doing things no one else really wants to do," Jason said. "Mom's trying to find out how to lift up our people and stop the generational low-class stigma."

Roman stood. "Why don't we have drinks around the pool?"

People stood. Mr. Butler, Aileen, and others stacked dishes

and brought them to the kitchen. They rinsed dishes and added them to the dishwasher. They scrubbed pans. Glassware rinsed and added to the top rack of the dishwasher. They finished the cleanup in a jiffy, and people went outside and claimed their chairs around the pool, or grabbed a chair from one of the stacks.

Sherm and Kevin manned the bar. Lonnie played bar-back, retrieved bottles from the bar closet, and lined up the glasses, rimming with salt when required.

"Everyone have what they want?" Sherm called out. "Bar's closing for now." He walked outside with his drink and grabbed one of the stacked lounge chairs. He found a vacant place near Ari, set it up and plunked down into it. "Someone needs to educate Sheila about shifter ways. You know, shredding clothes, the nakedness, things like that. I don't think Toby's thought about it."

Ari nodded. "You're right." She looked across the pool and saw Sheila in a deep discussion with Eddie that was causing Sheila's face to heat and change expressions. "I'm wondering if that's what Eddie is doing." Ari nodded in their direction.

Sherm honed in his hearing and got an earful. "Yup, the little one's taken the colonel under her wing."

Eddie, be gentle with Sheila, Ari sent. *We don't want her running out of the house screaming for a cab!*

Ari and Sherm saw Eddie huff up as the pint-sized shifter glared at her mother across the pool. *Honestly, Mommy, I do have SOME common sense!*

Ari and Sherm snorted out laughs.

"Do you think Sheila will be able to hear and communicate with Toby in mind-talk?" Ari asked.

"I'm not sure," Sherm said. "I wonder if Dr. Tanner and his wife communicate like that. I know he couldn't communicate with Roman or Gage when he was treating them, but it could be just a link between mates."

"Oh, someone also needs to explain about aging and moving," Ari said.

Roman and Toby joined them, followed by Gage.

"What are you two talking about? You look very serious," Roman said.

"We were discussing Sheila's shifter education, some of which Eddie is explaining," Ari said. "But what about how we age, and have to move from place to place so we aren't detected?"

Ari's eyes bored into Toby.

"We're going to have hours and hours of me explaining things," Toby said. "She's very astute, so she'll catch on, but there's so many things we take for granted in our everyday lives as shifters. All the nuances. The two worlds we walk through."

Ari stood suddenly, thrust her ginger ale glass at Roman, drenching his shirt, and turned to run. She didn't make it around the pool to the house. Her clothes shredded as she shifted to her liger, accidentally bumping Jason and Janina into the pool.

Cama stared at Ari's liger, her brows furrowing.

Sheila's mouth was fully open, but she didn't scream. Toby shifter-ran over to her. She had never seen him move that fast.

"These things happen, but with my queen, it's some strange unbalance due to her pregnancy," he explained.

"How did you get here so fast? You were on the other side of the pool with Roman," Sheila asked.

"I was going to explain that," Eddie said. "We're very fast... and quiet."

Cama grabbed Mr. Tran's hand, and all but dragged him over to the liger.

Roman and Gage were rubbing Ari's coat, trying to calm her.

"Mom, I really liked these shoes," Jason said as he climbed out of the pool, then helped pull Janina out.

I'm so sorry! I don't have any control over these shifts! Ari sent.

"Ari," Cama said, as she joined the group around the queen. "You should not be shifting like this."

"She can't seem to control when it happens," Gage said.

"I think there's something off balance," Cama said. She quietly conferred with Mr. Tran, then looked to the kings. "I'll mix up some herbs to help with this. She can drink this as a tea, either hot or cold."

"These herbs won't harm the babies?" Roman asked.

"No," Mr. Tran said. "You can look them up: vitex, raspberry leaf, black cohosh, dong quai. They are good for female hormone problems, and some women take them during the latter months of pregnancy."

Cama patted Ari. "I'm certain these herbs will stop your unpredictable shifts."

Across the pool, Toby had his hands full. It worried him that Sheila would walk away from their relationship. It was a lot to take in. Kenneth picked up on the anxiety and joined them.

"Sheila, Toby, I'd like to talk to you about my daughter," Kenneth nodded to Ari's liger. "And my wife, who was human, who ran away from Ireland to come to America to get away from her family of shifters."

Sheila listened attentively.

"We knew very little about each other when we married. Sometimes love is enough to glue together a relationship. But more often than not, sometimes there's not anything that can hold a couple together when one of them is so different,"

Kenneth said, sadness creeping into his voice. "When Alannah discovered I was a shifter—the very thing she thought she escaped—she left without a word. I didn't know she was expecting our child."

Sheila covered her mouth with her hand. "Oh, I'm so sorry to hear this. It must have been so difficult for you."

"I didn't find out I had a daughter until this year," Kenneth said. "When Ari's uncle Charles passed away, the attorney tracked her down and everything rolled out. She found her aunt Aileen, then Roman's Navajo friends found me."

"Thank you for telling me," Sheila said. She latched onto Toby's arm. "This is my man, and no matter what he is, I'll be at his side."

Kenneth nodded. "Good. You two belong together."

"I'm happy to hear that, Colonel," Toby said. "I'd hate to have to drag you back to my lair."

Sheila playfully punched him in the bicep.

Sherm wandered over. "Everything okay over here?" He zeroed in on Sheila.

"We're good," she said. "It's interesting that there's an integrated community of shifters and their humans. I want to learn as much as I can and see how I can contribute."

"Shifters age very slowly," Sherm said. "Kenneth is Ari's biological father. Ari is in her mid-seventies." He let that sink in.

Sheila stared at Kenneth. "How is that possible? You look like you're no older than me, and I'm forty-two. And Ari looks my age."

"Sometimes we have to pull up stakes and move," Kenneth said. "This is why I moved to the mountains, so I didn't have to interact with humans on a day-to-day basis. Having to come up with stories to support who I am at any given time or place— that can be a challenge."

Sheila stared, wide-eyed, at Toby. "How old are you?"

He stared back, wondering how he was going to explain this. "Two-hundred thirty-two."

"Two..." she flopped down into her chair. "How..."

"Sometimes I have to fake a death, become a relative, or just plain disappear," Toby said. "I know this is a lot to digest, but it will be okay."

"How could it? I'll be rotting in my grave..." Sheila said, close to tears.

"Actually, something happens," Kenneth said. "Humans in relationships with shifters—those that are bonded—their aging slows. It paces their shifter mate."

Sheila's sad tears turned into happy tears as she leapt into Toby's arms. "We can have a family!"

Sherm patted Toby on the back, then wandered back over to Roman, Ari, Cama and Mr. Tran.

Mr. Tran did a little bow. "I'm going to take my leave now. Thank you for such a wonderful evening. And, Ari, I think you will be able to resume a much more normal life once you begin drinking the herbal teas."

"I'll mix up a batch and bring it over in the morning," Cama said. She waved goodbye, then they left.

CHAPTER EIGHTEEN

E ddie skipped up to Roman and Sherm. "I have it all figured out."

"What's that, munchkin?" Sherm asked.

"The problem about the dragon's eggs, of course," Eddie said. "We can fly the eggs to the mainland, then take a boat to this one island that's uninhabited. Novi and Inggit's relatives can protect the eggs until they hatch. Then they can sort them and find out how many shifters there are. See?"

"Do you really think those people are going to want to live on a remote island without any of the typical comforts they're used to?" Roman asked.

"They can boat over to the mainland when they need to stock up on things," Eddie said.

"When people discover activity on an otherwise unoccupied island, it will bring undesirables," Roman said.

"Sherm can post signs that the island is private property, have cameras all over the place with big signs saying trespassers will be prosecuted," Eddie said. She acted as if they should have thought of this themselves.

Roman and Sherm thought it over while nodding at each other.

"It could work," Sherm said. "We'd have to present it to the dragons and see what they think. I don't know if mother Komodo dragons will give up their eggs so easily."

Eddie put her hands on her hips. "Once they understand the problem, and the danger they would bring to themselves and their eggs if the eggs stayed here, everything will be okay."

"You found an island?" Roman asked.

"There's lots of islands. You would just need to negotiate with the government to buy one or have unrestricted private use. Then we can have portable houses erected," Eddie explained. She skipped off to the stairs of the pool.

"I hate it when she's right," Sherm said.

"Which seems to be all the time," Roman said.

SHORTLY AFTER BREAKFAST, cars arrived at the office building with the new shifter recruits. Lonnie had Tommy and Doug outside directing the people where to park. Big Bear and Marcia were ready for them, with badges made ahead of time from Ari's list. They were ready to improvise and make a badge for anyone who decided to accompany a friend at the last minute.

Lonnie, Sherm, Roman, Gage, Toby and Sheila were in a mid-sized conference room when the shifters came through the door with Big Bear checking names off a list. When everyone was accounted for, the bear shifter handed the list to Sherm and exited back to the lobby.

They were a group of slackers. Only one recruit was dressed for a job interview. The rest were a rag-tag group, at best. They hadn't even bowed to their kings. Sherm's temper flared. "These two men are your kings. If you don't get down on one knee right now, I'll correct your infraction for you. Ladies, you will curtsey."

There was a sudden rustling of movement with the men dropping to their knee and the women curtsying and staying in the lowest position while wobbling.

"You may rise," Roman called out.

The general was ready for some fun. Sheila could hardly keep a straight face when she caught the stern look on his face. The Panther heads gave Toby his lead.

"TEN-HUT!" Toby boomed out.

The lackadaisical group of recruits became instantly alert. A couple snapped to attention, obviously from some sort of military experience. Others glanced around the room, trying to figure out what was going on.

Toby walked to the front of the group. "You will stand at attention with your eyes straight ahead, your shoulders back, and your mouth shut unless you are asked a question. Do you understand?"

The three former military recruits boomed out, "Sir, Yes, Sir!"

The others looked at them with questioning eyes.

"Did I not tell you just seconds ago to stand at attention with eyes forward?" Toby asked the group. "If you were in the army, you'd be on the ground giving me fifty pushups."

Several faces showed alarm. The rest of the crew stood at attention to the best of their ability. There were eight men and six women in the group. Sherm had Travis run background checks on all of them. Only two had arrest records, which were minor offenses. The rest of the lot were hanging on, barely making a living.

"I will now turn you over to Mr. Sherman Foo, the head of Panther Industries Security Division. Mr. Foo has a reputation for building this side of the company that is known worldwide for their teams of commandos who always get the job done. They have never failed," Toby said, still booming.

Sherm stepped forward. "Thank you, General Dickinson." He looked the recruits over. "The United States Army is one of our many clients. They trust us to provide the very best teams and to not bring any embarrassment back home to the United States. We have a code of honor, ethics, and discretion. We don't gossip like a bunch of old men and women. What we do and what we see while on assignment is never, ever talked about at the bar, a family dinner, or even in a dungeon. Do you understand?"

Some of the shifters boomed out the military *Sir, Yes, Sir,* and the others *Yes, Sir.*

"If you want to belong to this organization, you will train hard. You will change your life and you will always have a job with benefits. If you can't get your lazy asses to change your ways and you whine about how hard it is, this job isn't for you. Are there any questions?" he asked.

There was a resounding boom of "No" from all fourteen recruits. They only had one chance to turn their lives around and they got that. The only thing left for them if they didn't get this job, was sinking lower.

"You will be here at zero seven hundred every morning, Monday through Friday. Not seven-o-one, not seven-fifteen. Seven sharp. If your vehicle breaks down or your mother dies, you will call the front desk and speak with either Marcha or Big Bear Muchisky. Do you understand?

"Yes, Sir!"

"Be seated," Sherm said.

The group scrambled into the chairs at the two tables.

"My second in command, Lonnie Lyons, will discuss the

aspects of the different positions, but understand that you have to earn one of those positions," Sherm said.

Sherm, the general, colonel, Roman and Gage left the room. As the door closed, they heard Lonnie telling the recruits that lunch would be provided along with bottled water.

"Well, that was fun," Toby said.

"I was glad to see there were several women among your recruits," Sheila said. "They most likely have husbands or partners that can't provide very well. They all seemed poorly dressed, so I know they don't have a clothing budget."

"Hard to tell these days," Gage said. "The outfits I see when I go into town are questionable."

"Well, there is that," Sheila said. "I guess it's no worse than bell bottoms and tie-died clothing from the sixties and seventies."

They walked over to the house. Ari came outside and joined them.

"I hate to see you go, I barely had a chance to get to know you," she said.

Toby bowed down to her. "We'll be back, you can count on it, my queen. Thank you for your hospitality."

"Should I bow or curtsey?" Sheila asked, looking from one to the other, afraid she offended the royals by her lack of knowledge.

"Don't fret," Ari said. "Toby is showing his respect enough for the two of you. I hope you join us soon."

Cama's hippy VW Thing pulled up to the parking area.

"We'd better get back to the base so we can head out to DC," Toby said. "Have a rat's nest to sort out with Colonel Peterson, and I'm not looking forward to it."

They all shook hands.

"Thanks for everything, Toby," Roman said.

"Let us know how you're adjusting to our world, Sheila," Gage said.

Ari left the group and headed over to Cama.

"I can't stay," Cama said. She reached over and grabbed a bag from the passenger seat. "One cup in the morning, one in the evening. That erratic shifting should stop."

"I can't thank you enough!" Ari said.

"I'll check in on you in a few days," Cama said.

Ari waved as the Thing drove off. She walked over to the men, shaking the bag of herbal tea at them. "Hopefully, everything will settle down."

"I hope so, it's been very tough for you," Roman said.

"Oh, with everything going on, I almost forgot to tell you, the boxes from Reading arrived. I need to go through them and find those things that will help you with the timeline," Ari said.

ROMAN, Gage, Sherm, Butch and his assistant, Joe walked over to the area that Sherm had staked out as a good place for the jail.

"What you shared with me from Reading looked like a decent size," Butch said. "How many cells do you plan to have here?"

"Let's keep it to the four cells," Roman said. He looked to Sherm and Gage for their thoughts. "But here, we can have a different configuration. Back in Reading, we had one long row. We can have two cells opposite each other on each side of a very wide corridor."

"Very wide corridor," Gage reiterated.

"We also need to have the visitation area and the guard area," Sherm said.

Once again, Joe took notes on his iPad. "Separate bathroom for the guard and visitors, or can that be one bathroom?"

"Let's make that two separate bathrooms," Sherm said. "With locks."

"When will you fly to Reading to meet with Larry and Wendell?" Roman asked.

"We have a noon flight tomorrow," Joe said. "I've found two shifter welding shops here, but I'm not impressed. When we go to Wendell's forge, I'll be able to see if these two places can handle the work. That jail he constructed is first rate."

"Wendell Smith is going to be a hard act to follow, I'm afraid," Gage said. "Maybe he can supervise these locals. I know he had a lot of work back in Reading, but with Zoom, he could practically be in the room."

"Are you sure you really need this, King Roman?" Butch asked.

"Well, Butch, you tell me. There's the storm cellar, conference rooms, and apartments," Roman said.

Butch's face flamed at the memory of how he met his kings. "I know when to shut up."

"The jail may not get much use, but it's needed," Sherm said. "Make sure you get all the building permits in place prior to any work being performed."

RUSS GATHERED Butch and Joe from the Philadelphia airport and brought them to the Panther building, got them badged and assigned to a room. Then he drove them over to the jail.

Larry, the Kodiak bear shifter in charge of the jail, stood ready for action as the outer door opened and he watched the hidden camera. He relaxed as Russ ushered in the guests.

Russ used his badge to enter the concealed space that held the cells. Butch and Joe's eyes were all over the place. Typical for Joe, he was drawing and taking pictures with his iPad.

Then he realized there was a very large shifter in front of him. He swallowed. He had never seen such a large man in his entire one hundred fourteen years. He stuck his hand out and stuttered a friendly greeting.

"Uh, hi. I'm Joe," he said.

"I'm Larry. Nice to meet you," Larry said. "Our queen mentioned you."

Butch and Joe wandered over to the visiting area and took measurements, noting what was inside the glassed-walled visiting room. Then they made their way over to the cells where a shifter was curled up on a cot, back to the cell door.

They looked back at Larry in question.

"That's Greg McMahonas. He's off his meds again and we have to force the issue. Can't have a bear shifter getting into dumpsters downtown and shifting in public," Larry explained.

"Oh, no," Butch said. That brought back vivid memories of how off his rocker he had been prior to finally being diagnosed correctly and understanding what triggered his obnoxious behavior with auto-brewery syndrome. He had a lot of people keeping tabs on what he put in his mouth.

"I want to take a look at that keypad on the other side of the wall," Butch said.

"You only have the one monitor in here?" Joe asked.

"This place is self-contained," Larry said. "We want to see who's coming. It's not like someone is going to pull a jail break. Anyone would have to get through me. If I shifted, they'd be dead—possibly even before I shifted."

Larry walked over to the first cell, grabbed two bars and pulled them apart, then pushed them back together again.

Joe stumbled back and plowed into Russ, eyes filled with fearful respect.

"We've got Internet set up for the visiting room so people could contact their families out of town," Larry said.

Butch took one more look around. "This is a first-class facility. Let's take a look at that panel now."

Russ, Joe and Butch shook Larry's hand, then left through the only door. Joe took a picture of the panel that held the keypad and the audio button. Once he was finished, he closed the cover on his iPad.

"Let's go out to Wendell's place," Russ said.

PABLO BROUGHT NOVI and Inggit over to the warehouse, while Eyo and Sopan guarded the nests. Warman was on duty in Austin with Eddie and Phoebe. The female dragons were amazed at what looked like a furniture company storeroom.

"You can swap things you don't like, or won't fit," Pablo said, as he handed them sticky notes.

The women stuck together while meandering through the warehouse. They discussed each piece of furniture they considered for each room, and looked over lamps and whatnot. A couple of times they swapped sticky notes, or removed them when they found something they liked better. They finished up just under ninety minutes, and Pablo drove them back to the estate.

When they arrived back at the house in the woods, Eddie was waiting for them, along with Warman.

"Let's go over to your nests where Eyo and Sopan are so I don't have to repeat myself," Eddie said.

When the dragons were all together, Eddie laid out her plan for the eggs.

"But they'll be in danger of being stolen!" Novi exclaimed.

Eddie explained how the island would be set up with the cameras, signage and their dragon human relatives.

"When the eggs hatch, your family will determine which are animals and which are shifters," Eddie said. "The shifters would come here. If we kept all the eggs here, you're right back to where you were before. If people discovered Komodo dragons here, there'd be no safety. You wouldn't be able to shift. The estate would be overrun with dragons and outsiders."

The men nodded understanding. Novi and Inggit were fraught with indecision. Finally, Novi shook her head of black hair, then reluctantly nodded.

"It's a hard decision, but I understand. You're right," Novi said.

Inggit looked crestfallen. Finally, she came around. "We could build a dock for a boat. If we pool our resources, we can buy a boat to make it easier for the family to visit the mainland for supplies and visits with friends."

"Okay. I'll tell Roman. He'll put things in motion," Eddie said.

CHAPTER NINETEEN

I t had been two full weeks with no abrupt shifting. The herbal formula Cama and Mr. Tran mixed to stabilize Ari seemed to work, and she felt like she had her life back. As they were getting ready for bed, she looked over to her men.

"Roman, my liger wants to have sex with your panther," she said, casually.

Both Roman and Gage stood stock still and stared at her as if she had lost her mind.

What the fuck? Gage sent privately to Roman.

Where the hell did that come from? Roman sent to Gage.

"You don't mind, do you, Gage?" Ari asked. "It's not as if my liger can have sex with your eagle."

"Honey, what you're proposing is impossible," Gage said.

Ari looked at her life partners with a huge frown on her face. "Why?"

"First of all, you would never even feel my penis inside you because of our size differences. Second, I'd have to stand on a ladder," Roman said, perplexed.

"Are you dissatisfied with our lovemaking?" Gage asked.

His shattered ego wilted his dick, which had been preparing for a nice romp prior to this subject rising up.

"So, you don't want to then?" Ari asked, as if her partners' portion of the conversation never happened.

Gage and Roman looked at each other, wondering how to sort out this bizarre request. Did she not hear them?

"We could go into the woods so we wouldn't have to worry about breaking any furniture," Ari said, thinking things through.

They approached her with arms ready and folded her into a group hug.

"Sweetheart," Roman said, "I don't know why you would even suggest such a thing. Even though we're both cats, there are limitations."

"The mixed marriages of different shifters have the same limitations," Gage said. "If a beaver married a water buffalo, they sure don't have sex in their animal forms. They're more than happy with their human sex."

Roman nodded, enthusiastically. "Think about Leander and Trisha. He's a cobra, and she's a cougar. They sure as hell don't have sex in their animal forms—it's impossible."

Ari implored him with her eyes. "We could try, Roman!"

"No, we can't. My panther is dead set against it," he stated. His attitude and tone were final.

"Leave me, then," Ari said with frost.

"Leave you? Do you mean sleep in the other room?" Roman asked, confused.

"No, I mean leave! Go find another cat your panther can have sex with!" Ari stated. She turned and walked into the bathroom, slammed and locked the door behind her.

"What the fuck?" Roman all but shouted. He approached the bathroom door, a dangerous expression on his face. He raised a leg to bash in the door when Gage grabbed his arm and dragged him back.

"That's not going to help," Gage said. He yanked on his arm. "You sure as hell don't want her to shift. She'd tear you apart. Come on. Let's go get a drink and talk this through."

Roman glared at the locked door, then reluctantly nodded. He slipped into his pajama pants, then followed Gage out of the room. They entered the living room and went straight to the bar. Gage reached for the Blade and Bow 22-year Kentucky Straight Bourbon. Roman grabbed two rocks glasses and slid them across the bar to Gage.

They didn't bother with ice. They each took swift swigs of the bourbon to settle their nerves. Gage poured second shots.

"What the fuck just happened?" Gage asked. "Where did that come from? Ari's acting strange."

"I wonder if it's the herbs?" Roman asked. "Both Cama and Mr. Tran said there were no side effects."

"I don't know, but her thinking is whacked out," Gage said.

"She knows our bond can't be broken. Why would she even suggest that I leave?" Roman asked, devastated.

"That's not her talking," Gage said. "Something is definitely going on. She's not making any sense. It's as if she didn't even hear our arguments against her hairbrained idea. Should we call Cama and Mr. Tran?"

"I hate to bother them this late. Maybe Aileen and Kenneth can give us some insight," Roman said.

"Okay. I'll call out to Aileen, you call out to Kenneth," Gage said.

In under ten minutes, Aileen entered the big house by the kitchen door, and Kenneth tapped on the front door. Gage opened the door, and they walked to the kitchen.

"What exactly did you mean by this was a delicate discussion?" Kenneth asked.

"Ari told me I should leave and find a shifter my panther could have sex with in my animal form," Roman said.

Both Kenneth and Aileen stared dumbly at Roman.

"What?" Aileen squeaked out.

"She said what?" Kenneth asked.

"You heard him," Gage said. "It was a bizarre conversation that came out of left field as we were getting ready for bed, and it was as if she didn't hear our responses."

"Does that mean she wants to find another liger to have sex with?" Aileen asked.

Roman stepped back as if someone slapped him. The thought never crossed his mind. "No, no, no, no! She'd never even consider that!"

"I wonder if this pregnancy has triggered the same type of mental instability that her mother had?" Kenneth asked.

Gage and Roman stared at each other. They couldn't comprehend Ari not mentally fit. She was a brilliant woman. She ran her company and helped Panther Industries when Sherm or Lonnie had a project which required her keen insight and auditing.

"There's no way. This seems more like some type of imbalance. Maybe the herbs have tipped the scales somehow," Gage said.

"Let's think of everything she's eaten today," Aileen suggested. "There could be something that's throwing her off."

Roman opened the kitchen desk drawer and pulled out paper and pen. They made a list of everything they knew she ate at breakfast, lunch and dinner, including drinks and desserts. There wasn't anything new on the list, and she wasn't prone to snacking.

"What did she do today? Where did she go?" Aileen asked. "Maybe she was bitten by something and it affected her?"

"I'm pretty sure she worked on her spreadsheets, walked

over to the office building for a couple of meetings, then walked back home again," Gage said. "It's not like we vary from our daily schedules very often."

"Tomorrow, call Cama and Mr. Tran. If they don't know what's going on, call the doctor and the vet," Kenneth said. "There has to be a simple explanation."

"What do we do in the meantime?" Roman asked.

"What did her OBGYN suggest? Shut up and stay out of her way," Gage said.

Aileen and Kenneth left.

"Well, do we go to the bedroom and see if we're welcome there, or sleep in our offices?" Roman asked.

"Let's test the atmosphere in our bedroom," Gage said.

They walked down the hallway to the master bedroom. Ari was in bed, asleep. They undressed, then climbed onto the bed in their normal positions. She stirred.

"Where were you? How come you didn't come to bed with me?" she asked, groggy from sleep.

"We were in the living room having a drink and talking about a couple of things," Gage said. He blocked Ari. *What the fuck is happening? It's as if that whole freaky episode never happened!*

I hope to hell she isn't having some type of a nervous breakdown, Roman sent to Gage.

"Goodnight, we'll talk about it in the morning," Ari said. She yawned, cuddled into Roman and fell asleep.

Gage moved closer to Ari and placed his arm across her like he typically did. *Go to sleep. There's no point trying to figure this out tonight. We'll get help tomorrow.*

ROMAN EXTRACTED himself from their sleep pile and went into the bathroom. He relieved himself, then stood at the sink for a moment as he searched his eyes in the mirror. He didn't know what to expect when she woke. He left the bathroom and returned to the bedroom. Gage and Ari were still sound asleep. Roman stood beside the bed for a moment, staring at them.

He didn't know what he would do without them. Ari's statement last night practically shattered his heart. He didn't know how long he stood there when Gage lifted his head and raised his eyebrows.

What are you doing? What time is it? Gage sent.

Roman glanced over at the little clock on the nightstand. *Four-thirty.*

Come back to bed. We'll sort it out later, Gage sent.

Roman climbed back into bed, settled down and closed his eyes. When he opened his eyes again, the sun was shining into the room. Someone had opened the drapes. He noticed that Ari was up and getting dressed, and Gage was in the bathroom.

"Morning," Roman said, with a raspy sleep voice, testing the atmosphere.

Ari came over to his side of the bed, stooped down and gently kissed him on the lips. "Good morning. I didn't want to wake you because Gage said you didn't sleep well last night. Did you have a nightmare?"

Roman stared at her. "Yes... I had a nightmare."

"Do you want to talk about it?" she asked, gently.

"I'm not quite sure what it was about," Roman lied. He swung his feet over the edge of the bed.

"I'll see you in the kitchen," Ari said. She scooted out of the room and shut the door behind her.

Roman headed toward the bathroom. He stared at Gage in the mirror. *WHAT THE FUCK?* He ran his hands through his hair and down his face, not believing the complete turnaround from Ari.

Gage shrugged. *It's as if that conversation never happened.*

How are we going to bring this up to have her checked out? Roman asked.

We should have a private conversation with Cama and Mr. Tran and see what they have to say before we even open our mouths to Ari about this, Gage sent.

Roman nodded. *After breakfast. I think we should drive over to Cama's. I wouldn't want Ari to pick up on the conversation over the phone.*

Good idea, Gage sent. *I'll see you at breakfast.*

Roman headed for the shower.

GAGE DROVE the BMW while Roman brooded in the passenger seat. He pulled up and parked in front of Cama's place. Mr. Tran's vehicle was already there. He wondered if the herbalists were romantically involved. As a test, when he and Roman exited the car, Gage placed a hand on Mr. Tran's hood. It was cold.

I think Mr. Tran spent the night, or he got here a lot earlier because the hood is cold.

Roman scrunched up his face, holding back a snicker as he met Gage's eyes. They went to the door, entered without knocking and called out, letting Cama know they were there.

"Cama? Mr. Tran?" Gage yelled.

"Who goes there? Is that an eagle and a panther?" Cama yelled back. She and Mr. Tran entered the front room, smiling. When they saw Roman's downtrodden face and Gage's face filled with worry, they became serious.

"What's wrong?" Mr. Tran asked.

"Coffee?" Cama asked.

"Please," Roman said.

They sat at the round table.

"There's something radically wrong with Ari," Gage said.

"She's not shifting irregularly again, is she?" Cama asked, as she filled cups with coffee.

"Don't I wish," Roman said, in almost a whisper.

Gage detailed the conversation of last night with an emphasis on the part where Ari didn't even seem to hear their arguments. Then he mentioned her abrupt turnaround when they finally went to bed, and the waking conversation.

"Her mother had some mental issues," Roman said. "Kenneth is afraid that perhaps the pregnancy has pushed Ari in that direction."

"There is nothing wrong with Ari's mental stability," Cama said, emphatically.

Gage pulled a paper out of his slacks pocket and pushed it across the table. "We made a list of everything she had to eat yesterday. There's nothing new or unusual on the list. She doesn't snack between meals."

Cama stared at him.

"It's almost as if she was hypnotized," Mr. Tran said. Then he had a thought. "Are there any renovations going on right now? Any paint fumes or things like that?"

Gage and Roman shook their heads.

"Nothing," Roman said.

"How often is she drinking the tea?" Cama asked.

"I don't know," Gage said. He looked over to Roman for clarification. His life partner shrugged.

"Tell you what, you two be quiet, I'm going to call her," Cama said. She pulled her cellphone out of her pocket and placed the call. "Hi, Ari. It's Cama. How are you feeling? Is the shifting under control?" She listened, made some uh-huh responses. "How often are you drinking the tea?"

Cama's eyes opened wide. She glanced around the table, shook her head and continued. "That's way too much. Cut back to only two cups a day. No more." She listened some more. "No, it won't harm the babies, but it could have adverse reactions on your decision-making." She looked over to Roman and Gage. "For instance, you could say things you don't really mean, and become belligerent, almost like you would if, say, you were drunk. Do you recall any odd conversations? No? Okay then."

Roman let out a silent sigh and slouched down in the chair with his legs sprawled out under the table. Gage grabbed his head, elbows on the table, and almost cried.

"When's the last time you had a cup?" Cama listened. "Okay, no more for today. Tomorrow have one cup after breakfast, then the second cup after supper. Drink water in between to hydrate."

They said their goodbyes and Cama disconnected the call. "There you have it. She was drinking three times the amount I told her to. She's only had one cup today, so it should clear out of her system pretty fast."

Mr. Tran shook his head. "There's no reason for the reaction she experienced, no matter how much tea she consumed."

"You're forgetting that she's pregnant, and not a regular shifter," Cama said.

"All we can do is monitor her and see if any odd behavior crops up," Gage said.

"I pray to God that this will never happen again," Roman said.

CHAPTER TWENTY

S everal days passed with no strange conversations or behavior. Aileen, Mr. Butler, and Kenneth monitored Ari in addition to her life partners. They were all grateful that life returned to normal once again.

Friday night, Kevin and Tommy stopped by the house.

"Where are you off to?" Ari asked.

"We're meeting the gang downtown," Kevin said.

"Yeah, we're going dancing," Tommy said.

"Dancing?" Ari asked. She looked over to Roman, Sherm and Gage, her face lit up. "I want to go dancing! Where are you going?"

Kevin told them where they'd be.

Ari rushed out of the room toward her bedroom.

"Dancing?" Roman said. He looked over to Gage, then Sherm.

"Hell yeah," Sherm said. "I haven't been dancing in ages!"

Tommy and Kevin left.

Ari returned to the living room wearing a short skin-hugging dress in a brilliant blue that made her eyes spark. It shimmered in the light. She wore four-inch heels that made her legs look long and toned.

"Wow, you look great," Gage said. He and Roman stood and tried to kiss her.

"Don't mess with the makeup!" she scolded them. She gave them the once-over. "Go change your shirts. You too, Sherm."

THEY ENTERED The Girl with Fuchsia Eyes bar. It was an enormous open warehouse inside, with tiny colored Christmas lights at the high ceilings, and an enormous dance floor surrounded by tables and chairs. They looked around, getting the lay of the land. There were three bars and a platform where a band played.

Sherm spotted their larger group, and they headed over to the tables they had commandeered.

"Hot damn, Mom, you look fabulous," Jason said, kissing her on the cheek.

Ari kissed his cheek. "Thank you, son."

Gage went to the bar and ordered he and Roman bourbon on the rocks, and a Sprite for Ari in a champagne flute. He made his way back to their table.

Ari's eyes wandered all over the bar, taking in the people, the dancing, and the band.

The band played a slow, sultry tune. Roman and Gage stood. "Come on, let's show them how it's done." They each grabbed one of Ari's hands and they made their way to the dance floor. Gage let go of her hand while Roman twirled her slowly. She slid down his body, then Gage pulled her up and twirled her. They combined some ballroom style dancing in a very sexy way, commanding the floor.

People whistled and howled as they watched the threesome

on the floor performing perfect, choreographed moves in an ultra-sexy, mesmerizing dance. When the music ended, the place broke out with clapping and cheering.

As they made their way back to their table, several people stopped them. One young woman asked, "How did you learn to do that? It was beautiful! I want to learn how to dance like that."

"A lot of ballroom dancing classes, and lots and lots of practice," Ari said.

"Do you dance professionally," someone else asked.

"No, we dance for our own enjoyment," Gage said. "We're a team."

They made it back to their group.

"That's showing them, Mom," Kevin said.

"Yup, she still has it," Jason said.

A fast song started.

Sherm jumped to his feet, looking around. "Damn! That's my song! Who wants to dance?"

Ari grabbed his hand. "Come on, tiger."

They made their way to the dance floor and Sherm transformed. He was like John Travolta and Patrick Swayze all in one package. The man could dance. Ari never missed one of his moves, as if they'd been dance partners for years. Her hair swirled all around her with the fast pace.

When the song ended, they started to leave the dance floor. A four-pack of rough-looking men on the edge of the floor eyed Sherm.

"Hey, Chink, who taught you those moves?" one of them called out.

Sherm stopped dead in his tracks, turned slowly and looked over the group. "What did you call me?"

"I'll leave you to it," Ari said. She patted him on the cheek, then hurried over to their table. "The show's about to begin."

Everyone turned toward the dance floor where Sherm stood opposite the four thugs.

The rough guy smirked at Sherm. "You heard me. I didn't stutter." He elbowed one of his pals and they all laughed.

Sherm waved them over with three quick moves of his hand. "Let's see what you've got, you pile of pigs."

The four guys rushed Sherm. With moves that were hard to track, but as beautiful as a ballet dancer performing on a stage, the fight was over before it ever began. Four whining, sniveling not-so-tough guys were on the floor. It stunned the dance crowd. Then the crowd erupted with clapping, whistling and cheering.

Sherm brushed imaginary lint off his sleeves, turned and headed back to the table to join his gang.

Roman, Gage, and Ari were standing with the others.

"I'm ready to go home," Ari said. She looked from her partners to Sherm. "Had enough, or do you want to dance some more?"

"Nah, that was just what I needed," Sherm said.

"What, the dance or the fight?" Roman asked.

"What fight? That wasn't even a dribble of a bad-ass knock down drag out," Sherm said with a chuckle. "Great dance partner, Ari. Thank you so much for knowing how to dance."

"That was fun. You're a fabulous dancer." Ari turned to the larger group. "See you tomorrow." She waved them goodbye.

Roman draped his arm across Ari's shoulders, and Gage put his arm around her back at her waist. The three made their way through the crowd, with Sherm bringing up the rear. There were dozens of eyes on them as they walked to the exit of the bar.

The bouncer stopped Sherm at the door. "Great moves."

"Gotta know how to fight, man," Sherm said. "The world's a different place nowadays."

They fist bumped each other, then Sherm hurried to catch up with Roman, Ari and Gage.

THE NEXT MORNING as everyone ate breakfast and drank their coffee, Jason and Kevin came into the house.

"You're famous!" Jason said.

"Yeah, there's YouTube videos of you dancing, and your fight, Sherm," Kevin said.

"They've gone viral," Jason said. "You've had six hundred fifty thousand views so far."

"Listen to this comment, it sounds like a dance critic wrote it," Kevin said. "Perfectly choreographed moves from a bygone era."

"Here's another one," Jason said. "I've watched this video ten times! I want to learn how to dance like this."

"Sherm, this one's for you," Kevin said. "There was a non-fight at The Girl with the Fuchsia Eyes bar last night in downtown San Marcos, Texas. Four thugs jeered at an Asian professional dancer. In less than five minutes, all four were on the floor holding back tears."

"Sherm, you're now a professional dancer!" Gage said. "We'd better not hear about you sneaking out to go to dance competitions."

"He'd win them all," Ari said.

Aileen had her phone in her hand. She and Mr. Butler watched the videos. "Where did you learn how to dance like this, Ari?"

"Roman and Gage taught me," she said. "What we should ask, though, is where Sherm learned those moves."

All eyes swung over to Sherm.

"You can thank my mother and grandmother," he said. "They wanted me to dance gracefully at school events. I had years of dance coaching."

"It wouldn't surprise me if Hollywood didn't come sniffing around to sign you for the next dance movie," Roman said.

Sherm laughed. "That would be something. Can I take a leave of absence?"

"No!" Gage, Roman, Kevin and Jason shouted.

Once the silliness died down, Ari turned to her men. "How many recruits did you hire?"

"All fourteen," Roman said.

"I'm going to drive over to the tailor's shop and see about some uniforms," Ari said. "They all looked to be in the medium to large size range. If their pants require hemming, they can bring them to Mr. Patel's shop."

HER MEN HAD a private conversation before Ari left the house. Kenneth begged to go with her, saying he needed to get out. He offered to drive. They were all still worried about the unknowns regarding her actions, behaviors, not to mention the shifting.

Kenneth found a convenient parking place in front of Mr. Patel's shop. They went inside and rang the bell on the counter.

Mr. Patel scooted around the curtain on a rolling stool. "Hello, Ms. Davis! I'll be right with you." He rattled out some orders to his workers, then hurried to the counter. "How can I help you today?"

"Hi, Mr. Patel. This is Kenneth. We've hired more people, so we're going to need fourteen sets of uniforms, sizes medium and large, for men and women. Some of them may require hemming, but I'll let them make their own arrangements to come in."

Mr. Patel nodded. "The regular uniforms?"

"Yes," Ari said.

"Would you want half long-sleeved and half short-sleeved?" he asked.

Ari turned to her father. "What do you think? Some of these guys will be outside."

"Lonnie will rotate them, so I'd stick with the half and half," Kenneth said.

Ari nodded. "Okay, go with the half and half. If it looks like we need more of one or the other, I'll let you know."

Mr. Patel wrote up the order. Ari got out her checkbook and wrote him a check for the material, then she and Kenneth left.

"Oh, there's the ice cream place! Want a sundae?" Ari asked.

Kenneth knew better than to say anything other than *yes*. He pulled the car over in front of the place and they got out. There were several people inside, enjoying their treats. They walked up to the counter.

"I'll have a hot fudge sundae with pistachio and butter pecan, with all the toppings," Ari said. "Heavy on the toppings will get you a good tip." She winked.

The kid looked to Kenneth. "I'll have a butter pecan cone."

"Is that all?" Ari asked, as she looked at her father.

"We just finished eating, Ari," he said.

She laughed. "Some of us have special needs." Ari dug into her sundae. After she patted her lips with a napkin, she looked around the shop, satisfied. She did a doubletake when her eyes fell on a little blonde girl that could have been Eddie's twin.

"Dad, that little girl looks just like Eddie!" she whispered.

Kenneth spotted the child with her family. He frowned. "The resemblance is way too close to be a coincidence."

"What should I do? I have to know who they are. They must be related," Ari whispered.

"Why don't we go start a conversation, find out who they are, if they live here or are on vacation?" Kenneth suggested.

Ari nodded, almost in a fog. They stood and walked over to the table of four. "Hi, I'm sorry to interrupt, but your little girl could be my daughter's twin."

The mother and father stared at Ari.

"Oh, I'm sorry, I'm Ari Davis and this is my brother, Kenneth," she said.

The man stood. "I'm Gerry Sullivan. This is my wife Kate, and our two kids, Denver and Summer."

"Sullivan?" Ari asked. "Eddie's natural mother was Clariss Sullivan. Is she a relative of yours?"

"Clariss?" Gerry appeared shocked. "That's my sister! I haven't seen her in at least ten years! What do you mean, natural mother? Did she have a baby and gave her up for adoption?"

Call out to Roman and Gage—get them here! Ari sent to her father.

Ari gently gripped Gerry's arm and tugged him a few feet from the table. "Gerry, I'm sorry to tell you, but your sister passed away several months ago."

His eyes widened and filled with tears. "Oh, no! She ran away from home when she was sixteen, but she called me every so often. What happened, do you know how she died?"

Ari took a deep breath. "She was attacked by a pack of wolves back where we used to live in Pennsylvania. It was out by our vacation home, and someone was driving by and discovered Eddie all by herself at the side of the road, crying. She was three. Animal control never found the wolf pack."

He just stared at her, trying to digest what she said. Ari led him back to his table. He quietly told his wife the tragic news.

Roman and Gage entered the shop, saw Ari and Kenneth and headed their way.

"Hi, honey. We needed some office supplies, and you didn't answer your phone, so here we are," Gage said.

"Roman, Gage, this is Gerry Sullivan, Eddie's uncle, and his wife Kate. This little guy is Denver, and this is Summer," Ari said.

"Wow, she's the spitting image of Eddie," Roman said.

"I just told Gerry about Clariss."

"We're very sorry for your loss, it was tragic," Gage said. "Do you live here in San Marcos?"

Gerry was at a loss for words, so Kate took over. "We've just relocated here. Gerry's going to be teaching at the college."

"You'll love it here. Everyone is friendly, and the best part is, no snow!" Roman said.

"I know this is a shock, learning about a family member's death from a complete stranger. When you meet Eddie, you'll understand why Ari was so stunned when she saw Summer," Gage said. He dug into his pocket and pulled out a business card. "Please contact us so we can get together. We have a lot of questions about her family, medical history—things like that."

Kate clutched the card. "Gerry needs to call his folks. It's going to be tough, but when they hear they have another grand-daughter, they most likely will be on the next plane."

"What part of town are you in?" Roman asked.

"We're in the Embassy Suites hotel while we look for a house," Kate said.

"We'd better get back home," Ari said. "I'm so sorry, Gerry. Please call if you need anything and let us know when we can all get together."

Gerry stood. "Sorry, I'm just shocked. Thank you so much for being here. I would have wondered for the rest of my life what happened to my sister. Now, I can let it go a lot easier."

The men shook hands, then Ari, Kenneth, Roman and Gage left the shop.

CHAPTER TWENTY-ONE

They stood on the sidewalk by their cars for a few minutes in silent conversation.

They're human! Ari sent.

Maybe someone else in the family has the gene, Kenneth sent. *They're going to have to be told. They can't be left to their own devices like you and the boys were, Ari.*

Let's talk about this at home, Roman said.

They got in their vehicles and drove home.

When the men garaged the cars and they all walked back to the house with Ari between them, the door opened and Eddie came running out, followed by Phoebe.

"What's wrong? I could feel waves of stress coming off you when you drove up the driveway," Eddie said.

Roman grabbed Eddie and carried her into the house. "Honey, Mommy discovered that you have an uncle, an aunt and two cousins in town."

"I have an uncle? Is he my blood uncle, or is my aunt my blood aunt?" Eddie asked, eyes wide with excitement.

"Your uncle is your blood relative, and they have two kids.

A boy named Denver who looks to be around six, and a girl named Summer who looks just like you!" Ari said.

Eddie squirmed to get down. "When are they coming to visit? Are they coming for lunch or supper?"

"Unfortunately, Mommy had to tell your Uncle Gerry that his sister, your natural mother, died," Ari said. "He is very upset right now, and he has to call his parents and tell them."

"I have a grandma and grandpa?" Eddie all but shrieked, giddy with excitement.

"Yes, you do! Isn't that wonderful?" Gage said.

Eddie looked her parents over. "What's wrong with them?"

"They're human. They don't know about our kind," Roman said.

Eddie thought about that. "I don't understand. How could they not know?"

They walked into the kitchen and sat at the table. Mr. Butler came out of the pantry. "Can I get you anything to nibble on, or to drink?"

"No, we're good," Gage said.

"Ari, Jason and Kevin didn't know until they shifted a couple of years ago," Kenneth said. "People make terrible mistakes hiding this information from their families."

"I went to college with a girl who didn't have a clue," Phoebe said. "I sensed her animal, but I also sensed that she didn't have any shifter knowledge whatsoever."

"What happened?" Ari asked. "I know something must have happened. You look pensive."

"She went to a beach party down at Corpus Christi. From what I've pieced together, she must have gotten drunk, manhandled, and shifted into a bear and mauled the guys who were attempting to rape her, behind a dune," Phoebe said. "It didn't end well. I don't think she knew how to shift back. Animal control, the police and a bunch of civilians with guns went on a hunt. They shot and killed the bear. It shifted back to the girl as it died, but they just thought she must have been standing in back of the bear, and it got away."

Roman shook his head. "I wish there was a way to find everyone with the gene and educate them. That is one tragic story."

"The Sullivans are headed in that direction unless someone has a conversation with them," Gage said. "Perhaps when the grandparents come to meet Eddie, we can ask them?"

"If I had been around when Ari was born, she would have seen me shift multiple times. I would have had that conversation with her through stories when she was little. There are different ways to make children understand when they grow up, that one day they might also shift," Kenneth said. "It is completely irresponsible for someone to not do their duty and leave their family members without any knowledge of their genetic abnormality."

"Maybe my new grandma and grandpa are shifters," Eddie said.

"Hopefully, they will visit soon," Ari said.

TWO DAYS later Gage's phone rang while he was in his office. He didn't recognize the number. "Stryker," he said, answering brusquely. "Oh, Gerry, I'm so glad you called." He got up, opened the connecting door to Roman's office and stood in the doorway.

Roman stopped what he was doing and waited.

"Are your parents okay?" Gage asked. "That's understandable. It's a tragic loss. Are they flying in soon?"

Roman gave Gage the thumbs up sign.

"Tomorrow?" Gage and Roman thumbed up each other.

"We'd love for you to come to dinner." He gave Gerry the address. "I'll text you a map so you can find the place easily."

SIX O'CLOCK THE next day brought two vehicles to the house. The front door of the house opened, and the family piled out. Eddie could hardly be contained. She was so excited to meet her blood relatives. She ran over to the cars, jumping, waving and screaming in childish delight.

Gerry opened the driver's door, got out and scooped her up into a tight hug. He could not stop himself from crying as he held his niece. He set her back on the ground and wiped his eyes. "Hi Eddie, I'm your uncle Gerry."

"Hi Uncle Gerry!" Eddie squealed.

Everyone else got out of the cars. Eddie and Summer stared at each other for a quick second, then they were jumping and screaming with delight. It was like looking in a mirror; they were so similar.

Denver stood by and watched his sister and cousin. He was too shy to join in their private moment.

Kate came around the car and stared. "Oh, my goodness! They could be twins!"

Gerry's parents hurried over from their car.

Roman, Gage and Ari joined them, then the rest of the clan swarmed the visitors.

"This is my mother and father, Charlene and Stuart Sullivan," Gerry said.

Roman took charge. "I'm Roman Davenport, this is Ari Davis, Gage Stryker, Kevin and Jason Davis. Janina is Jason's fiancé. Phoebe is Eddie's nanny-slash-tutor. This is Ari's aunt Aileen, Ari's brother Kenneth, Sherm, one of our best friends, and Mr. Butler." He looked around. "Did I get everyone?"

"I'm so happy you could come to dinner so we could get acquainted," Ari said. "We realize this is a happy and sad day for all of you. I wish we had known about you sooner, but things tend to work out the way they are supposed to."

Eddie and Summer calmed down. Eddie rushed over to her new grandparents.

"You're my grandma and grandpa!" she shrilled with excitement.

Charlene squatted. "Come here, you little imp." She enfolded Eddie into her arms. They had a quiet moment. "You look just like your mother when she was little." She turned to Stuart. "Don't you think Eddie looks like Clariss when she was this age?"

"Yes, it's remarkable." Stuart turned to his other grand-daughter. "Summer, come over here and stand by Eddie."

The little girls stood side-by-side, holding hands.

"I can't get over it," Stuart said.

"Why don't we all go inside where it's nice and cool," Gage said. He ushered the visitors into the house to the large living room.

Mr. Butler carried a tray of finger food snacks, while Dirdjo carried a tray of glasses and a pitcher of iced tea.

"Dinner will be in an hour," Mr. Butler announced. He knew there would be emotional conversations that could spill over into the dinner hour.

Phoebe stood. "Eddie, why don't we show your cousins your hop scotch place and the swings?"

Eddie squealed, excitedly. She looked from Summer to Denver. "Do you like hop scotch? We could play a game. And we have swings! They're very strong ropes. Pablo hung them and my daddies and Sherm tested them out to make sure they were strong enough for me and my friends."

Denver looked over at his parents. "Can we go outside and play?"

"Yes, but don't wander off," Charlene said.

"They won't," Phoebe said. "I'm like a pit bull! They're not going anywhere that I'm not there with them."

Gage and Sherm smirked. Ari kicked Gage and gave Sherm a look.

When the kids left the house, there was a momentary tenseness among the Sullivans.

"What really happened to my daughter?" Stuart asked.

"It was what Ari told Gerry," Roman said. "We dug into your daughter's background and it was obvious that she was living on the edge, barely surviving."

Sherm leaned forward. "When we arrived at the scene, well before the police did, we found her vehicle. It was filled with garbage bags of clothes and very few personal effects. One of my people ran a background check, and we discovered she had been evicted from her apartment. She didn't have a bank account, and her driver's license was expired."

"Eddie told us they slept on a stinky sofa, then in the car. Her mother tried to make it an adventure by telling her it was like camping," Gage said.

"How did you get there before the police?" Gerry asked.

"When our acquaintance called Roman, we flew to the scene by helicopter," Sherm said.

The four Sullivans stared at their hosts, faces filled with questions.

"Let's back up a bit, shall we?" Gage said. "Roman and I are the heads of Panther Industries. It's an international company. Sherm is our head of Panther Industries Security Division. We are very, very wealthy. Ari's uncle Charles left her this estate. She's wealthy in her own right. Any questions?"

Stuart's mouth wiggled as he took it all in. "I noticed an office building as I drove up."

"That's where my uncle's company and the Texas Panther offices are located. My uncle's company used to be called O'Briain's, but I renamed it O'Briain Petroleum and Energy Resources Amalgamated when I took over. The acronym is OPERA," Ari explained.

"Explain how you came to be Eddie's new family," Charlene asked.

"We found her father," Roman started. "He's a totally worthless piece of shit. He had another family, turned his back on Clariss and Eddie. Left town after we found him. He's nothing but a coward."

Charlene covered her face with her hands and cried silently. Stuart comforted her the best he could.

"Our daughter had some problems when she was a teenager. She wouldn't confide in us, and she ran away from home," Stuart said. "She contacted her brother every once in a while, but she never called us. It broke our hearts that she wouldn't come back home. We would have tried to help her, but we never knew what was wrong."

We need to tell them, Kenneth sent to the shifters in the room.

Not yet, Roman sent. He stood. "Stuart, could I see you outside for a minute?"

Stuart stood, unsure of the situation.

Roman led him out the French door to the pool area.

Stuart stared at Roman, hard, disgust written all over his face. "You're one of them, aren't you?"

Roman stared back even harder. "You knew of our kind but didn't tell your children?"

"That's not something anyone should talk about!" Stuart fumed.

"If you had told your daughter, she wouldn't be dead now. She would be in the bosom of your family, where she belonged. Gage, Ari, and I are royalty of our kind. We are Tothars. We are responsible for all shifters around the globe." He let that sink in. "When someone doesn't know their heritage, they could shift at an inappropriate time. It could forever scar them, as it did your daughter. As it stands, your son or his children could shift. They need to be told. Today. Now."

Stuart shook his head, crestfallen. "What would my wife think? My daughter-in-law? How could I possibly tell them?"

"We will tell them. You *will not* leave here today without them knowing," Roman said. "As the royalty of our kind, it is our responsibility to make sure all of our people are safe. Do you understand?"

Stuart nodded, dumbfounded. He let Roman lead them back into the house.

All the shifters in the room knew what was coming. They didn't know how these strangers would receive it though.

Roman let Stuart sit on the sofa by Charlene before he took the floor. "What I have to say is going to be shocking, even unbelievable, but no one will leave this house without the full knowledge of what truly happened to Clariss."

That had their attention. Waves of fear rolled off the Sullivans as they stared at Roman.

"There are things in this world that you have never heard about, except, perhaps, in novels or movies. The people who write these things come up with ideas, but they have no basis from which to pull the information. It's all make-believe, and most of it is entirely wrong. However, there are people who walk among you that are not human. They look just like you and me, but they are genetically different. Clariss was one of those people. She was a shape-shifter, and her animal was a tiger. Eddie's animal is also a tiger."

Kate jumped to her feet, freaked out. "My children are playing with a mutant? She won't kill them, will she? What if they provoke her?" She was ready to launch herself out of the living room.

"Sit," Roman commanded in a booming voice. "Your children are not in any danger. Do you feel as if you are in danger?"

Kate looked at the new strangers around the room, her husband, then in-laws. She slowly shook her head.

"The reason I'm telling you this is because Gerry and your children could carry the gene. Everyone needs to be aware of the crisis that would occur if one of you shifted into your unknown animals at the wrong time," Roman explained.

He looked over to Stuart. "Stuart was aware of this genetic abnormality, but chose not to have the discussion with his children." He turned to Charlene. "Did you know about this?"

She looked like she was staring into headlights. "He joked about something when we were dating, but I never took it seriously, otherwise I never would have married him."

Stuart fully understood the error of his way. He lowered his head in shame. "I'm so sorry to bring this on our family. Please don't hate me."

"Listen to me, all of you," Roman said, with a tight control on his anger. "You didn't *bring this* on your family. Did your parents or grandparents never discuss your heritage with you?"

Stuart shook his head.

"Some people discover their animals when they are young. I didn't know about my panther until I turned twenty. Gage discovered his eagle at that age as well. Ari and her sons didn't know they had shifter genes until a couple of years ago, and she's in her seventies. Sherm just recently shifted when his mother and grandmother visited us in Reading." Roman stared at Stuart. "You could still shift. At least your daughter prepared her daughter. Eddie shifted into her tiny tiger cub when her mother was attacked by the wolves."

"Why don't we show you our faces?" Gage asked.

The Sullivans nodded, slowly. They were still in shock over the shared information.

The shifters showed their animal faces.

Mr. Butler raised his hand. "Human."

"There's so much you need to know," Ari said.

They told them what really happened to Clariss—how she really died, and as the rulers of their kind, how they dealt with the wolves.

"We are fair and just rulers," Gage said. "But there's a line that we will not allow any of our people to cross. If they do, they will pay the consequences, and they won't like it."

Kate looked around the room, then set her eyes on Mr. Butler. "You said you were human, aren't you afraid?"

Mr. Butler let out a laugh. "This is the safest, and the most dangerous place anyone could live or work, but I wouldn't change my decision. I love living and working here. This family and their extended family are the most honorable and loyal people I've ever known. They tell it like it is. They go out of their way to help people. But, if you do them or one of their loved ones wrong, you won't be able to hide. They will find you."

"Just so you understand, you can't *catch* something from a shifter. If you were scratched by a shifter, you wouldn't become one overnight. It has to be in your genetic makeup," Roman said. "One of the things we would like to put into place is how to find our kind, so they are educated to understand their heritage. This is a secret that should never be kept."

CHAPTER TWENTY-TWO

The front door opened, and the kids ran through the rooms to Eddie's bedroom. Phoebe followed, glancing at the people in the living room. She sensed a mixture of high stress and resignation. She reached Eddie's room and softly closed the door behind her.

"One of the things we wanted to find out, if we ever found Eddie's people, is about intelligence levels," Ari said. "She's very, very smart. Do you have any gifted people in your family?"

"Gerry's smart," Charlene said. "He breezed through high school and college without cracking a book. Clariss had been smart, as well. We thought maybe school was too slow for her, and that it was one of the reasons she left home. Guess not."

Ari looked over to Kate. "What about your kids? Are they showing signs of being smarter than other children their ages?"

"Yes, Denver is in special classes. Summer won't start school for a while yet," Kate said.

Ari explained Eddie's intelligence.

"PhD?" Stuart blurted.

"She taught the class when her professor was out sick," Gage said. "You wouldn't believe it unless you saw it. We have it on a DVD if you want to watch it sometime."

Dirdjo came to the living room. "Dinner is ready."

The Sullivans looked relieved. Roman determined they were at their peak of digesting information and were in overload.

Ari went to Eddie's room and tapped on the door, then opened it. "Dinner's ready."

"I'm starving!" Eddie exclaimed. "We have to wash up before we can sit at the table." She led her cousins to the bathroom.

Phoebe stole a glance at Ari. "How'd it go? I didn't hear any outright screaming—close though."

"People are so irresponsible. I hope Kate and Charlene don't walk away from their husbands," Ari said. "There's going to be some tough personal conversations in that group, along with fear and constantly watching for any signs of shifting."

"You did the right thing," Phoebe said. "No one should ever be in the dark about our heritage."

The kids rushed out of the bathroom, hands and faces washed, hair brushed. Eddie led her cousins to the big dining room, with Phoebe and Ari following.

"Slow down!" Ari yelled.

"What's the point?" Phoebe asked.

"You're right. They're excited. Did Eddie say anything to her cousins?" Ari asked.

"No, but I noticed she was listening to those conversations in the living room, even when she was outside," Phoebe said.

They arrived at the dining room and took their places. The table was laden with food. The kids table was set up in the corner. Eddie was advising her cousins on napkin etiquette at her house. She placed her napkin across her lap and they followed suit.

Kate and Charlene took note.

"Eddie appears to be quite the influencer," Kate said, "I've drilled Denver and Summer about napkins, but most of the time they either ignore me or forget."

"We have strict rules at the table in this house," Gage said, with a knowing look.

"It smells wonderful," Charlene said.

"Don't be shy. We typically pass things around the table. If the dishes are too hot, Roman will serve," Ari said.

After everyone had their food choices on their plates, and they had served the little table, there was quiet eating time. Roman kept an eye on their guests, sensing the emotional levels. He felt the turmoil among them, especially in the women. They were the true humans in their family, and the most upset about the deception.

Little by little, conversations formed around the table.

"How did you make this chicken so tender?" Kate asked Mr. Butler. "It's delicious."

"I'll email you the recipe if you like," he said. "It's an easy recipe, and never fails."

"Share that with me also," Charlene said. "I could eat this for a week and never get tired of it."

Roman determined everyone was more settled. "Have any of you experienced hearing anyone else's thoughts? Maybe thinking you read someone's mind?"

Denver raised his hand. "I do that all the time, don't I, Mommy?"

Ari thought Kate would pass out. She got up and went to her side. "It's going to be okay. That's one sure sign of his genetic makeup. Now you know where it comes from and you'll be prepared for when he shifts, which could be soon, or twenty years from now."

Eddie piped up. "Denver and I just talked in our heads! Can I show him my kitty face?"

"I don't think..." Charlene started.

"Sure, go ahead," Gage said, overriding the grandmother.

Eddie let her tiger kitten face show.

Denver grinned from ear to ear. "Wow, you're a tiger!"

Summer stared at Eddy. "Can I do that?"

"Maybe one day you could, but I don't think you can right now," Eddie said. "I don't sense your animals yet."

Gage looked at the Sullivan parents and grandparents. "Your children now know about their heritage. You need to provide them with more information. They are not too young to accept any of what we have discussed."

Sherm pushed his chair back a couple of inches and crossed his leg over one knee. "Let me explain. All my life I thought I was one-hundred percent pure human. I became aware of shifters when I began to work for Roman and Gage, way before they met Ari and her boys. I couldn't read their minds or anything, but I was always highly tuned into things around me. In my line of work, I've been infallible, always seeming to know what was the best line of action we should take ahead of time."

Roman and Gage nodded.

"I always suspected Sherm had to have some shifter genetics hidden away because he was so good in the field," Roman said.

"Then, last year, my mother and grandmother flew to Reading for a surprise visit—they called it an intervention," Sherm said. He glanced over at the little table and smirked. "Wouldn't you know we were having dinner just like we are now, but in Reading before the little table was even thought about, and Eddie dropped the bomb. She asked my mom and grandma if they were bears."

"So, you're a brand-new shifter?" Stuart asked, surprised.

"Turns out Sherm is a wolverine," Gage said. "I don't know who was more shocked, Sherm, or Roman and me. He was always just one step ahead of any other human and could gather intelligence so quickly. Then he shifted, and that was the end of his being left out of conversations."

"Yeah, we have a lot of private discussions in our heads," Sherm said. "For years I felt left out. When I woke from that first shift the next morning, I had all these voices flying around in my head until I learned how to tune them out."

"It's really handy to mind-talk with people," Ari said. "You can learn how to block anyone you don't want in on your conversation. The only thing you have to remember is if you are out in public having a private mind-to-mind discussion, it will cause people to think you're not quite right in the head."

Roman and Gage glanced at each other, chuckling.

"We've both experienced that," Gage said. "Roman and I were at a bar once, having a very long silent conversation, making all the normal nuances and gestures. People were staring at us, although we didn't pick up on it. The bartender happened to be a shifter and made us aware of the errors of our ways."

Roman stood. "Why don't we go into the living room and have a drink? You could probably use one right about now."

Sherm's phone dinged a text. He pulled his phone out of his pocket and returned the text. He made eye contact with Roman, then Gage. "Travis is coming over. There's been some unusual movement with the wolves."

They all went into the living room, and Roman and Gage manned the bar. Once everyone had a drink—whisky for the

men, wine for the women, except for Ari. She had ginger ale—
they settled into the seating where they had sat before dinner.

A tap sounded on the front door, and Sherm got up and let
Travis and Lonnie in.

"Oh, you've got company. Want us to come back later?"
Lonnie asked.

"Nah, come on in. This has been an unusual day," Sherm
said.

They went back to the living room.

"What's up with the wolves?" Roman asked.

"That lone wolf, Dovensky, looks to have met up with Lisa
Hamilton," Lonnie said.

"What?" Sherm belted out.

"I've run some tracking from their chips, Sherm. They're at
the same location," Travis said.

"This isn't anything I would have expected," Roman said.

Gage looked at the Sullivans and filled them in. "Edmund
Dovensky is Eddie's biological father. Lisa Hamilton is a cougar
that we cast out for plotting with her late uncle, an old Italian
Tothar king. He kidnapped Roman and practically starved him
to death."

"Oh, no! This doesn't sound good," Gerry said.

"Is that Dovensky the guy who murdered my daughter?"
Stuart asked.

"Yes," Sherm said.

"Why didn't the police arrest him? Why isn't he in prison?"
Charlene wailed.

"Because your daughter died from an animal attack,"
Roman said. "Humans don't know about shifters unless they're
married to one. It's critical to keep our kind a secret. We would
be hunted and killed, or in government labs. Is that what you
want for your family?"

Charlene sputtered, then decided it was best not to respond.

"As the kings and queen of our kind, we know how difficult some things can be. But I won't see our people slaughtered because humanity fears us. If the government found out about shape-shifters, everyone would be undergoing DNA testing. Would you want your children stuck in a lab?" Roman asked.

Gage stepped in, a tad angry. "Look, Roman and I have had to take some very harsh actions against a few bad apples. We now have a committee in place so we're not judge, jury, and doling out punishment. However, I should tell you that we recently found out that Ari's uncle served justice ten years ago that no one will ever forget."

The Sullivans were quiet.

"What happened?" Gerry asked.

"Three shifters raped a human. She later committed suicide. A fourth shifter didn't participate, and he told Charles, Ari's uncle. He hung the three shifter men. We found the tree with the ropes and the graves," Sherm said.

"Our people have two sets of rules to follow: human and shifter," Ari said. "Sometimes shifters end up in human prisons for crimes. We don't know if they stay in captivity or manage to shift and escape. But we won't tolerate criminals."

"What should we do about this current situation?" Lonnie asked Sherm.

Sherm stood. "I need to go take care of this problem."

The Sullivans stood.

"We should get going," Stuart said.

"When we have an online community meeting or an event, we would like to see you attend," Ari said. "It might be helpful to understand our world better. I'll need your email addresses and phone numbers. I know we have Gerry's phone number, but that's all."

"I'll send you everyone's info," Gerry said.

Eddie's bedroom door opened, and the kids came marching out.

"Do we have to go?" Denver asked, whiny.

"Yes, you've been playing with your cousin for hours now," Kate said.

"Can we come back again soon?" Summer asked, with pleading eyes.

"We'll see," Kate said.

Ari didn't like that response, but she buttoned her lips. She didn't want to sound forceful, and she was worried that she used the wrong wording about the Sullivans attending events. *Oh well,* she sent to no one in particular.

It's not like they can hide, Roman sent. *We have their scents.*

Please! We're not going to turn all predator on them. They're Eddie's biological family, Gage sent.

They all walked toward the front door.

ARI, Roman, Gage, Eddie and the rest watched the two cars drive away.

"That was intense," Jason said. He and Janina had been quiet as mice during the entire debacle.

"Mom, you sounded a little forceful with the whole *attending events* thing," Kevin said.

Ari sighed. "I realized that after the fact. There's no making amends right now, so there's nothing I can do about it."

"It will be okay, you'll see," Eddie said.

"I sure hope so," Ari said.

Sherm led the breakup when he started walking to the office building. Jason kissed Ari on the cheek, then he and Janina, Kevin, Lonnie and Travis walked that way.

"We should go and see what's going on with the wolves and Lisa Hamilton," Gage said.

"Okay, I'll leave you to that," Ari said. "I'm going to take a nap. This wore me out."

They kissed her in their usual cluster, turned and strolled off to the Panther offices.

"Want me to read you a story so you can fall asleep?" Eddie asked Ari.

"That's so sweet of you to think about me, but I'm just going to lie down for a little bit," Ari said.

They walked into the house. Ari stopped at the kitchen for a moment.

"If you need anything, I'm going to take a short nap," she said.

Mr. Butler and Aileen nodded.

"That was intense," Aileen said.

"Would you like a cup of chamomile tea?" Mr. Butler asked.

"I'll be okay. There's never a good time to discover your entire life is a lie," Ari said. She left the kitchen, went to the master bedroom and flopped down on the bed and kicked off her shoes.

CHAPTER TWENTY-THREE

Panther Industries Security Division was a hub of activity. The big monitors along the wall showed Travis closely tracking Edmund Dovensky and Lisa Hamilton.

"Do we know anyone up there?" Sherm asked Lonnie.

Lonnie shook his head. "Have to look on the spreadsheet."

"Ari's napping. I don't want to disturb her. Don't you have an older version you can use?" Roman asked.

"Got it," Kevin said. He sorted the gigantic database by state. He found the Montana shifters. There were only a dozen in the entire state. "Whereabouts are they in Montana?"

"Billings," Travis said.

"Okay, we've got three people up there," Kevin said.

"Let me have their phone numbers," Sherm said. He turned to Roman. "Want me to call?"

"Yeah. I'm not feeling too charitable right now," Roman said.

Sherm dialed a number. "Is this Jeff Tudor?" He listened, bristled. "Listen, you piece of shit, this is Sherman Foo, Panther Industries Security. Recognize that name? Or do you want the wrath of your kings down your throat? Didn't think so. We need your help. Would you be able to contact the other two shifters up there... ah... Francis Lapine and Billy Tender... do you know them?"

Sherm shook his head about the guy on the phone. "Okay, great. There are a couple of new shifters in your territory. A wolf named Edmund Dovensky. Goes by Mundy, and a cougar named Lisa Hamilton." He listened. "Yes, they were. That's why we need you to gather some intel for us. We want to know if they're together now, as in a small pack, or what's going on. Would you be able to do that for us?"

Sherm nodded toward Roman and Gage and gave a thumbs up. "Did my phone number come across your screen? Make sure you save it to your contacts. We appreciate it. Call or text anytime when you have an update."

He disconnected the call. "Should find out something soon. Seems odd that they would be in the same place at the same time."

"I can't imagine it was a planned meeting," Gage said. "They're two outcasts who would draw much more attention together with the branding on their foreheads."

"They probably had someone tattoo a design or something to cover it up," Travis said.

"What are we going to do about this other problem? We can't have people with shifter genetics walking around unaware of their heritage," Roman said.

"Honestly, I don't see what we could do, unless everyone's DNA was checked," Gage said.

"Why don't you have a world-wide meeting and ask people if they know anyone, or suspect someone has shifter blood?" Kevin asked. "That might be a good place to start."

His step-fathers and Sherm nodded.

"That might work. Maybe we could get DNA samples," Roman said.

"How?" Gage asked. "That's the big question. People aren't going to give samples of their DNA to anyone."

"We may have to be underhanded in collecting them," Roman said.

"There's always a way," Sherm said. "If they're friends, or even just acquaintances, they could go for coffee or share a dessert and swipe the fork or spoon when they finish."

Sherm's phone rang. He glanced at the screen. "It's our guy in Billings. Hello?" Sherm listened, then switched to speaker. "I've got you on speaker so our kings can hear. Go ahead."

The guy stuttered and stammered. *Oh! King Roman. King Gage. Franny, Billy, and I did some recon for you. That Mundy guy and Lisa had a knock-down-drag-out in the Crazy Mary's Fish and Chips parking lot. She's got a mean left hook, knocked out one of his front teeth.*

"Did you hear what they were fighting about?" Roman asked.

Franny got there first. He said Mundy wanted her to join up with him so they could share resources and save money on rents and things, Jeff said. *Lisa didn't want anything to do with a murderer, especially one who killed his girlfriend and left his little kid by a highway. When I got there, they were cussing each other out. He told her she was just as bad for setting you up with her uncle, who almost killed you.*

"Did they part ways?" Gage asked.

Yeah, after the fist fight. She kicked him in the nuts so hard I don't think he'll ever have any more kids, Jeff said. *She got in her car and took off. Someone called the cops. We didn't hung around after that.*

Sherm huffed out disappointment. "So, you don't know if the cops stopped Lisa, or if they took Mundy to jail?"

They heard a discussion in the background.

Billy said a cop car pursued Lisa. There was a crowd at that parking lot. Probably going to charge her with assault, Jeff added.

"Mundy would have to press charges. I don't think he's in a position to do that," Sherm said. He eyed Roman and Gage.

Roman made a slice movement with his hand to end the call.

"Okay, thanks for the intel. Appreciate it," Sherm said. He disconnected the call. "Well, it appears we worried for naught. Doesn't look like a planned meeting."

"One less thing we have to worry about," Gage said. "I think we have enough on our plates."

TWO WEEKS ZIPPED by without any word from the Sullivans. After everyone was settled at the dinner table, Eddie nonchalantly dropped a bomb.

"Denver said they found a house," she said.

Forks stopped midway to mouths as everyone stared at her.

"You've been talking to your cousin?" Roman asked.

"Uh-huh," Eddie said, without elaborating.

"When did this begin? Why haven't you mentioned it?" Ari asked.

"He and Summer are upset that everyone's being so stupid," Eddie said. "Our grandma wants to sue for custody of me."

"WHAT?" Gage roared. His fork clattered to his plate. "Don't worry, Eddie. You're not going anywhere!"

Eddie calmly ate her broccoli, then twirled a fork of spaghetti and shoved it in her mouth. "I know. Grandma is just upset dealing with the unknown. I can sense grandpa is trying to calm her down, but that's not working out right now."

"Let them throw their money down the toilet," Roman said. "If they think they can match us with attorney funds, have at it." He was steamed.

"What could she possibly say to justify a court of law taking Eddie from you?" Mr. Butler asked. "She can't bring up shifters. They'd think she was crazy."

Eddie stared into space for a moment. "Denver said Uncle Gerry is on his way over here."

"Is he trying to be the peacekeeper?" Sherm asked.

Eddie shrugged. "We'll find out when he gets here."

They ate in silence for a little while.

"I wonder if Kate has chosen sides yet," Aileen said.

"If Stuart or Gerry would just shift!" Ari said. "Then they would have better communication and things would settle."

"Well, that's not anything someone can force you to do," Gage said.

Roman scrunched his face. "Actually, I think that might work. If someone threatened them within an inch of their lives, they might shift, like you and the boys did in Italy, Ari."

There was complete silence around the table as people digested Roman's suggestion.

"How would we even go about that?" Gage asked.

"It can't be Ari—I think it has to be an outsider that they don't know," Roman said, thinking aloud. "What about Big Bear? He'd scare someone senseless."

"That's all find and dandy, but how are we going to get them all here for that experiment to happen?" Aileen said.

"We command them here!" Gage said. He was still peeved about the audacity of Charlene taking them to court.

The doorbell rang.

Mr. Butler jumped up. "I'll get the door. Why don't you all go to the living room?"

He hurried out of the kitchen and opened the front door. Gerry and Stuart were on the stoop. "Hello! Won't you come in, please?"

Mr. Butler stepped back, opened the door wider and let the two men inside. He escorted them to the living room.

Remember, you're not supposed to know this news, Eddie reminded everyone.

Everyone stood, smiles plastered on their faces.

Denver said his mother, grandmother, he and Summer are in the car. Grandma's mad that her husband and son came over here, Eddie said.

Okay, this is working out better than I expected, Roman said. *When everyone is in the room, we can have Big Bear come over.*

"Hello Gerry, Stuart, it's so nice of you to stop by," Ari said. "Won't you sit down?"

The visitors sat. Stuart looked regretful.

"Charlene is very upset about this whole shifter thing, and that wolf gang that killed Clariss," Stuart said.

The front door opened, and Kenneth joined everyone in the living room. He looked at the two men. "Oh, nice to see you again." Stuart and Gerry stood and shook Kenneth's hand.

"We were going to sit around the pool. Would you mind sitting outside?" Gage asked.

"We've been getting used to the climate. Today is beautiful, not too hot," Gerry said.

They all walked to the French doors that led to the pool area, and plunked down into chairs.

"Have you started your job at the college yet?" Ari asked.

"I won't begin for another two weeks," Gerry said. "We just

found a house and we're going through all the paperwork for a mortgage."

"Oh, whereabouts is it?" Roman asked.

"On Overland Drive," Gerry said.

"Oh, that's only around a mile away," Sherm said. "Eddie will like that."

"About Eddie..." Stuart said.

Denver and Summer came running through the doors to join Eddie. This time, Denver joined in the jumping and screeching.

Charlene and Kate followed. Kate looked guilty. Charlene appeared furious.

"Honestly, Stuart. Where is your sensibilities these days?" Charlene put on a dignified expression, stood tall. "I'm suing you for custody of my granddaughter."

Roman stood. He towered over the woman and used his height and his kingly stature to intimidate her. "Good luck with that. There's no court in the land that will remove Eddie from our care just because she's your granddaughter."

The French doors opened again and Big Bear marched through. He bowed. "My Kings. My Queen." He straightened up, found Sherm. "Sherm, I wanted to let you know that one of the recruits called. His mother did, in fact, pass away today—I verified it, so he won't be joining us right away." He looked around, seeing the visitors and sensing the tension. "Oh, I'm sorry, I didn't realize strangers... uh, visitors were here."

"Big Bear, these people are Eddie's relatives," Gage said.

The adult Sullivans stared at the huge man, fear wafting off them.

Denver grinned from ear to ear. "You're a shifter, aren't you?"

"Yes, I am," Big Bear said. He inhaled. "I don't detect a strong shifter scent from you."

Charlene went into full rage mode. "My grandson is not a filthy shifter!"

"Mom! What's the matter with you?" Gerry roared.

"Filthy? What do you know about our kind? If I recall, your daughter was a shifter, and so is her daughter," Big Bear said, indicating Eddie.

"That's all a mistake that a good psychiatrist can cure!" Charlene ranted. "When my granddaughter comes to live with me, she'll be much better off."

Big Bear twitched. One minute he was holding back his anger, the next, his clothes went flying, and he shifted into his enormous grizzly bear and roared.

Charlene and Kate screamed for all it was worth. Stuart and Gerry pushed their wives behind them. Then Stuart shifted into a black-maned lion. He stepped forward and roared. Charlene screamed, eyes wide as she watched her husband approach the grizzly.

"Stuart, NO! He'll kill you!" She yelled. She started forward, but stopped herself, remembering she was supposed to hate these creatures.

Big Bear let out an answering roar.

Gerry shifted. His lion was a golden-maned cat. He startled for a moment, then tried out his own voice and roared.

My job is done here, Big Bear said. *The death of the recruit's mother wasn't made up. The call came in just as I was heading over here.*

"I'll see what they need," Ari said.

Big Bear shifted. Typical of their kind, he was naked as a jailbird.

Kate turned her back, rushed over to Summer and covered her eyes.

Summer shook off her mother. "What is wrong with you, Mommy?"

"It's very inappropriate for you to see a naked man, honey," Kate said.

"We're shifters, Mommy. This happens," Summer said.

Roman approached Stuart. "Think you can shift back?" He turned to Gerry. "How about you, Gerry?"

"Think your human form," Gage said. "You should pop back when you ask it of yourself."

Gerry was the first to shift back. Shortly after, Stuart shifted. They each placed their hands in front of their penis'.

"After a while, you will get used to shifting and will have a better opinion of your body—you won't hide anything," Sherm said. He raised an index finger. "However, always carry a change of clothes in the car."

"This is how my daughter and her sons shifted. They were threatened with their very lives by the Italian Tothar king in Italy," Kenneth said.

"Your daughter? I thought you were Ari's brother?" Charlene asked.

"I know it's hard to take in, but you'll discover that this shifter world is pretty amazing. Now that your men have shifted, you human women should be able to share thoughts with your mates," Roman said. "Bonded couples have a lot of perks."

"Your aging will slow," Ari said. "Maybe reverse. I'm in my mid-seventies. Roman and Gage are in their hundreds—very young for our kind."

"Seventies?" Charlene squeaked out. "That's not possible. You look Kate's age." She plopped into a chair, thoughts swirling.

Mr. Butler came through the French doors and handed a t-shirt and a pair of shorts to the naked men. "These should fit." He looked around the pool. "Is everyone ready for a drink?"

"Good idea," Sherm said. "I'll man the bar."

Gerry and Stuart dressed. Stuart looked around for his shoes and discovered that they were shredded.

"Oh, no... my shoes," Stuart said.

"About that... always remember to step out of your shoes prior to shifting," Gage said.

Stuart picked up his wallet and phone. He looked at the ground and started gathering his pocket money.

Gerry held up his wrecked shoes. "I hate buying shoes."

"Well, Kate and I will have to go shopping. Better pick up several pairs," Charlene said. She followed Stuart, picking pieces of clothing off the ground.

They all went inside where Sherm had glasses lined up at the bar. He poured whiskey.

The front door opened. Jason, Janina and Kevin came inside. A moment later, Tommy joined them. Jason took in the barefooted men.

"What did we miss?" Jason asked.

"We had an intervention and Stuart and Gerry shifted," Ari said.

"Yeah, Big Bear scared them out of their human shells," Gage said.

"You didn't!" Kevin said.

"Damn, we missed the show!" Jason said.

Janina elbowed him in the ribs. "That's very private."

"No, it isn't. My mother and step-dads probably planned the whole thing," Jason said.

"We did," Roman said. He held out his hand at the two men "Black-maned lion, and golden-maned lion. I expect maybe one of the kids will be a tiger. There's bound to be both lions and tigers in their heritage since Eddie is a tiger, as was her mother."

"Come get a drink; settle your nerves," Sherm told the Sullivans.

Charlene approached the bar, took a rocks glass and tossed the whiskey back, shocking the bartender. She turned to Kate. "You're driving." She turned back to Sherm. "I think I need one more."

He smiled like a Cheshire cat and poured.

CHAPTER TWENTY-FOUR

Afer they all sat and pulses slowed, conversations started. "About that lawsuit," Charlene said. "I'm so very sorry. Don't worry, I didn't call a lawyer."

Ari studied her. "We understand. It's not an easy transition to believe that something you thought were fairy tales and romance stories were not made up. Just the idea of a supernatural world around you can be quite creepy until you get used to it, then you notice things."

"It may take some practice before you can mind-talk with your wives," Roman said. "But you two men could have dialogs between yourselves. Just remember, when you are out and about, there could be other shifters around. If you want to have a private conversation, you have to learn how to block others out."

"Stuart, why don't you try to say something to Gerry?" Gage suggested.

Stuart stared at his son. *Can you hear me, Gerry?*

Gerry started. *Yes! I can hear you, Dad.*

Both men smiled like fools.

"Okay, we all heard you—that is, all the shifters in the room heard you. Try to say something while blocking everyone else," Ari said.

"I'll try first," Gerry said. He stared intently at his father. *Everyone who hears me, raise your hand.*

Stuart raised his hand. He looked around the room. No one else raised their hands. "That looked difficult. You were staring very hard at me."

"Don't worry, it will get easier the more you practice. It will become as second nature," Gage said.

"There isn't a handbook of instructions," Roman said. "Just understand that you are responsible for your actions. Never, ever shift in public—I don't care what the circumstances are. It is strictly forbidden. And no shifting in front of anyone to show off. If you are being attacked by humans in a remote place, or in the dark, shift to protect yourself. Make sure no one escapes that will be able to identify you. As your kings, we will take severe action against you for being irresponsible."

"Same goes for you ladies. You can't discuss this with your friends or relatives, unless you know for a fact, they are shifters, in which case they will most likely introduce that fact," Gage said. "You must think about the safety of your children, who may, in all probability, shift at some point. Denver is already showing signs of his shifter heritage with his ability to read minds. Summer may not have inherited the gene."

The little girl frowned. "I want to be a shifter!"

Eddie took her hand. "You just have to wait and see. I don't sense anything off you right now, but maybe it will come later."

"Okay," Summer said, downcast.

"Honey, Mommy and Grandma aren't shifters, so don't worry about it," Kate said.

"Charlene, are you and Stuart going to move here? If not, we can connect you with local shifters in your area," Ari said.

"We were thinking about it when Gerry got the job offer, but hadn't decided," Charlene said. "Now that we've discovered Clariss' daughter in the same city besides our new secret, we'd better start planning. I'm pretty sure Gerry and Stuart will want to be close by to share this new world of ours."

"We can share our corporate real estate person with you. She'll only charge a four percent commission fee if you buy something through her," Roman said. "Gage made the arrangements when we moved from Reading. Several from our shifter community made the move as well."

"Would you be able to text that realtor information to Charlene?" Stuart asked.

"Be happy to," Gage said. "You're part of our family. We'll do whatever it takes to help you adjust to your new lives."

Charlene stood. "I think we'd better get going. We've got a lot to discuss, and plans to think about."

The Sullivans stood and started for the front door.

Stuart stuck out his hand to Roman. "Thanks for what you did. I know it must have been very frustrating dealing with us." He gave a little bow of his head. "Guess I need to learn the correct protocol."

"Make sure you send all contact information to Ari for her spreadsheet. When we call a meeting, you will get the notice electronically, and mentally," Gage said.

"Will do," Gerry called out. He got in the driver's seat in his father's car, and Kate drove the kids and her mother.

The household waved goodbye as the Sullivans drove off.

"That went well," Sherm said.

"I'm going to buy a gift certificate so Big Bear can take his entire family out to eat," Ari said.

A black car pulled up in the driveway by the group. A soldier stepped out and saluted. He looked them over. "Sherman Foo?"

"Yes, what's going on?" Sherm asked, suspicious.

"Urgent communication from Colonel Jenkins, Sir," the soldier said. He handed over an envelope. He looked back at the group. "Roman Davenport?"

"Me," Roman said, as he stuck his hand out.

The soldier handed over the second sealed envelope, saluted, got back in the car. He made a U-turn and drove off.

"A new contract?" Gage asked.

"Never received one in this manner before," Roman said. He carefully opened his envelope and perused the document. "Fuck. Toby's in the hospital. Colonel Peterson is on the loose." He pulled out a photo of the colonel.

Sherm opened his envelope, pulled out an identical photo, then looked his docs over. "We have the contract to find and neutralize him. You should share the photo with the entire shifter community. Let me go call this number." He hurried off toward the building.

"You'd better call Sheila. I hope she's okay," Ari said.

They hurried into the house.

SHERM, followed by Big Bear, mentally called out to his entire team, and the OPERA leads as he entered the Panther Security Division domain on the third floor in the building.

Lonnie stood as Sherm and Big Bear entered the office. His forehead wrinkled in thought as he approached his boss. "What's happened?"

Sherm held up a hand. "Let me say it once."

Both elevator doors opened and people poured out of the cars and swiped themselves into the office space.

Sherm took inventory: OPERA, dragons, Lonnie, his people. They were all shifters except for Lonnie and Doug, Mr. Tran's son, so he figured he'd better use thought and voice. The stairwell door opened and Jason, Janina, Kenneth and Mr. Tran entered the room.

"What's happened?" Jason asked.

Sherm brought everyone except Lonnie and Mr. Tran up to date mentally. He sent a visual picture to all the shifters in the room, along with holding up the picture for them to see.

"This is Colonel Raphael Peterson. He is armed and dangerous. We have the contract with the United States Army to apprehend the colonel in any way possible," Sherm said. "Colonel Peterson has shown an unhealthy interest in Eddie." He looked to the dragons. "Warman, I want your team to guard her around the clock, including trips to the university. Use deadly force if you have to."

The dragon leader nodded.

Sherm focused on Lonnie. "All my commandos, suit up. Be ready for action at a moment's notice. Our good friend, Major Dickinson, is in critical condition in a hospital. I don't have the details yet. Roman will share information when he gets it from Colonel Jenkins. The royals will send a bulletin out to the world-wide community to be on the safe side, since we don't know where he escaped to yet. I'll be updating everyone after I make this phone call. In the meantime, be vigilant."

ROMAN, Gage, Ari, Phoebe, Eddie, Mr. Butler, Pablo and Aileen stood in the kitchen, tense. Ari held Eddie's shoulders, holding her against her body.

Roman eyed Mr. Butler and Pablo. "You two carry weapons on your person at all times. Shoot to kill, understand? This is a very skilled military man and he won't stop to chit chat. He has an agenda, and it's getting a hold of Eddie and most likely selling her to the highest bidder."

"I have marksman skills," Mr. Butler said. "But I don't own any weapons here."

"I'll have Lonnie contact you about choices," Gage said. He worked his phone.

"I have my forty-five," Pablo said, as he patted his pocket. "I use it to shoot rats."

"The rest of you, if you have weapons, keep them on you— not nearby. If your gun is out of reach, it can't do you any good in a faceoff," Roman said. "Ari, you've had lessons with Sherm, so I feel you can protect yourself. Phoebe, what about you?"

"Besides my pit bull, I am exceptionally skilled with knives," the nanny-slash-tutor said.

Roman nodded. "We need to alert the entire shifter world-wide community."

They noticed that there was a shifter stationed at each entry door, including the French doors. Gage recognized a new recruit at the patio door. He looked very serious on the job.

Everyone was on high alert as the group broke up. Roman, Gage, and Ari headed to her office.

"I'll send out an email alert to the world-wide community," Ari said. She walked over to her scanner and placed the photo of Colonel Peterson on the glass and pushed the button. "Give me a minute to put this together, then you two can blast out the message. I wish Atsa, Yiska and their boys were here now."

Eddie entered the room, Phoebe on her heels. "Do you want me to call grandma and grandpa, Uncle Gerry and Aunt Kate, to let them know about this? I'm worried because Summer and I look alike."

"Fuck!" Gage spewed out.

"Language!" Ari blurted.

"Honestly, Mommy, I've heard worse—from you, whether or not you realize it," Eddie said, her hands on her hips.

Ari's mouth opened to deny it, but she shut it and sighed. "Oh, okay. No language barriers."

Gage, Sherm and Roman smirked.

"Maybe we should have them stay here since there's no high-level security at the hotel," Eddie said.

Gage nodded. "Good idea. This is all too new to them. I'll get Stuart on the phone."

He pulled his phone out and found Stuart's name in his contacts. "I think I should go over to the hotel with some of our team to make sure there's no problem getting them here."

"Good plan," Roman said.

Gage placed the phone call. On top of learning they weren't human, he knew this might set Charlene off again. Stuart took the news in stride. "Pack up a week's worth of clothes. We don't know where this guy is, so we don't know how long it will take to apprehend him. I'll be there in fifteen minutes, tops."

He ended the call and tapped Ari's desk. "I'll take the Navigator, with Lonnie's team following in another vehicle."

"Better get our guns out of the gun safe," Roman said. He and Gage left Ari's office and headed to the master bedroom where they had discovered Uncle Charles had a stash of weapons in two different places. An authentic gun safe, and a concealed weapons closet.

Bruce sent Gage a message. *We've got the Navigators out front when you're ready. What's the destination?*

Embassy Suites hotel, Gage sent. He turned to Roman. "Gotta go. Bruce and his team are out front."

"Be vigilant. Peterson might think Summer is Eddie, like she suggested," Roman said.

They parted at the front door.

THE NAVIGATORS PULLED up to the hotel pickup area and parked. Gage and Bruce, in his commando uniform, went inside and rode the elevator up to the seventh floor. Bruce's team stood at the vehicles, one on each side of each Navigator. People probably thought they were military, but their commando uniforms sported the Panther logo.

Stuart and Charlene were in 705 and Gerry, Kate and the kids were in 710. Gage sent Bruce's picture to both Gerry and Stuart just to be on the safe side. He sent Bruce to 710.

When they had the entire family in the hallway at Stuart's door, Gage took charge. "Stuart, Gerry, use your minds and senses to feel for any threats around you. This colonel doesn't know about our kind, so even though you are new at this, you have a great advantage over him. Bruce is human."

They headed to the elevators and rode down to the lobby. Bruce halted them. "Everything looks okay, but let me check in with the team." He pressed his earpiece. "Any threats?"

No.

Nothing here.

Everything's okay.

No.

Bruce nodded to Gage. "All set. Let's proceed. Keep the kids in between you," he said to the Sullivan adults. He opened the front door of the hotel and preceded the group outside, hand on the grip of a gun hidden inside a pocket. Gage brought up the rear.

They got the family into the big Navigator with the luggage

in the second one. Gerry and Stuart started, were quiet, then amazed.

"I just got a message from King Roman," Gerry said.

"Me too," Stuart said.

"I heard King Roman!" Denver said.

"You did?" Charlene asked. She and Kate stared at the little boy.

Summer grumbled about being left out.

"That's good to know you can hear us," Gage said. "Sometimes it's critical, like this information that has gone out to all of our kind."

Gage drove the vehicle and Bruce rode shotgun. They were followed by the second Navigator with Bruce's team, ready to take action.

They made it back to the house without any incidents. Everyone piled out of the vehicles and they ushered the family to the front door. Bruce's team brought the luggage.

Gage took charge. "Everyone, go to the living room." He nodded to the team. "Put the luggage here for now." He indicated to the room at the right of the front door.

Ari came out of her office, and Mr. Butler came out of the kitchen.

"We decided it was safer for you to stay in the house instead of the apartments in the building," Ari said. "We can't chance you walking over here for meals."

"I feel as if we're putting you out," Charlene said.

"You're just not used to us yet, but you're Eddie's blood relatives, and therefore our family," Gage said.

The front door opened. Roman and Sherm came inside and joined everyone in the living room.

"I heard you in my head!" Denver said, as he ran up to Roman.

"You did? That's a good sign, Denver. You'll be able to help keep your sister, mother and grandmother safe with your shifter instincts," Roman said. He walked up to Ari and gave her a quick smooch on the lips. "Sherm and I are going to drive to San Antonio. Peterson shot Toby. Barely missed his heart."

"Oh, no!" Ari wailed. "He's got to get out of that hospital so he can shift and heal."

CHAPTER TWENTY-FIVE

Roman drove while Sherm manned his phone.

"You know, if Sheila wanted to get him out of there, we could always put down one of the king mattresses on the floor in the gym," Sherm said.

Roman took a quick look at his best friend. "That's not a bad idea. You can broach that subject to Sheila when we get there."

Roman's phone rang. He glanced at the caller ID on the app through the dashboard and answered on speaker.

What the hell is going on there? Atsa boomed out.

Sherm let out a snorted laugh. "You leave us alone for a minute and shit flings out all over the place."

Seriously, what's going on with this manhunt? Atsa asked.

"Sherm and I are on the road to San Antonio to see a friend of ours that lunatic colonel shot," Roman said.

Is he going to make it? Atsa asked.

"Took three in the chest," Roman said. "I was hoping he'd retire so he could come work for Panther."

If you want us there, say the word. Yiska and I will hop on a plane, Atsa said.

"I think Ari misses the boys, she mentioned them earlier," Roman said.

Don't go getting yourself or Sherm shot, Atsa said.

"We're only going to see Toby and Sheila, and see if there's any other details other than what we blasted out," Sherm said.

Yeah, that might be the plan, but you, Roman and Gage are a magnet for trouble, Atsa said. *Let us know if you need us there.*

Atsa disconnected the call.

The phone rang again.

King Roman? It's Donatello and Marco here. Can you hear me?

"Donatello? Is everything okay over there?" Roman asked.

We are fielding calls from the European community, Russia and the Far East. People want to know if we should come with force to help protect you and the royal family.

Marco interjected: *Would it be okay if we took some treasure from in the vault and bought a jet? It would be better to have something available at a moment's notice. There's a Russian shifter who could pilot it.*

"Let me think about it," Roman said. "That's not a bad idea, but we should discuss what assets we should use. You don't want to flaunt jewels, gold or other valuables that would raise questions."

Oh, right... right. Donatello and I will look at the inventory and see if there's anything that we could dispose...

They heard Donatello talking in the background.

Donatello said it might be better if we paid for it from one of the bank accounts or the boxes.

"We're driving to see our friend who was shot. Let me get back to you a little later, after we talk it over," Roman said.

Okay, King Roman. I hope your friend recovers.

"Thanks, Marco. I'll talk to you and Donatello soon," Roman said, as he ended the call.

"At least we know the message went out, and was received in the US and overseas," Sherm said. "Might want to consider keeping a helicopter at the palazzo to make it a quick trip to the airport."

Sherm's phone rang with a blocked call. He eyed it suspiciously, then answered with the speaker on. "Sherman Foo."

Commander Foo? This is Dimitri Alexeyev. My team will come from Russia to defend your compound.

"Dimitri? I haven't heard from you in ten years, since that rather awkward mission," Sherm said. "What are you up to? And, no, don't come unless we call."

We've been staying very busy in Moscow, as you can guess. Everyone requires a security team here. Are you sure you don't need help to take down that colonel?

"We don't have any intel as to where the colonel is at this point," Sherm said. "But we're working on it. It's good to know you received the message."

People have been checking in with me, and I let Donatello and Marco know what's going on. If that bastard shows up over here, he's dog meat.

"Thanks, Dimitri," Sherm said. He disconnected the call.

"Guess we know who that pilot is that Marco mentioned," Roman said.

"Good old Dimitri," Sherm said. "He's the reason we added *No seducing the help* to our training. Remember that mess? He and that dignitary's wife—but she seduced him."

"Okay, no more about Dimitri. Keep your eyes peeled; we should be coming up to Fort Sam Houston any minute now," Roman said. "We need to go to the visitor center to get access to where Toby is at Brooke Army Medical Center Hospital. Sheila will meet us there."

"I'll text her we're close," Sherm said. "Take the second exit."

Roman took the exit ramp, followed all the signs, and finally pulled up to a parking place at the visitor center. They went inside, showed their IDs, and got visitor badges. A few minutes later, Sheila came through a door and waved at them.

"How are you holding up?" Roman asked. He hugged her.

"It's been tough, but Toby will pull through. He's a strong man," Sheila said.

Roman lowered his voice and leaned toward her ear. "If he could shift, he'd heal a lot quicker."

Sheila looked up at him, then over to Sherm. "Really?"

"Yes, our healing abilities are phenomenal. You can either fly him home and call on the shifter community for help, or we can accommodate him. We have medical equipment and a hospital bed from when Ari recovered from her situation," Roman said.

"Plus, there are shifter doctors and veterinarians in San Marcos, along with our two herbalists," Sherm said. "Just think about it."

"Maybe that's why he's asking for you," Sheila said.

"He must be too weak to send a silent message," Roman said.

They walked over to the hospital, went through protocols and took the elevator up to the ICU where Toby was.

"You can only stay for ten minutes," the nurse said. "And only two can visit." She did not look apologetic when delivering the news.

They nodded.

Roman and Sheila entered the room.

Roman called out silently to Toby. The wounded shifter opened his eyes.

Difficult to concentrate to talk this way.

Understand, Roman sent.

"Roman can only stay for ten minutes," Sheila said. Her unspoken message was for Toby to get on with it and tell Roman what he needed to relay.

"Need to get out of here," Toby said.

Sheila swiped the hair off his forehead. "We were just discussing that. Do you want to go back to DC, or do you want to recover at Roman and Ari's?"

"Stay in Texas. Closer. People we know," Toby said.

"Toby, what do you know about Peterson's plans?" Roman asked.

"He's been working with a foreign government on handing over Eddie," Toby said. "We didn't find out who that was when he escaped."

"Sheila can fill us in. If we get a hold of him, Sherm and Lonnie will extract all the information, so don't worry about it. We just need to set a trap to catch him," Roman said. "The good thing is, he knows nothing about the shifter world."

Toby closed his eyes.

The nurse must have had eyes on the glassed-in room, because the door quietly popped open.

Sheila leaned in and whispered into Toby's ear. "We'll make arrangements to transfer you. Rest up. I'll be back in a little while."

He didn't respond.

They left the room and joined up with Sherm.

"We need to arrange to get Toby discharged and get him to San Marcos," Roman said. "Let's talk to the attending physician and find out what equipment is required. If there's something we don't already have, Jason will order it."

"It would most likely be better to fly him to home base by helicopter," Sherm said.

"All that sounds like a lot of money," Sheila said.

Roman patted her hand. "Not to worry. Panther Industries owns a couple of jets and a helicopter. We have all the equipment. The most difficult problem would be to get him discharged. We might have to use our resources in DC to override protocols."

"Why don't we go to my hotel room so we can talk more privately," Sheila said.

They turned to go, and a man hurried up to them.

King Roman!

Who are you? Roman sent. The man wore scrubs, so he assumed he was a doctor.

I'm Doctor Sondheim, General Dickinson's attending physician, the doctor sent.

As he approached, he nodded his head in a modest bow, and switched to verbal communication.

"Doctor Sondheim," Sheila said. "This is Roman Davenport and Sherm... Foo?"

Sherm winked at her. "That's correct."

They shook hands.

"I don't hear many shifter communications here, so when I heard you and General Dickinson, and your discussion with Colonel Jenkins, I wanted to get involved," Dr. Sondheim said.

"Is it going to be difficult discharging the general?" Roman asked.

The doctor spoke to both Roman and Sheila. "It's a highly unusual request to move someone in such critical condition, but Colonel Jenkins has the authority as the general's partner, to make those decisions."

"Okay. Would you speak with my stepson, Jason, to tell him if we require any other equipment than what we already have?" Roman asked.

Roman silently sent the doctor Jason's phone number.

"I'll contact him so he can pull up the list of what we have on hand," Roman said.

The doctor nodded in a low head-bow. "It's an honor, King Roman. I will make myself available to check in on the general's progress."

The doctor shook Roman, and Sherm's hands, and he patted Sheila on the back. "Everything is going to be okay. Once he can shift, he will heal remarkably fast."

"Thank you, Doctor Sondheim," Sheila said.

"Now, let's go somewhere we can talk," Sherm said.

THEY DROVE to the Holiday Inn Powless House hotel and entered Sheila and Toby's suite.

"Can I get you a drink?" Sheila asked. She pointed to the counter in the kitchenette where a bottle of bourbon, gin, and scotch waited.

"I'll man the bar," Sherm said. "What can I get you, Sheila?"

"I'll have scotch, neat," she said.

"Roman, you want bourbon?" Sherm asked.

Roman nodded. He wandered over to the living area and sat on the sofa. "Sheila, sit down and try to relax."

Sherm handed Sheila her scotch, then carried his and Roman's bourbon to the living area. He sunk into an over-stuffed chair after handing Roman his drink.

There was a quiet moment while everyone partook of their beverages. Sheila let out a long sigh.

"I needed that," she said. "I'm so happy to know the doctor is a shifter. He didn't tell me in any of the conversations we had."

"It's not something you blurt out to someone, regardless if

one person is a shifter and the other isn't. It would be like *outing* someone," Roman said. "He had no idea you knew of our kind."

Sheila stood. "I'll be right back." She went into the bedroom and returned with a briefcase. "Toby had gathered intelligence on Peterson. I can't even focus right now, but you will most likely gain some important intel by looking through some of these documents."

She set the briefcase on the coffee table and unlocked the locks with the spinning lock tumblers.

Roman reached out and grabbed a manilla folder. He nudged Sherm to dig in.

They both sat quietly sifting through the papers.

"Looks like my daughter has a bounty on her head of twenty million dollars," Roman said. "When Ari and Gage hear this, they will freak out."

"What exactly do these people think she can do?" Sheila asked. "She's not a super being. She can't turn rocks into gold as far as I know. She's just super smart."

"They'll most likely want to use her for scientific formulas," Sherm said. "Think of formulas that have stumped scientists for years. She most likely could solve the problems with her math skills."

Sheila's phone vibrated an incoming call. She checked the screen, rose and started for the bedroom. "Toby's family. Be back in a little while."

Sherm set the briefcase on the floor, then spread out several documents.

"Find something interesting?" Roman asked as he leaned over to look.

"Yeah, Peterson was communicating with people in three countries: Iran, Arab Emirates, and Nigeria. Make that four. Here's something from China."

Roman put his pile of pages down and scooted over to the end of the sofa to sit by Sherm. "Why don't we take pictures of these and have Lonnie and his team track activity with these people. That might lead us to Peterson. These only show who was bidding on Eddie. I don't see any indication that someone actually paid him, but who knows what's transpired since they apprehended him, and he escaped."

Sherm snapped pictures while Roman put the next doc front and center.

"We'd better keep going through these files. I'm surprised the Russians aren't included in this bidding war," Roman said.

Sheila returned to the living area. "That was Toby's sister and brother. I mentioned having him moved to a private residential facility. I don't know if they're shifters, so I didn't want to say anything more."

"Are they flying in?" Sherm asked.

"Yes, they'll be here tomorrow," she said.

"We'll find out their status when they get here," Roman said. His phone rang. "Hey, Jason. Did you talk with the doctor about the equipment?" He listened. "Okay, that's good. I forgot that the hospital bed was back in Reading. Think you can get one delivered tomorrow?" He listened some more. "Tell your mom we'll be back tonight sometime."

He turned to Sheila. "Everything is all set for Toby at the house. All the equipment we ordered from when Ari was recovering is everything he requires."

Sheila's forehead scrunched in thought. "What happened to Ari? Toby hasn't mentioned anything."

"She was almost murdered by a serial killer," Sherm said.

Sheila sucked in a breath as her hand flew to her chest. "Oh, no! Obviously, you rescued her in time."

"It was a very tense year," Roman said. "She was in a coma for a long time, then on edge for many months after she regained consciousness. We almost lost her, more from the trauma she experienced than anything else. She had deep psychological scars."

"I'm so sorry to hear this. She seems like such a strong woman; I can't imagine her succumbing to psychosis. But I've experienced nothing even close to that, so I can't relate on a personal level," Sheila said.

"Do you get along with Toby's family?" Sherm asked.

"They're stand-offish with me," she said. "I almost get the feeling they look down their nose at me."

"I bet they're shifters," Roman said. "Once they discover you are now aware of their kind, they will most likely be more accepting of you."

Sheila started. "That sounds like racism, if you ask me! I'm pretty sure I'm not the only human in their circles."

"Toby should have had his *reveal* party with you long ago," Roman said. "Once you two bond, you will be able to share thoughts, as we've already mentioned. That will change things drastically in his family structure."

They returned to the paperwork but didn't discover any other clues.

"No decisions in all of this," Sherm said. "We'll see what Lonnie comes up with tomorrow."

Sherm gathered up all the paperwork and placed it back into the briefcase. He and Roman stood.

"Will you be okay by yourself tonight?" Roman asked Sheila.

"Oh, sure. I'm going to go back to the hospital," she said. "They've been pretty good about me staying there."

"You shouldn't have any problems, now that Doctor Sondheim is on board," Roman said.

CHAPTER TWENTY-SIX

Sheila walked them over to the visitor center and they turned in their badges. She returned to the hospital, and they hit the road.

Roman called Gage while Sherm manned the Navigator. "Any problems crop up?"

No, we've had dozens of calls about the message we sent out. Ari and I've had to stop people from getting on a plane more than once.

"Yeah, I understand. We've had several calls. Tell Ari that Atsa is ready to bring the whole reservation of shifters if necessary."

Let people know when you're hitting the driveway. Everyone's on edge.

"Will do. We should be there in a little over a half hour," Roman said. He disconnected the call. "I'm going to check in with Lonnie."

"My bet's on the Arab Emirates," Sherm said. "They have more money than they know what to do with. I'm not feeling the Nigerians for this, but the Chinese and the Iranians would be my second and third choices."

"Lonnie, we're almost back home. Anything on those docs Sherm sent?" Roman asked.

Travis has set up alerts with those specific names, emails and phone numbers that were in the paperwork. We'll have a good trail by morning, Lonnie said. *If Peterson is using a different phone or email, this will find him. He's going to want to make sure he gets his cash.*

"Tell Travis he doesn't have to stay at the office if he has alerts set up," Sherm said. "Neither do you. Go see Melly."

She's irate over this. She's learning how the security part of Panther works and appreciates how well we do our business. Says she's never felt safer and can't believe how lax OPERA was before Ari came on board.

"We're in San Marcos, so I'll let you go," Roman said.

They drove through the town and headed to Bradon Gorge Road, on the north side of the Spring Woods Preserve. Roman called out to the shifters in the area.

This is King Roman. Sherm and I are pulling into the driveway.

A dozen responses came through acknowledging him.

Sherm pulled up to the garage and pressed the garage door fob for the third door. He pulled the Navigator into the slot, then he and Roman got out, exited the garage and listened as the door slid down. They walked over to the house and were greeted by Ari and Gage.

"Our big dragon men are rearranging the gym so the hospital bed and equipment will fit," Ari said. "Is Sheila coping okay? Were you able to see Toby?"

Gage pulled Roman and Ari into a hug. He waved Sherm in.

"These are tough times. We'll get through this like we get through everything else," Gage said.

They went inside. Sherm headed straight for the bar and lined up glasses without asking. He poured the whiskey. The men each grabbed a glass and drifted to the sofas.

Eddie shuffled down the hall in her pajamas into the living room, rubbing sleep out of her eyes. "Daddy Roman, you're home! Sherm, you're back! I was worried about you. Is Sheila okay?"

Roman scooped up Eddie and kissed her cheek. "Everything is under control, honey. Go back to bed and get some more sleep."

"Okay," she said that stretched out with a wide yawn. She shuffled out of the room and they heard her door close quietly.

The dragon men sauntered down the hall into the living room.

"We've moved the gym equipment so that the medical equipment can go against the wall with ample space for the bed, side table and visitor chairs," Warman said.

"Go get some sleep," Gage said.

The alpha dragon shook his head. "We're going to walk the property."

"We have three shifts walking the property," Sherm said. "Keep yourselves rested."

"Don't worry, we get plenty of rest. We just like to walk the property. It's peaceful, and we want to make sure it stays that way," Eyo said.

"Tell Novi and Inggit I'll be over to see them tomorrow," Ari said.

The dragons nodded, then left. The door closed quietly with a snick.

"So, what haven't you told me?" Ari asked, drilling Roman and Sherm with her eyes.

Roman dove in. He figured there wasn't any possible way to ease into the mess. "Peterson has a bidding war in progress."

Ari interrupted him. "What kind of bidding war?"

"For Eddie," he said.

For once, Ari was silent. He could see her mind working.

There was a tap on the front door, then Kenneth entered. At nearly the same time, Stuart came down the hall and sat on an overstuffed chair.

"Want a shot of bourbon?" Sherm asked both men.

"Yeah, after the day I've had, I could use one," Stuart said.

"I'll join you," Kenneth said.

Sherm got up and manned the bar, poured the drinks and handed them out. He sunk back into his seat.

"We have to keep the girls under lock and key," Ari said. "If by some freak chance, someone got a hold of Eddie, she could survive. I'm not so sure about Summer—she's just a little girl. She's not a shifter, or if she has the gene, it hasn't manifested yet."

"Kate and Charlene are freaked out," Stuart said, as he swiped his hand down his face.

"What we have to focus on is that none of these factions know anything about shifters, so that will be to our advantage," Sherm said. "We'll hear them coming. They might keep their approach quiet on foot, but I'll bet they won't quiet their minds."

Gage sat quietly, tapping his thumbs together. "Colonel Peterson must have started working out a plan as soon as those government guys left the university after Eddie gave her presentation."

"Could have been right after her scores were posted to that gifted and talented website," Kenneth said.

"That makes more sense. He would have had more time to

think it through, make contact and start the process," Roman said.

"We really fucked up royally," Gage said. "Never in my wildest dreams did I think there was any danger in that one action!"

"No point in flogging yourself any longer," Sherm said. "None of us thought that through, and it's my job to be security-minded."

"If anyone so much as sets foot on this property, I will not hold my liger back," Ari said, with a chilling calm.

TRAVIS' eyes popped open. He lay in his comfortable bed in his room over the garages and listened for whatever woke him. He wasn't sure if it was something in his room, in the garage apartment—maybe one of his roommates was in the refrigerator again, or an external sound.

Two rapid dings sounded. He sprung from his bed and grabbed his phone and woke the screen. The Colonel was receiving messages from the Arab Emirates and Beijing. Travis looked at the World Clock icon he set up on his phone. It was three in the morning in San Marcos, noon in Abu Dhabi, and four o'clock in the afternoon in China.

He texted Lonnie, then he slipped into clothes and headed over to the office building to check his computers. Sanderstonn was on duty.

"What's up?" Sanderstonn asked. "Any problems we should know about?"

"You'll know when I know," Travis said as he rushed past the guard toward the elevators. He swiped his badge and entered the car. When he slid his badge through the card-reader beside the Panther Industries Security Division door, he saw Lonnie pacing.

They both rushed over to Travis' area and looked at the huge wall monitors where the tracking maps showed activity pinging around.

Travis had given Peterson a green Frankenstein icon, and it was stationary.

"Where's Peterson right now?" Lonnie asked, as he stared at the maps.

Travis clicked a few keys. "Looks like he's in Mexico." He zoomed in. "Garcia, Nuevo Leon. Six and a half hours from here."

"I can't believe he's stupid enough to use his phone," Lonnie said. "How the hell did he get his phone if he was in lockup on an army base?"

"He obviously had help to spring him out of there," Travis said. "We should ask Roman and Sherm if they found out who his accomplice is, so I can set an alert for him."

"Can you check the messages? See if we have a positive identity of who he's selling the information to," Lonnie said.

Travis rolled his chair to a different keyboard and desk monitor. Within several clicks, he pulled copies of messages from Peterson's phone. He and Lonnie studied the screen.

"No names mentioned here. No decisions have been made yet. Looks like they're still haggling over money. Too bad he won't ever get the chance to spend any of it," Travis said.

"Let's hope the hell he doesn't," Lonnie said. "Go back to bed."

They exited the Panther offices and went in different directions. Travis down to the lobby; Lonnie upstairs to Melly's apartment.

MR. BUTLER and Dirdjo had help with breakfast for the large group which Roman tried to get a correct headcount for. At the current moment, thirteen were present, half of which were in the kitchen helping out.

People carried stacks of plates, silverware, cups and glasses to the table, freeing up kitchen space when those individuals left for the dining room. Eddie, Summer and Denver sat at the little table watching the activity and staying out of the way.

The doorbell rang.

The kids were out of their chairs and racing to the front door.

"No!" Ari boomed out. "Go back to your table and sit. You don't know who is at the door—it could be the enemy playing a trick!"

The Sullivans appeared stricken when they heard Ari.

The three children crept back to their table, wide-eyed.

Ari scented Travis. She opened the door. "Good morning, Travis, come in. Do you have news for us this morning?" She closed the door, but not until she drew in a deep breath from outside.

Sherm, Roman and Gage approached their tech guru.

"What's up?" Sherm asked.

Travis brought them up to date from the early morning activity.

"Nothing further?" Roman asked.

Travis shook his head. "Do you know who Peterson's accomplice was to get him out of jail, and hand him his phone?"

"We don't know, but Toby will be here today. When he recovers from the transfer, we can see if he has any insight. We didn't think to ask Sheila last night," Sherm said.

"Would you like to stay for breakfast, or were you having bachelor smorgasbord?" Gage asked.

"Smells wonderful in here. I'll stay if you have enough. You have a full house right now," Travis said.

"We need one more place setting," Gage called out.

Aileen brought the extra plate, silverware, and napkin to the table. Kenneth poured juice. Charlene carried a platter of buttered toast to the table, followed by Kate with a plate piled with two packages of cooked bacon.

"This is the three-minute warning. Everyone take your places," Aileen sounded.

"Come on, Travis. I'll show you where you can sit," Ari said.

Before long, they filled the circumference of the table to the brim with occupied chairs.

Mr. Butler and Dirdjo brought out trays of bowls: scrambled eggs, fried potatoes, and fruit salad.

Gage filled Eddie's plate and set it in front of her, while Kate and Gerry prepared plates for their kids.

"Does Lonnie have the instructions and coordinates to land the Sikorsky?" Roman directed to Sherm.

"He's on top of it," Sherm said. "We're just waiting on word from Sheila telling us when Toby's being discharged."

"Has the hospital bed arrived yet?" Roman asked.

"Let me check in with Jason," Gage said, as he sent Jason a silent message.

It should be here within the next half hour, Jason sent.

"Should be here soon," Gage said, for the benefit of the non-shifters in the room.

"I don't know how he gets things done so quickly," Ari said.

"Whatever he's doing, I hope he keeps doing it," Sherm said. "That boy has some kind of magic going on."

It was quiet for several minutes as everyone ate.

"You should start calling this place *The Compound*," Stuart said, as he grabbed another piece of bacon and chomped away.

Roman and Gage glanced over to Ari, eyebrows raised to get her take on the suggestion.

She turned her head this way and that as she tossed it around mentally. "I like that. This place is a compound. Apartments over the garage, in the building, gardens, livestock at the farms. Very self-contained."

"Good call, Stuart," Gage said. "Welcome to The Compound."

"We need to call Duke and Humberto," Ari said. "They should check out Toby when he arrives."

"Good idea," Roman said. "I'll let you handle that. See if they're available sometime today."

The rumble of a truck coming up the driveway pulled their attention away from food and chatter.

Hospital bed's here, Jason called out.

"Bed's here. We need to direct the driver and crew to the gym," Ari said.

Kenneth put his napkin on the table. "I'll show them where to put it. Keep eating." He got up and went outside.

Eighteen minutes later, the truck rumbled back down the driveway. The bed was set up, plastic removed and thrown in the back of the truck. Ari and Aileen put linens on the bed.

"They were going to include linens, but I've always found them scratchy, so figured it was best to use our own. Toby has enough problems without having to lose sleep over itchy bedsheets and pillowcases," Ari said.

As Aileen and Ari walked back to the kitchen, they heard a tap on the front door.

Mr. Butler popped his head out of the pantry. "Is someone at the door?"

"Don't worry, we'll get it," Aileen said.

She and Ari went to the front door. Aileen opened the door to Lonnie.

"Hey, Lonnie. You heading out?" Ari asked.

"Yeah. Is Roman, Gage, and Sherm around?" he asked.

Lonnie's here. He wants to talk to you, Ari sent to her men.

"They'll be here in a jiffy. Come inside," Ari said.

Roman, Sherm, and Gage walked toward the door as Lonnie stepped inside.

"I'm heading over to the airport. Do any of you want to come along?" Lonnie asked.

"Sherm, you'd better stay here," Roman said. He glanced at his life partner.

"I can go," Gage said. "You both have things to catch up on." He pecked Ari on the lips, gave the thumbs-up to Roman and Sherm, then left with Lonnie.

Ari rushed into her office and picked up the phone to call the shifter doctors.

LONNIE LANDED the Sikorsky in the middle of the parking area between the house and garages. After the rotors and engine shut down, the doors opened on the temporary airlift. Lonnie, Dr. Sondheim, Gage, and Sheila climbed out.

A few minutes later, two cars pulled into the driveway and parked away from the helicopter. Humberto and Dotty got out of one vehicle, and Duke exited the second car.

The house door opened. Ari, Mr. Butler, and Aileen ventured outside. Roman, Sherm, Jason and Mr. Tran hurried from the office building.

Lonnie opened the rear doors. Gage stood opposite Lonnie.

"Getting ready to move you, Toby," Gage said. "We'll try to keep it as smooth as possible."

"Glad to be out of the hospital," Toby said, weakly.

They slid the power stretcher out of the back and the rear

legs unfolded. Roman and Sherm grabbed the stretcher and rolled it until Lonnie and Gage had a firm grip on the front of the power stretcher. The front legs lowered to the ground.

Sheila hovered, fretting silently.

Ari placed her arm across Sheila's shoulders. "It's okay. Everything is under control."

"We're so grateful for your offer to let Toby convalesce here at your home," Sheila said. "We'll try to be inconspicuous."

"Sheila, you're part of the family. Roman and Sherm have known Toby for a long time. They wouldn't hear of him staying in that hospital. Just like they converted the spare room back in Reading when I went through my ordeal," Ari said. "You're not a bother or an inconvenience. You need to decompress some of that stress."

Sheila squeezed Ari's fingers. "Thanks."

The four men rolled the power stretcher toward the house. Within a short time, they had Toby transferred to the new, oversized hospital bed.

He sighed. "Feels good."

Two king-size mattresses from the garage were on the floor, and they had moved a queen bed in from the warehouse so Sheila could be close by.

Dr. Sondheim, Duke, Humberto, Dotty and Mr. Tran huddled in a conversation about Toby's care.

"I feel confident that you can keep me up to date on his progress," Dr. Sondheim said. They shook hands and the doctors, Dotty and Mr. Tran approached their patient. They connected all the diagnostic equipment.

"How do you feel, General?" Dr Sondheim asked.

"Good. Nice and quiet here," Toby said.

CHAPTER TWENTY-SEVEN

After letting the general recover from the transfer for a few hours, Roman, Gage and Sherm entered the gym. Sheila stood.

"Is he awake?" Roman asked quietly.

"He's been restless," Sheila said.

"Might be ready to shift to his lion," Gage said. He approached the bed. *Toby, do you want down on the mattresses on the floor so you can shift?*

The general opened his eyes. *Yes. What about the equipment?*

"He wants down on the mattresses. Should we disconnect the equipment?"

Ari walked into the gym. "Dr. Sondheim said he should stay connected. Can we roll the equipment while he's moved?"

"Maybe we should call the dragons?" Sherm asked.

"Good idea," Roman said. "They're much better at this because of their size."

Warman, can you and your dragons help move the general?

Yes, we'll be right there.

"They're on the way," Roman said.

Ari gazed through the floor-to-ceiling gym windows and noticed the recruits along the side and back window walls. "Looks like the new recruits are on the job."

"They're doing a great job," Sherm said. "It's good that we could employ these people, and they were eager to learn."

The dragons entered the gym and approached the royals and Sherm.

"King Roman, Gage, Queen Ari," Warman said, with a nodding bow of his head.

"We need you to move the general to the mattresses on the floor so he can shift," Ari said.

"We'll roll the equipment with you—he has to stay connected even after he shifts," Gage said.

The dragons nodded. They approached the hospital bed.

"How should we go about this?" Eyo asked.

Sopan looked over the general. "Two of us can handle the legs while supporting his lower back, and two can handle his upper torso while supporting his upper back."

Everyone nodded at the plan. The dragons moved into place.

Sheila fretted as she moved the chair out of the way. Roman, Gage, Sherm and Ari stood by at the equipment, ready to roll with the dragons.

The whole procedure went smoothly. As the dragons stood over the king-sized mattresses, they lowered Toby evenly.

He let out a sigh. In less than two minutes, Toby shifted into his lion. The four hundred twenty pound animal stretched across the two mattresses.

Sheila was at his side within moments. "Toby, make sure you are very careful not to pull out the tubes to the monitoring equipment."

I'll be careful, he said.

"He said he'll be careful," Warman said.

"I'm not going to be able to hear him," Sheila said, somewhat in a panic. "Someone will have to stay here with me." She started. "Did you say something to me, Toby?"

Can you hear me? Toby sent.

"Yes! I heard you in my head!" Sheila said.

"Oh, that's good! You've bonded," Ari said. "Things will be a lot easier now that you can communicate. You should be able to talk back with your mind, Sheila."

"Oh! I'll try," Sheila said. She focused really hard. *Toby, can you hear me?*

Yes!

Sheila's eyes teared up. "He heard me."

"We'll go back to work," Warman said.

The men all shook hands.

"Thanks for helping," Gage said.

The four male dragons nodded, then left the gym.

Roman and Sherm approached the mattresses.

"Toby, do you know who helped Peterson break out of jail?" Sherm asked.

Lt. Everston. Sheila can get you his profile.

Okay. Rest up, Roman said.

"Sheila, do you have Lt. Everston's profile? We need to have the basics: a photo, phone, email and physical address," Sherm said.

"Yes." She stood and retrieved her briefcase and set it on the hospital bed. She pulled out a handful of papers, flipped through several, and snagged a couple of sheets of paper. "Here you go."

Sherm pulled out his phone. "Travis, here's the accomplice. Lt. Anson Everston." He rattled off the cell phone and address. He disconnected the call and turned to his people. "He's on it."

SUMMER AND DENVER were taking a nap. Eddie strong-armed Phoebe into going outside for a game of hopscotch.

Warman and three recruits hovered nearby, two of which were in the trees camouflaged.

"Want to play with us, Warman?" Eddie asked.

The big dragon chuckled. "You have fun. I'm okay."

"Did you ever play hopscotch when you were a little boy?" Eddie asked him.

"Yes, I did. It's a lot of fun," Warman said.

"I'm going to run inside to the bathroom," Phoebe said. "I'll be right back."

PHOEBE CAME BACK OUTSIDE. Warman and Eddie were nowhere around. She walked over to the swings. They weren't there. "Eddie? Warman? If you're playing hide and seek with me, you're in big trouble!"

When no one responded, concern set in.

She called their names verbally and silently, mildly pissed off.

She let her senses stretch, determined to find them. Phoebe walked over to the hopscotch game. One of Eddie's flip-flops was on the ground. She grabbed it, then flipped out in a full-blown panic.

EDDIE! WARMAN! Phoebe screeched in wild-eyed terror.

ROMAN, GAGE, ARI, SHERM! I CAN'T FIND EDDIE AND WARMAN!

Phoebe sprinted down the driveway and screamed bloody murder at the sight before her.

"WARMAN!"

The giant dragon was face down on the ground in a pool of blood, a knife sticking out of his back.

Feet thundered to her.

"EDDIE! EDDIE!" Ari screamed out, over and over, waiting to hear a response.

EDDIE! EDDIE! Roman and Gage called out, trying and failing to keep the panic out of their silent voices.

Sherm dropped to the ground and searched for a pulse. "Faint pulse. Get him to the house on the hospital bed. Someone go get Mr. Tran. He's the closest. Call Cama and the shifter doctors."

Jason gulped a breath, turned and ran to the building. "I'm on it!"

"WARMAN!" Novi wailed.

The dragons dropped to the ground near their fallen comrade, helpless.

Sherm took in the crowd. "Big Bear, help the dragons with their brother. Everyone else, take to the woods. Carefully look for evidence—try not to trample any. Have the security team check all our cameras and find out how they got in here and got out."

Phoebe came undone. "They have Eddie! It's all my fault! They took her by the hopscotch area." She sobbed as she clutched Eddie's shoe to her chest.

Kenneth wrapped his arms around her. "No, it isn't. She was guarded. We don't know yet how they managed this." He led her away toward the house.

Mr. Butler ran ahead of the men carrying Warman.

Aileen wrapped her niece into her arms. "We'll find her. Take a deep breath." She tried to steer Ari to the house, but her niece wasn't moving.

Kate and Charlene Sullivan hovered close, wanting to lend a helping hand with Ari.

Janina was the one who stepped in and calmed her future mother-in-law.

"Come into the house, Ari. I will make you some hot tea." She wrapped her arm across Ari's shoulder and nudged her forward. "Come into the house."

Ari nodded numbly and let herself be led away.

Kevin and Tommy came out of the woods. They ran up to Sherm, Roman and Gage.

"We found two of the recruits. Their throats were slashed. We don't know where the third one is," Kevin said.

King Roman! A voice silently yelled out. *We found a recruit by the road! He's... he's dead!*

Pain rushed across Roman's face. *Bring him back here.*

"We'll need to notify the next of kin," Gage said. "The authorities will treat these deaths as murder. They'll want to know about Eddie's kidnapping."

"We don't have to tell them anything..." Roman spit out.

Sherm placed his hand on Roman's shoulder. "Stay focused. We will start with the basics—we'll find out who is related to our dead. We can't have the cops near the gym. How would we explain a four-hundred-pound African Lion, or a Komodo dragon with a knife in his back, if Warman shifts?"

The doctor's cars sped up the driveway, followed by Cama's VW Thing.

Sherm pointed them to park at the house, then he, Roman, Gage, Kevin and Tommy hurried up the driveway.

EDDIE WOKE UP. It was dark... pitch black. Her shifter eyes tried to adjust, but there was no light whatsoever. She reached out in front of her and felt a cold structure. She got on her knees and used both hands, trying to determine where she was.

She reached over her head and felt the same cold structure six-inches above her. She continued with her hands along the wall. She determined she was in some sort of a metal box.

There were no sounds on the outside of the box as far as she could detect. She shivered.

MOMMY!

DADDY!

SHERM!

GRANDPA!

Eddie strained to hear a response. She was greeted with a cold, dead silence.

To be continued...

SNEAK PEEK

If you thought I was finished with my shifter family, get real! Here's Chapter 1 of Book 5.

———————————— 🍃 ————————————

The large Indonesian Komodo dragon shapeshifter lay unconscious on the hospital bed in the private home gym of his benefactors, the royal family of the shapeshifter kingdom. The extra-large hospital bed almost accommodated his enormous form that stretched to approximately eight-feet. Someone had wrapped the top sheet under his dangling feet, probably to keep them warm since his feet protruded off the end of the bed.

More than a dozen people stood quietly nearby watching as two shifter doctors, one a veterinarian and the other an OBGYN, attended to him along with two herbalists.

"The knife did not damage any organs," Dr. Duke Cavendish stated for all to hear.

"When he wakes up, he may shift unconsciously, unaware

of his surroundings, or the circumstances," Dr. Humberto Rosas said. "I'm concerned about that, because he may open the wound if he were to fall, or leap off the bed."

Dotty, Dr. Rosas' human nurse, monitored the medical equipment.

"We'll stay close by," Eyo said.

The Indonesians were all Komodo dragons. The two females were less than a head shorter than the huge males in their human forms. They were all shell-shocked at their fallen brother, the alpha of their group.

Several feet away, a tawny African Lion was sprawled on two king-sized mattresses on the floor, recovering from gunshot wounds to his chest. A human woman hovered close by, attending to him.

Two separate incidents, but both from the same perpetrator.

Roman Davenport and Gage Stryker, kings of the entire shapeshifter world and life partners, stood close by with their queen and their bonded life partner, Ari Davis. They kept her between them in a protective cluster. They were surrounded by family and close friends, waiting for the news of the dragon.

Roman's fingers morphed into panther claws, then back into fingers again. He could barely control himself from shifting because he was beyond furious at the turn of events. He wanted to rip someone apart to satisfy both his and his panther's bloodthirsty need for revenge. Deep fear coursed through his body at the kidnapping of Eddie, their adopted four-year-old daughter.

He met Gage's eyes. The eagle shifter suffered the same difficulty with his rage. Feathers sprouted, then retracted. This time he couldn't take to the skies to search. Their security team was pouring through video of all the cameras on the property, searching for faces and vehicles to identify, track down and capture.

The gym door opened and Pablo, the groundskeeper, entered carrying a piece of wood and some linens. He approached the bed. "I think this will do, but we should pad this with more towels or something, then wrap this sheet around it before we slide it under the mattress."

Mr. Butler looked over the board, gaged that it was the right size. "This should work just fine." He and Pablo wrapped the board and towels. "Someone lift up Warman's feet so we can slide this under the mattress."

Sopan and Eyo leapt forward and took hold of each of Warman's legs. They lifted the mattress with their other hands.

Pablo and Mr. Butler slid the board under the mattress. Sopan and Eyo lowered Warman's legs. His feet were now stabilized on the padded board.

Roman nodded his approval.

The medical team moved away from their newest patient.

"Everyone needs to go back to your business," Duke said. The veterinarian nodded to the dragons. "You can take turns looking after your wounded brother, but he needs his rest."

Eyo nodded. He was second in command and would take the first shift.

As everyone left the gym, the doctors went down on their knees to check out General Dickinson, the African lion. He had been shot in his human form—three bullets to the chest while in San Antonio, Texas. It was a miracle his heart and lungs were spared.

Lt. Anson Everston had helped the power-hungry Colonel, Raphael Peterson, escape while detained at the military base and awaiting transport back to Washington, DC. They were both now at large.

"How's he doing?" Dr. Rosas asked.

"He's in and out of consciousness," Colonel Sheila Jenkins said. She and Dotty were the only humans in the room.

Duke examined the wounds and was satisfied with what he saw. "His shifter genes have kicked in and launched his healing ability. Those wounds are nearly healed."

Dr. Rosas patted Sheila's shoulder. "Remember to alert him of the catheter and other tubes and connections. He shouldn't stand—he's going to be disoriented and may stumble and fall."

Sheila nodded, numb.

Roman paced in the living room. "We need to call a world-wide mandatory meeting. We have to find Eddie!"

"Should it be one-hundred percent virtual, or do we want locals to come here to the compound?" Gage asked.

"There's no conference room large enough for that crowd," Jason reminded them. "They'd have to stand outside."

Kenneth, Ari's father, sat beside her on the sofa, his arm around her shoulders, keeping her calm.

Roman nodded. "Okay, then virtual. Let's get over to the building."

Stuart Sullivan, Eddie's newly discovered grandfather, approached. "What can we do to help?"

Roman patted Stuart on the shoulder and shook his head. "There's nothing you can do. It will be good for all of you to experience the meeting, but you can do that from the house. Aileen or Mr. Butler will take charge of that when we get everything together."

Roman, Gage, Jason, Kevin and others who worked in the office building on the property, filed out of the living room and out the front door.

———————————— ❧ ————————————

Eddie pounded on the cold, steel wall of the box she was in. She was hungry, thirsty, and had to go potty. Even after all the hours she huddled inside the box, her eyes could not find any source of light. It was ink black. She wondered if this was what it was like to be blind. She shuddered.

She sat on her butt and rubbed her shoeless foot. It was icy cold. She switched her silent shifter mind-calling from mommy, daddy, Sherm and grandpa to their names.

ROMAN!

GAGE!

ARI!

SHERM!

KENNETH!

Nothing seemed to penetrate her prison.

———————————— ❧ ————————————

Roman, Gage, Jason and Kevin stood on a stage in the recently renovated meeting room in the OPERA/Panther Industries building in San Marcos, Texas. The six-story office building that contained two floors of apartments was behind the garages by several hundred feet.

Sherm made his way through the people in the room who worked in the building. He joined the royal family, minus Ari, onstage a moment later. "All the emails have been sent. You got the verbal message sent out?"

Gage nodded. "Started to get a lot of confirmations. Had to switch my phone to vibrate. No point in repeating myself a hundred or more times. They'll just have to show up to the online meeting."

Three large meeting room screens were mounted on the

wall. The royals and Sherm stood facing the screens. Roman's phone alarm beeped, alerting him it was time to start the meeting.

Communities from around the United States and the world began populating the large monitors on the wall.

"Let's give it another minute," Sherm said.

They watched as their Italian Panther office came online. The palazzo looked crowded. After Sherm glanced at his watch, he nodded to Roman. It was six minutes after the hour. Any other communities would join in as their internet connections allowed.

Roman faced the shifter community. "This is an emergency meeting. We are calling on all shifters across the United States and the world. Our daughter has been kidnapped. The kidnappers are not seeking ransom money."

Sherm pressed a button on the overhead slide projector. A recent picture of Eddie appeared on the screen.

"Eddie is four-years-old. An Army colonel named Raphael Peterson shot our friend General Toby Dickinson three times in the chest. Luckily, all his major organs were missed. He is recovering."

Roman inhaled a deep breath, trying to calm himself. Gage placed his hand on his arm.

"Colonel Peterson escaped with the help of Lt. Anson Everston from the army base in San Antonio, Texas. We don't know if anyone else is helping them, and we don't know how they infiltrated our property without being detected. They murdered three of the shifters that were guarding Eddie," Gage said. "The fourth was knifed in the back, but he is recovering."

Pictures of the colonel and the lieutenant appeared on the screen.

"We are calling out to the world for help. We know that the

colonel has been in negotiations to sell Eddie to the highest bidder. We are aware of bidders from Iran, Arab Emirates, China and Nigeria. All shifters in those areas are called upon to do your duty to help your royal family," Gage said.

Roman's face distorted into pure rage. He snatched the microphone from Gage. "If I discover one of our kind is involved in this treacherous act of kidnapping, murder and attempted murder, I can guarantee that he will be charged with treason. I will be judge, jury and hangman." He pounded a finger into his chest with the word I.

Sherm took hold of Roman's upper arm. Roman tried to shake him off, but Sherm held firm. "Calm down. You have to keep it together to move our people into action."

Roman let out a shallow breath. He nodded.

Sherm stepped back.

Gage sent a questioning expression to Roman.

Roman rolled his shoulders.

Kevin stepped forward. "Our family needs your help. My little sister is out there somewhere. Put your ears on alert. Listen to the thoughts of humans and shifters alike—all around you—that might be in a position to help the kidnappers. Panther Securities has teams all over the world. If anyone hears of anything remotely connected to the kidnapping, please contact us as soon as possible."

Jason took the mic from his brother. "For those over in Europe, Russia or the Far East, contact Donatello or Marco at the Fuiggi office in Italy immediately. They will contact the Panther teams. Are there any questions?"

There were a multitude of hands raising and people blurting out questions.

Sherm stepped up and grabbed the mic. "People! Be orderly. One at a time." He noticed a man from Russia arguing with several people and recognized him. "Dimitri?" The man grabbed a microphone and stepped closer to the screen.

"Sherm! Where do you want my team? We can gear up and be airborne within an hour," Dimitri said.

Sherm had a silent conversation with Roman and Gage. Then he turned back to the screen. "Dimitri, I'll call you after the meeting. Who's next?"

A British man captured their attention by waving his hand. "Why won't these people be seeking a ransom?"

Gage took the microphone. "Our daughter is very intelligent. She was tested, and it was determined that she has the highest IQ of anyone known to have been tested."

The British man nodded. "So, they will want to enslave her for war and other purposes."

Gage lowered his head, trying to control his emotions. He looked back up. "Yes."

A German woman stepped forward. "Is Queen Ari okay?"

"Yes, she's with her father. She's very distraught, as you can imagine," Sherm said.

The questions continued for several minutes more, then Sherm ended the meeting. The screens went dark. He checked to make sure all connections were closed.

The locals that attended the meeting filed out of the room, talking quietly among themselves.

Roman, Gage, Kevin, Jason and Sherm stepped off the stage and sat at a table.

"Where can we best use Dimitri and his team?" Sherm asked.

"I think whoever the Arab Emirates contact is will be the winning bidder," Roman said. "They have more disposable cash than anyone else."

"China would be a close second," Jason said.

"So, should we have his team go to the Arab Emirates?" Sherm asked.

Roman and Gage faced each other, just looking at each other, no silent conversation going through their heads. Slowly, they nodded.

"Yes, have Dimitri and his team fly to Arab Emirates," Gage said.

ABOUT THE AUTHOR

DG Ireland writes full time. She lives among dreams and fantasies with two cats. Her head is filled with stories. She doesn't suffer from writer's block. If you buy her books and products, and sign up for her newsletter, she'll love you forever.

I'm on Patreon! Please help support me while I create fabulous content!

Made in the USA
Middletown, DE
15 February 2021